Joanna Fulford is a compulsive scribbler, with a passion for literature and history, both of which she has studied to postgraduate level. Other countries and cultures have always exerted a fascination, and she has travelled widely, living and working abroad for many years. However, her roots are in England, and are now firmly established in the Peak District, where she lives with her husband, Brian. When not pressing a hot keyboard she likes to be out on the hills, either walking or on horseback. However, these days equestrian activity is confined to sedate hacking rather than riding at high speed towards solid obstacles.

A recent novel by the same author:

THE VIKING'S DEFIANT BRIDE*

*Part of the *Mills & Boon Presents...* anthology, featuring talented new authors

To Vee Leighton
for her insight and encouragement
throughout the writing of this book.

**Praise for
Joanna Fulford's
debut novel:**

THE VIKING'S DEFIANT BRIDE
'Fulford's story of lust and love set in the
Dark Ages is reminiscent of Woodiwiss'
THE FLAME AND THE FLOWER.'
—*Romantic Times BOOKreviews*

Chapter One

'Gartside! Alight here for Gartside!'

The guard's voice roused Claire from her doze. Feeling startled and disorientated, she looked about her and realised that the coach had stopped. She had no recollection of the last ten miles of the journey to Yorkshire and had no idea what hour it might be. At a guess it was some time in the midafternoon. Her cramped limbs felt as though they had been travelling for ever, though in reality it was three days. For more reasons than one it would be a relief to escape from the lumbering vehicle. Further reflection was denied her as the door opened.

'This is where you get down, miss.'

She nodded and, under the curious eyes of the remaining passengers, retrieved her valise and descended onto the street in front of a small and lowly inn.

'Can you tell me how far it is to Helmshaw?' she asked. 'And in which direction it lies?'

The guard jerked his head toward the far end of the street. 'Five miles. That way.'

'Thank you.'

After a grunted acknowledgement he closed the door of the coach and climbed back onto the box. Then the driver cracked his whip and the coach moved forwards. Watching it depart, Claire swallowed hard, for with it went every connection with her past life. Involuntarily her hand tightened round the handle of her bag. The latter contained all her worldly possessions, or all she had been able to carry when she left, apart from the last few shillings in her reticule. The rest of her small stock of money had been spent on the coach fare and the necessary board and lodging on her journey. Her last meal had been a frugal breakfast at dawn and she was hungry now, but the inn looked dingy and unprepossessing and she felt loath to enter it. Instead she hefted the valise and set off along the street in the direction the guard had indicated earlier.

It soon became clear that Gartside was not much of a place, being essentially a long street with houses on either side, and a few small shops. As she walked she received curious stares from the passers-by but no one spoke. A few ragged children watched from an open doorway. A little way ahead a small group of men loitered outside a tavern. Uncomfortably aware of being a stranger Claire hurried on, wanting to be gone. She hoped that Helmshaw would prove more congenial, but a five-mile walk lay between her and it. Massing clouds threatened rain. Would it hold off until she reached her destination? And when she got there, what would be her welcome? She hadn't set eyes on Ellen Greystoke in seven years, and nor had there been any correspondence between them apart from that one letter, written to her aunt's dictation, not long after Claire had removed there. Seven years. Would her old governess remember her? Would she still be at the same address? What if Miss Greystoke had moved on? Claire shivered, unwilling to contemplate the possibility. She had nowhere else to go, no money and no immediate prospect of earning any. Moreover, there was always the chance that her uncle would discover where she had gone.

For the past three days it had been her constant dread. Each time a faster vehicle had passed the public coach her heart lurched lest it should be he. Every feeling shrank from the scene that must surely follow, for he would not hesitate to compel her return. After that she would be lost. She had no illusions about her ability to resist her uncle's will: those had been beaten out of her long since. His maxim was: *Spare the rod and spoil the child*, a policy he had upheld with the utmost rigour. He would have her submission all right, and would use any means to get it.

At the thought of what that submission meant her stomach churned. Within the week she would become Lady Mortimer, married against her will to a man old enough to be her father, a portly, balding baronet with a lascivious gaze that made her flesh crawl. The memory of his proposal was still horribly vivid. She had been left alone with him, an occurrence that had set warning bells ringing immediately. Her aunt and uncle were usually sticklers for propriety. After a few minutes of stilted conversation Sir Charles had seized her hand, declaring his passion in the most ardent terms. Repelled by the words and the feel of his hot, damp palms she had tried to break free, only to find herself tipped backwards onto the sofa cushions. Claire swallowed hard. Almost she could still feel his paunch pressing her down, could smell the oily sweetness of hair pomade and fetid breath on her face as he tried to kiss her. Somehow she had got a hand free and struck him. Taken aback he had slackened his hold, allowing her to struggle free of that noxious embrace and run, knowing she'd rather be dead than married to such a man. How her refusal had been represented to her uncle afterwards she could only guess, but his anger was plain.

'You stupid, ungrateful girl! Who do you think you are to be refusing such an offer? Do you imagine you will ever get another as good?'

All her protestations had counted for nothing. She could see her uncle's cold and furious face.

'You have until tomorrow morning to change your mind or I'll know the reason why. By the time I've finished with you, my girl, you'll be only too glad to marry Sir Charles, believe me.'

She had believed him, knowing full well it was no idle threat, and so she had run away the same night.

'Now there's a fancy bit of muslin.'

'Aye, I wouldn't mind ten minutes behind the tavern with her.'

The voices jolted Claire from her thoughts and, as their lewd import dawned, she reddened, recognising the group of loafers she had seen before. From their dress they were of the labouring class, but dirtier and more unkempt than was usual. Uncomfortably aware of their close scrutiny Claire kept walking, determined to ignore them, but as she drew nigh the group one of them stepped in front of her blocking the way. When she tried to go round him he side-stepped too, blocking the path again. He looked to be in his early twenties. Taller than her by several inches and sturdily built, he was dressed like the others in a brown drab coat and breeches. A soiled green neckcloth was carelessly tied about his throat. Lank fair hair straggled beneath a greasy cap and framed a narrow unshaven face with a thin-lipped mouth and cold blue eyes. These were now appraising her, missing no detail of her appearance from her straw bonnet to the dark blue pelisse and sprigged muslin frock. Although she had dressed as plainly as she could to avoid attracting attention, there was no mistaking the fine quality and cut of her garments.

'Can you spare a coin, miss?'

'I'm sorry, no.'

'Just a shilling, miss.'

'I have none to spare.'

'I find that hard to believe, a fine young lady like yourself.'

'Believe what you like.'

She made to step round him again, but again he prevented it.

'Suppose I take a look for myself.'

Before she could anticipate it he grabbed her reticule. Claire tried to snatch it back, but he held on. His four companions gathered round, grinning. Seeing herself surrounded she fought panic, knowing instinctively it would be a mistake to show fear.

He shook the reticule and heard the chink of coins. Her last few shillings!

'Sounds like money to me,' he remarked with a wink to the general audience.

'Give that back.'

He grinned. 'What if I don't, eh?'

Claire glared at her tormentor. She had not risked so much and come all this way merely to fall victim to another bully. Resentment welled up, fuelling her anger, and without warning she lashed out, dealing him a ringing crack across the cheek.

'Give it back, you oaf!'

In sheer surprise he let go of the reticule while his companions drew audible breaths and looked on in delighted anticipation. Claire lifted her chin.

'Get out of my way!'

She would have pushed past, but he recovered and seized her arm in a painful grip.

'You'll pay for that, you little bitch.'

Glaring up at him, she forced herself to meet the cold blue eyes. 'Unhand me.'

'High and mighty, aren't we? But I'll take you down a peg or two.'

'Aye, that's it, Jed,' said a voice from the group. 'Show her.'

A chorus of agreement followed and with pounding heart Claire saw them move in closer. Jed smiled, revealing stained and decaying teeth.

'Since you won't give a coin I'll take payment in kind. Perhaps we all will, eh, lads?'

A murmur of agreement followed. Her captor glanced toward the alley that ran alongside the tavern. Claire, following that look, felt her stomach lurch.

'Let go of me.'

She tried to twist free, but his grip only tightened. In desperation she kicked out. The blow connected and she heard him swear, but it was a temporary victory. Moments later she was dragged into the alley and shoved up against the outer wall of the inn. Then his arm was round her waist and his free hand exploring her breast. She could feel his hot breath on her neck. Claire struggled harder.

'Aye, go on, fight me. I like it better that way.'

'Let me go!'

'Not before I've given you what you need, lass.'

'Save some for us, Jed,' said a voice from behind him.

He grinned appreciatively. 'I reckon there's enough here to go round. You'll get your turns when I'm done.'

More laughter greeted this. Claire screamed as Jed's hands fumbled with her skirt.

'Let her go!'

Hearing that hard, cold command, the group fell silent, turning to look at the newcomer who had approached unnoticed. Claire swallowed hard, her heart pounding even as her gaze drank in every detail of her rescuer's appearance. An arresting figure, he was a head taller than any present. His dress proclaimed the working man, but there the similarity ended: if anything his upright bearing smacked more of a military background. The brown serge coat had seen better days but it was clean and neat and covered powerful shoulders; waistcoat, breeches and boots adorned a lean, athletic figure that had not an ounce of fat on it. Dark hair was visible from beneath a low-crowned felt hat. However, it was the face that really held attention, with its strong bone structure and slightly aquiline nose, the chiselled, clean-shaven lines accentuated by a narrow scar that ran down the left side from cheek to jaw. The sculpted mouth was set in a hard, uncompromising line, as uncompromising as the expression in the grey eyes.

For a moment or two there was silence, but the hold on Claire's arm slackened. With pounding heart she glanced up at the newcomer, but he wasn't looking at her. The hawk-like gaze was fixed on her persecutor. The latter sneered.

'This is none of your business, Eden.'

'Then I'll make it my business, Stone.' The quiet voice had the same Yorkshire burr as the others, but it also held an inflexion of steel.

'We were just having a little fun, that's all.'

'The lady doesn't seem to share your idea of amusement.'

'What's it to you?'

The reply was a large clenched fist that connected with Stone's jaw. The force of the blow pitched him backwards and sent him sprawling, stunned, in the mud of the alley. Before he could stir, one of his companions threw a punch at Eden. He blocked it and brought his knee up hard into his attacker's groin. The man doubled over in agony. As he staggered away a third stepped in. Eden ducked under the swinging fist and landed his opponent a savage upper cut that lifted him off his feet and flung him backwards to lie in the mud with Stone. Seeing the fate of their fellows, the remaining two men hesitated, then backed away. Eden threw them one contemptuous glance and then looked at Claire.

'Are you hurt, miss?'

'No. I…I'm all right,' she replied, hoping her voice wouldn't shake.

'Good. Then I'll set you on your way.'

He looked round at the others as though daring them to challenge the words, but no one did. Instead they avoided his eye and moved aside. Seeing her bag lying nearby, Eden picked it up. As he did so, Stone came to, propping himself groggily on one elbow, his other hand massaging the lump on his jaw. Blood trickled from a split lip.

'You'll get yours, Eden, I swear it!'

If the other was in any way perturbed by the threat he gave no sign of it save that the glint in the grey eyes grew a shade harder.

'I'll look forward to that, Stone.'

Then, placing a firm but gentle hand under her elbow, he led Claire away from the scene.

For a few moments they walked in silence and she was grateful for the respite because it allowed her time to regain her self-control. She was trembling now with reaction and the knowledge of how narrow her escape had been. Moreover she was ashamed to the depths of her soul to have been seen in such a situation. Respectable young women did not travel unaccompanied and would never place themselves in circumstances where they might attract the attentions of such brutes as those. Her face reddened. What must he think?

She stole a glance at her protector, but the handsome face gave nothing away. Nor did he venture a comment of any kind. Instead they walked on in silence until they were well clear of the tavern, she all the while aware of the warmth of his hand beneath her elbow. It was a gesture that was both comforting and disturbing at once. Yet the nearness of this man was not threatening as those others had been. How much she owed him. She stole another look at his face.

'Thank you, sir. I am most grateful for what you did back there.'

The grey eyes regarded her steadily a moment.

'I beg you will not regard it, madam.'

Claire knew a moment's surprise for the Yorkshire burr had disappeared to be replaced with the pure modulated diction associated with a very different social rank. However, fearing to seem rude, she did not remark on it.

'Who were those men?' she asked then.

'Scum. They needn't concern you further.' He paused. 'May I ask where you're going?'

'To Helmshaw.'

'Helmshaw. That's a fair walk from here.'

'Yes, I believe so, but the public coach doesn't go there.'

'You came on the coach?'

'Yes.'

'Alone?'

Her cheeks reddened. 'As you see.'

'You have family in Helmshaw perhaps?'

'A friend.'

'But your friend is not expecting you.'

'No, not exactly.'

'Not at all, I'd say, or you would have been met at the coach.'

Not knowing what to say, Claire remained silent. A few moments later they reached the end of the street. There he paused, looking down at her.

'Yonder lies the road to Helmshaw. I'd walk along with you, but I've important business requiring my attention here. However, I think you'll not be troubled again.'

She managed a tremulous smile. 'I'm sure I shan't be. You've been most kind, sir.'

'You're welcome, Miss, er…'

'Claire Davenport.'

He took the offered hand and bowed. For one brief moment she felt the warmth of his touch through her glove. Then he relinquished his hold.

'Farewell, Miss Davenport.'

'Farewell, Mr Eden. And thank you again.'

He handed her the valise and touched his hand to his hat. Then he turned and walked away. Feeling strangely bereft, she watched the tall departing figure with a rueful smile. In all likelihood they would never meet again, though she knew she would never forget him. With a sigh she turned and continued on her way.

As the man Eden had predicted she met with no more trouble on the road, but half an hour later it came on to rain, a thundery summer shower. The open roadway offered no shelter and in a very short time she was soaked through. It was with real relief that she saw the first houses on the edge of the village. An enquiry of a passing carter directed her to a grey stone house set back from the road in a pleasant garden. Claire paused by the gate, feeling her stomach knot in sudden apprehension. What if Miss Greystoke had moved on? It had been seven years after all. What would she do then? Where would she go? Taking a deep breath, she walked up the paved pathway to the front door and rang the bell. A maidservant answered. On seeing Claire's bedraggled and muddied appearance she eyed her askance.

'The doctor's not at home,' she said.

Shivering a little now, Claire stood her ground.

'It is Miss Greystoke I seek, not the doctor.'

Before the girl could answer another voice spoke behind her.

'Who is it, Eliza?'

Claire's heart beat painfully hard. The woman's elegant lavender-coloured gown was different, but everything else was familiar from the light brown hair to the blue eyes now regarding her with shock and concern.

'Claire?' The woman came closer, wonder writ large in her expression, and then a beaming smile lit her face. 'Oh, my dear, it really is you!'

'Miss Greystoke.'

'What a wonderful surprise. But what am I doing talking here on the doorstep? Come inside, do.'

Only too happy to obey, Claire stepped into the hallway and for a moment the two women faced each other in silence. Then Ellen Greystoke opened her arms and drew her visitor into a warm embrace. Knowing herself safe for the first time in days, Claire began to shake.

'Good gracious! How cold you are! We must get you out of those wet clothes at once. Then we shall sit down and have some tea and you can tell me everything.'

Claire was escorted to a pleasant upstairs bedroom, provided with hot water and towels, and then left in privacy. Shivering, she removed her bonnet and then stripped off her wet things. How good it was to be free of them at last and to be able to bathe again and tidy her hair. Having done so, she donned a clean gown. It was one of two that she had been able to bring. Apart from those, a russet spencer, a few necessary personal items and her sketchbook, the valise contained nothing of value. Involuntarily Claire's hand sought the locket she wore around her neck. It was her sole piece of jewellery and it bore the only likeness of her parents that she possessed. She had inherited her mother's dusky curls and hazel eyes and her face had the same fine bone structure. Her father too had been dark haired with rugged good looks. It was not hard to see why her parents had been attracted to each other or why Henry Davenport should fly in the face of his family's disapproval and marry a young woman with only a pretty countenance and a hundred pounds a year to recommend her. Goodness was not a marketable quality in their eyes. Yet, contrary to all predictions, the marriage had been a success. Claire had fond memories of her early years, days filled with sunshine and laughter when she'd been truly happy and carefree. How long ago it all seemed and how like a dream.

An outbreak of typhus changed everything: her father had sickened first and then her mother, the fever carrying them off within three days of each other. At a stroke she was an orphan. Miss Greystoke had taken it upon herself to inform her father's family and in due course Uncle Hector had arrived. Her thirteen-year-old self could see the likeness to her father in the dark hair and grey eyes, but there the similarity ended. The tall, unsmiling man in black was a stranger whose cold expression repelled her. She hadn't wanted to go with him and had sobbed out her grief in Miss Greystoke's arms. In the end though there had been no choice and she had been taken to live at her uncle's house.

From the moment of her arrival she knew Aunt Maud disliked her and resented her presence there. At first she had not understood why, but as time passed and she grew from child to young woman the contrast between her and her much plainer cousins became marked. To be fair her cousins showed no resentment of her good looks, but then they were so timid that they never expressed an opinion on anything. Claire, outgoing and high-spirited, found them dull company. Moreover she found the educational regime in the house stifling.

From the start Miss Greystoke had always encouraged her to think for herself and to read widely and Claire's naturally enquiring mind devoured the books she was given and easily assimilated what she found there. She loved learning for its own sake and enjoyed gaining new skills, whether it was drawing or playing the pianoforte, speaking in French or discussing current affairs. In her uncle's house everything was different. Independent thought was discouraged, and only the most improving works considered suitable reading material. They were taught their lessons under the exacting eye of Miss Hardcastle, a hatchet-faced woman with strict views about what constituted a suitable education for young ladies, and an expectation of instant obedience in all things. In this she was fully supported by Aunt Maud and any infraction of discipline was punished. Claire, loathing the constraints imposed on her, had been openly rebellious at first, but she had soon learned the error of her ways. Remembering it now, she felt resentment rise in a wave. She would never return no matter what.

Some time later she joined Ellen in the parlour where she was plied with hot tea and slices of fruit cake. When she had finished she favoured her friend with an explanation of why she had fled her uncle's house. Ellen listened without interruption, but the blue eyes were bright with anger and indignation. Claire swallowed hard.

'I'm so sorry to impose on you like this, Miss Greystoke, but I didn't know where else to turn.'

'Where else should you turn but to me? And let us dispense with this formality. You must call me Ellen.'

'You don't know how I missed you all these years.'

'And I you. My brightest pupil.'

'Did you receive my letter?'

'Yes, I did.'

'I wanted to write again, but my aunt would not permit it.'

'Then you did not get my other letters?'

Claire stared at her. 'What other letters?'

'I wrote several, but there was never any reply, so in the end I stopped sending them.'

'On my honour I never received them.'

'No, after what you have told me I imagine you did not.'

Anger and indignation welled anew and Claire bit her lip. To think that all that time her aunt had lied to her, if only by omission.

'It was the saddest day of my life when I had to leave you. Your parents' house was such a happy place and they were always so good to me. I felt more like a member of the family than a governess.'

'I feel as though I have been in prison for the past seven years. And then this. I could not do what they wanted, Ellen.'

'Of course not! No woman should ever be compelled to marry a man she does not love and esteem. What your uncle did was shameful.'

'But what if he finds me?'

'He shall not remove you from this house.'

'I wish I were not so afraid of him, Ellen.'

'I am not surprised that you are. The man is a perfect brute.'

'If my aunt read your letters, she will have seen the address and may guess where I am.'

'She probably burnt them without reading them. In any case it was a long time ago. It is most unlikely she kept them.'

'I pray she did not.' Claire's hands clenched. 'If only I might reach my majority and be out of their power for good.'

'That day cannot be so far away now. How old are you?'

'Four months short of my twenty-first birthday.'

'No time at all. It will soon pass and then you will be a free woman.'

'Somehow I must earn my living and I am not afraid to work, provided it is honest employment. I do not wish to be a burden.'

Ellen smiled and squeezed her hand gently. 'You could never be a burden to me.'

'But what will your brother say when he returns?'

'You leave George to me.'

Doctor Greystoke returned some time later. In his early forties, he was a little over the average height and had a strong athletic build, which made him seem younger than his years. His face was pleasant and open rather than handsome and, as yet, relatively unlined save for the creases round the eyes and mouth. Like his sister he had light brown hair, in his case greying a little at the temples and lending him a distinguished air. Claire thought he had a kindly face. Even so there was no way of knowing how he would respond to having his home invaded by a stranger—and a penniless stranger to boot.

She need not have worried. Having been apprised of the situation, he seated himself on the sofa beside his unexpected guest, regarding her keenly.

'My sister has told me everything, Miss Davenport. I confess I am deeply shocked to learn of the reason for your coming here, but can in no way blame you for leaving. To force a young woman into marriage must be in every way repugnant to civilised thinking.' He smiled. 'You are welcome to remain here as long as you wish.'

'Thank you. May I also ask that my reason for being here remains a secret?'

'You may rely on it. Neither my sister nor I will divulge it to a soul.'

Claire's eyes filled with tears and a lump formed in her throat.

'Indeed, sir, you are very good.'

To her horror tears spilled over and ran down her face and she dashed them away with a trembling hand. Seeing it his face registered instant concern.

'Don't cry,' he said. 'You're safe here.'

Claire drew in a shuddering breath and fumbled for a handkerchief. Before she could find it he produced his own.

'Here, try this. I prescribe it for the relief of tears.'

It drew a wan smile and he nodded approvingly. 'That's it. Now dry your eyes and let us have no more of this. I absolutely forbid you to be sad here.'

Ellen rose and rang the bell to summon the maid.

'Shall we have some more tea?'

Her brother looked up and grinned. 'I thought you'd never ask.'

Chapter Two

Gleams of moonlight shone through flying rags of cloud, its pale glow illuminating the moor and the winding road along which the wagon made its steady progress. Drawn by four great draught horses it lumbered on, its load a dark mass concealed beneath a heavy tarpaulin. Apart from the driver and his companion on the box, six others accompanied the wagon, big men chosen for their physical strength. Two walked in front with lighted torches; the others rode on either side of the vehicle. All were armed with clubs and pistols. Conversation was kept to a minimum. The only sounds were the wind and the muffled rumbling of iron-rimmed wheels over the track. For it was more track than road, an ancient drovers' trail that crossed the hills above Helmshaw. As they walked the men kept a sharp look out, their eyes scanning the roadway ahead and the pooled shadows to either side. No other sound or movement revealed any more human presences. The little convoy might have been the last living things upon the face of the earth.

'All quiet so far,' muttered the driver, 'but I'll not be sorry to see journey's end.'

His companion merely grunted assent.

'If it weren't for t'money you'd not catch me out here with this lot,' the other continued. 'I thought long and hard about it I can tell thee. A man should be at his fireside of an evening, not wandering t'moors to be prey to scum.'

Another grunt greeted this. Seeing his companion wasn't in a responsive mood, Jethro Timms gave up the attempt at conversation. From time to time he eyed the other man. A taciturn cove, he thought, and no mistake. However, what he lacked in amiability he made up for in sheer physical presence for he was tall and well made with a lean, athletic figure that had about it something of a military bearing, though nothing about his clothing suggested it. Coat, breeches and boots, though strong and serviceable, had seen better days. Still, the driver reflected, that was not surprising. Since Napoleon went to Elba there were lots of ex-soldiers roaming the land looking for work, though heaven knew it was in short supply. If a man was desperate enough he might volunteer to ride guard on a wagon in the middle of the night.

He gave his companion another sideways glance, but the other seemed unaware of it, his gaze on the way ahead. Dark hair was partly concealed under a hat which shadowed the strong lines of brow and jaw. Down one cheek the faint line of a scar was just visible. It might have been a sabre slash, but the driver didn't care to ask. Something about those steel-grey eyes forbade it. Nevertheless, he thought, Eden was a comforting presence tonight, not least for the blunderbuss he held across his knee and the brace of pistols thrust into his belt.

Timms made no further attempt to break the silence and the wagon lumbered on. Gradually the scenery began to change, the open heath giving way to more rugged terrain as the track passed through a deep valley. On either hand the dark mass of the hillsides was just visible against the paler cloud above, but to one side the ground fell away in a steep drop to the stream. As it passed through the declivity the track narrowed. Suddenly Eden sat up, his expression intent.

Timms swallowed hard. 'What is it?'

'I thought I heard something. Stones sliding.'

'I can't hear owt.'

For a moment or two they listened, but the only sounds were the wind through the heather and the chuckling water below.

'Tha must have imagined...'

The driver's words were lost as the darkness erupted in a flash of fire and the sharp report of a pistol. A linkman cried out and fell, his torch lying unheeded on the path. As though at a signal a dozen dark shapes rose from the concealing heather and rushed forwards. Cursing, Timms reined in his startled team as a masked attacker reached up to drag him from his seat. Beside him the blunderbuss roared and a man screamed, falling back into the darkness. On the other side of the wagon two others launched themselves at Eden. He swung the blunderbuss hard and felt it connect with bone. His attacker staggered and fell. The other came on. Eden kicked out at the masked face and heard cartilage crunch beneath the sole of his boot. A muffled curse followed and the would-be assailant reeled away, clutching his ruined nose. Eden drew the pistols from his belt as his gaze took in the chaos of struggling shadowy forms in the roadway. As another masked face loomed out of the dark he loosed off a shot. The ball took the man between the eyes and he fell without a sound. Several others swarmed toward the wagon.

Timms, struggling to control the restive horses, cried a warning as hands reached up to drag him from the box. Eden heard it and, turning, fired the second pistol. He heard a yelp of pain and saw a man go down, but almost immediately another shot rang out and Timms swore, clutching his arm. A moment later he was dragged from the box and lost to view. Other hands caught hold of Eden. Instead of resisting them he threw himself forwards, diving off the wagon to land on top of his assailants in the road. Fists and feet connected with flesh amid muffled cries and oaths. Then he was free. Leaping to his feet, he spun round to find himself staring at the mouth of a pistol. Pale moonlight afforded a swift impression of cold eyes glinting above a mask, and below it a soiled green neckcloth. For one split second something stirred in Eden's memory. Then there was a burst of flame and a loud report. Hot lead tore into flesh and he staggered, clutching his shoulder. Blood welled beneath his fingers and then vicious pain exploded in a burst of light behind his eyeballs and he fell.

He lay in the dirt for some moments, aware only of the pain that seemed to have replaced all other sensation. The sounds of fighting receded. With an effort of will he forced back the threatening faintness and became aware of a voice issuing instructions. Moonlight revealed dark figures round the wagon, some unhitching the horses, others loosening the ropes that held the load, flinging back the tarpaulin to reveal the crate beneath. Eden's jaw tightened as the figures swarmed aboard and levered it off the wagon. As in slow motion it crashed onto the road and rolled forwards down the slope, tumbling over and over, gathering momentum until it came to rest, smashed and broken on the rocky streamed below. A ragged cheer went up from the wreckers. At that a man stepped forwards to face the remaining members of the escort. Like his companions his face was covered by a scarf and his hat pulled low.

'Tell Harlston his machines are not wanted here,' he said. 'Any attempt to replace this one will result in more of the same.'

With that he jerked his head towards his companions and the whole group made off into the darkness. Eden tried to rise, but the pain scythed through his shoulder. Crimson bombs exploded behind his eyes and then blackness took him.

He had no idea how long he lay there; it might have been minutes or hours. For some moments he did not move, aware only of cold air on his face and the dull throbbing ache in his shoulder. Instinctively he lifted his hand to the wound and felt the stickiness of blood. Then the details began to return. As he became more aware of his surroundings the first thing that struck him was the eerie silence, a hush broken only by the wind and the stream. The sky was a lighter shade and the stars fading so dawn could not be far off. Experimentally he tried to rise; pain savaged him and he bit back a cry. With an effort of will he dragged himself to a nearby boulder and used it to support his back while he forced himself to a sitting position. The effort brought beads of cold sweat to his forehead and it was some minutes before he could catch his breath. Then he looked around. In the predawn half light he could make out the dark silent shapes that were the bodies of the slain. Grim-faced, he counted half a dozen. Where were the rest? The wreckers were long gone, but surely some of the wagon escort had lived. He could see no sign of the wagon or the horses. Had the surviving members just abandoned their fellows to their fate and saved their own skins?

Anger forced Eden to his knees and thence to his feet, using the rock to steady himself. Agony seared through the injured shoulder. His legs trembled like reeds. Gritting his teeth against the pain, he drew in a few deep breaths. As he did so he glanced over the edge of the hillside. Among the rocks that lined the stream he saw the smashed remains of the power loom and with it the wagon. At the sight his fists clenched, but he understood now why he had been left behind in this place. The survivors had taken the horses for themselves and the injured. He had been mistaken for one of the dead. The thought occurred that if he didn't find help soon he might well be among their number. The nearest town was Helmshaw: Harlston's Mill was located on its edge. It was perhaps two miles distant. Mentally girding himself for the effort and the coming pain, Eden stumbled away down the track.

His progress was pitifully slow because every few minutes he was forced to rest. The sky was much lighter now and the track clear enough, but pain clouded his mind until he could think of nothing else. Moreover, the darkened patch of dried blood on his coat was overlain with a new scarlet wetness that spread past the edges of the original stain. He had tried to stanch the bleeding with a wadded handkerchief, but that too was sodden red. His strength was ebbing fast and only sheer will forced him to put one foot in front of the other. He had gone perhaps half a mile when the level track began to rise at the start of a long steady climb up the next hill. Eden managed another fifty yards before pain and exhaustion overcame his will and he collapsed on the path in a dead faint.

Claire was woken just after dawn by heavy pounding on the front door. Her heart thumped painfully hard and for one dreadful moment she wondered if her uncle had discovered her where-abouts and was come to drag her away. Forcing herself to take a deep breath, she slipped from the bed and threw a shawl about her shoulders. Then she crept to the bedroom door and opened it a crack, listening intently. The pounding on the door increased and was followed by Eliza's indignant tones as she went to answer it. Then a man's voice was heard demanding the doctor. Claire breathed a sigh of relief. Not her uncle, then.

'What's so urgent that the doctor must be dragged from his bed at this hour?' demanded Eliza.

'There's half a dozen injured men at Harlston's Mill,' the man replied. 'Some bad hurt.'

'Good gracious! Not another accident?'

'No accident. They were escorting a consignment of new ma-chinery for t'mill. Seems they were attacked on their way over t'moor. There's been some killed an' all.'

'Heaven preserve us from such wickedness! Wait here! I'll fetch the doctor.'

Within a quarter of an hour Dr Greystoke had left the house. Claire heard the sound of horses' hooves as the men rode away, and in some anxiety digested what she had heard. Her limited knowledge of the machine-breakers' activities had been gleaned from newspaper accounts: here evidently it was far more than just a story of distant industrial unrest. Here the violence was all too real. Could it be true that men had lost their lives? The thought was chilling. What could make men so desperate that they were prepared to kill?

It was a question she put to Ellen when they met in the breakfast parlour some time later.

'When the war with France cut off foreign trade it caused a lot of hardship hereabouts,' her friend replied. 'Even now that Napoleon is exiled the situation is slow to change. The advent of the power looms is seen as yet another threat to men's livelihoods.'

'Then why do mill owners like Harlston antagonise the workforce in that way?'

'They see it as progress and in a way I suppose it is. The new machines are faster and more efficient by far than the old looms. All the same, it is hard to reconcile that knowledge with the sight of children starving.'

Claire pondered the words, for they suggested a world she had no experience of. In spite of recent events her life had been sheltered and comfortable for the most part and although she had lost her parents she had still been clothed and fed and there had always been a roof over her head. Other children were not as fortunate. For so many orphans the only choice was the workhouse. If they survived that, it usually led to a life of drudgery after. For a young and unprotected girl the world was hazardous indeed. Recalling the scene in Gartside, she shuddered.

'Are you all right, Claire? You look awfully pale.'

'Yes, a slight headache is all.'

'No wonder with all you've been through.'

Claire managed a wan smile. She hadn't told Ellen about the incident with Stone and his cronies. She had felt too ashamed; the memory of it made her feel dirty somehow and she wanted nothing more than to forget about it. Yet now it returned with force and with it the recollection of the man who had saved her.

'Why don't you go for a walk this morning?' Ellen continued. 'I'm sure the fresh air would do you good.'

'Yes, perhaps you are right.'

'There is a gate in the garden wall that leads out onto the moor. It is quite a climb, but the views from the top are worth the effort.'

'I could take my sketchbook.'

Ellen smiled. 'You have kept up your drawing, then?'

'Oh, yes. It is one of my greatest pleasures.'

'You were always so gifted that way. I shall look forward to seeing your work later.'

'Will you not come with me?'

'I wish I could, but this morning I have an engagement in town. Never fear, though, we shall take many walks together in future. The countryside hereabouts is very fine.'

Looking out across the sunlit moor an hour later Claire could only agree with her friend's assessment. From her vantage point she could see the town below, and the mill, and then the wide expanse of rolling heath and the hills beyond. Far above her a skylark poured out its soul in song. Listening to it, Claire felt her spirits lift for the first time and suddenly the future seemed less threatening. Smiling, she walked on, revelling in the fresh air and exercise.

She had followed the track for another mile or so when she saw the figure lying on the path. It was a man and he was lying very still. Claire frowned. What on earth was he doing there? How had he got there? She approached with caution but he did not move. Her gaze took in boots, breeches and coat and the dark stain on the shoulder. It was unmistakably blood. Swallowing hard, she drew nearer and then gasped.

'Mr Eden!'

In a moment she was beside him, her fingers seeking his wrist for a pulse. For a moment she couldn't find one and her heart sank. Her fingers moved to his neck and in trembling relief she found it at last, a slow and feeble beat. His face was very pale, the skin waxy where it showed above the stubble of his beard. When she spoke to him again there was no response. Claire gently lifted the edge of his coat and her eyes widened.

'Dear God,' she murmured.

Shirt and waistcoat were soaked, as was the wadded handkerchief thrust between. He had been shot. Shocked to the core, she stared a second or two at the scarlet stain. Who could have done such a thing? Unbidden, the memory of their first meeting returned and she heard Stone's voice: *'You'll get yours, Eden, I swear it.'* Feeling sick and guilty, Claire bit her lip. Was this her fault? Had his earlier action brought this on him? There was no time for further reflection; he needed help and soon. She looked around in desperation, her mind retracing her route and the length of time it would take to get back and wondering if she would find Ellen or her brother returned yet. In the midst of these thoughts her eye detected a movement further down the track. Straightening, she shaded her eyes and strained to see, praying it might be a rider. In fact it was several riders and in their midst a cart. Almost sobbing with relief, she waved frantically.

'Help! Over here!'

It seemed to take an age before they heard her. Then two of the men spurred forwards to investigate. Claire stood on the track and watched them come. They reined in, regarding her with open curiosity. Then they noticed the still form lying at the edge of the path.

'What's happened here, lass?' demanded the first.

'He's badly injured. He needs a doctor and soon.'

'Have no fear. Help is at hand.'

The first rider dismounted and hastened over to the injured man. Then Claire heard a muffled exclamation.

'Merciful heavens, it's Mark Eden.'

'What!' His companion edged his mount closer. 'I heard he was missing, believed dead.'

'He soon will be if we don't get him to a doctor. Help me get him onto my horse.'

Claire eyed the approaching vehicle. 'Would it not be better to put him on the cart?'

The men exchanged glances, then shook their heads.

'Better not, lass.'

'I don't understand.'

They gave no further explanation and she could only watch in helpless bewilderment as they lifted Eden and put him on the horse. Then one mounted behind, holding the inert form so it could not fall. They had no sooner done so than the lumbering wagon drew nigh. Seeing what it contained, Claire went very pale.

'Come away, lass, it's no sight for a woman's eyes.' The man's voice was gruff but kindly. 'I'll take thee up on t' horse behind me.'

'Those men in the cart, are they…?'

'Dead? Aye. Killed last night in the attack on Harlston's machines.'

Claire drew in a deep breath and then glanced at the slumped form on the other horse, praying they had not come too late.

When Eden came round it was to the sound of voices and hurrying footsteps. Through a fog of pain he had an impression of walls and floor and ceiling. He didn't recognise the room. It had a strange and yet familiar smell too, something vaguely chemical that resisted identification and yet one he thought he ought to know. He shifted a little and winced as pain knifed through his shoulder.

'Don't try to move.'

He looked up and saw a face bending over his. His mind registered a girl—no, a young woman. Twenty years old or thereabouts.

Dark curls framed a face with high cheekbones and beautiful chiselled mouth. But it was the eyes one noticed most: huge hazel eyes deep enough to drown in. They seemed familiar somehow.

'Where am I?'

'At the doctor's house.'

His brows knit, unable to comprehend how this had occurred, but having to trust the evidence of his eyes. Before he could say more he heard another voice.

'Lift him onto the table. Gently now. That's it.'

He stifled a groan as hands raised him, felt the hard, flat surface under his back. Then he heard the same voice speak again.

'Fetch me hot water, Claire, and clean cloths.'

A swish of skirts announced her obedience to the command. Her quiet voice brought the two erstwhile assistants after her. As their footsteps receded a man's face swam into view, a pleasant clean-shaven face with clear-cut features. It was framed by light brown hair, greying a little at the sides. The eyes were blue and now staring as though they had seen a ghost. The same shock was registered in the grey eyes of the injured man.

'George,' he murmured. 'George Greystoke.'

'Marcus?' The doctor looked closer, taking in every detail of the pale face and resting on the scarred cheek. 'Marcus Edenbridge. By the Lord Harry, it *is* you. But what in the name of—?'

He broke off as a hand closed over his in silent warning.

'No, it's Mark Eden at present.'

For a moment the blue eyes narrowed and then the doctor nodded. Then he took Eden's hand in a warm grip.

'Tell me later. Right now I must get that ball out of your shoulder or the wound will fester.'

Before either of them could say more the girl returned. With her was an older woman who seemed to resemble George. They set down the bowl of water and the cloths and then came to stand by the table. George glanced round.

'Help me get his coat and shirt off, Ellen.'

They were gentle, but nevertheless Eden bit his lip against the pain. Once the task was accomplished George laid out his instruments and, selecting a probe, held it in the flame of a spirit lamp before dousing it in alcohol. He did the same with the forceps. Then he put a thick strip of leather between the patient's jaws.

'Bite down on this.'

Eden obeyed. A moment or two later the probe slid into the wound. Sweat started on his skin. Greystoke frowned in concentration and the silence stretched out. The probe went deeper. Eden's jaw clenched. Then he heard the other speak.

'Ah, here we are. Hand me the forceps, Ellen.'

Eden's fists tightened as the pain intensified until it dominated every part of his being. Then the light in the room narrowed to a single point and winked out.

Claire watched Greystoke extract a wad of bloody cloth from the wound and drop it into a metal bowl. Then he returned for the ball. It dropped into the receptacle with a metallic clink. After that he swabbed the area liberally with alcohol before covering it with a thick pad of gauze and bandaging it securely in place.

'Will he be all right?'

'Time will tell,' replied Greystoke. 'He's lost a lot of blood and is much weakened by it. There is also the chance of fever.' Then, seeing Claire's white face he gave her a gentle smile. 'But he's young and strong and with God's grace and good nursing he may recover.'

Eden was riding down a dusty road. It was hot, very hot. He could feel the burning sun on his skin and the rhythm of the horse beneath him, could hear the hoof beats and the jingling harness of the mounted column behind. The air smelled of dry earth and dung, spice and horse sweat. Above him the sky was a hard metallic blue. Then he heard shouting and the clash of swords, he saw the mêlée in the road ahead and the litter, its curtains a vivid splash of colour in the midst of all. Women screamed. Then his sword was in his hand and the column swept like a tide onto the dacoit raiders and washed them away or drowned them quite. And then there was silence and the curtains of the litter parted and he saw her: Lakshmi. For a moment he was struck dumb, unable to tear his eyes away. He thought he had never seen anything so beautiful in his life, a living dream and lovelier than a fairy-tale princess, though a princess in all truth. Unable to help himself he smiled and she smiled too, though shyly. And he spoke to her in her language and she to him in his and he offered her his protection for the remainder of her journey home. Four days and four nights. Nights of velvet starlit skies and air fragrant with jasmine and frangipani, warm nights of firelight and shadow, cushioned with silk, scented with sandalwood and patchouli; nights made for love. Four nights. That was all. He had prayed that the fourth one might last for ever, but the daylight came anyway and brought with it the end of their road. He could see her face and the sadness written there and then the yawning palace gateway that swallowed her up. He thought his heart would break.

'Lakshmi!'

Later he lay on his hard bed in the sweltering heat of the barracks, too hot even for a sheet, hearing the whine of mosquitoes in the sultry air while the sweat trickled down his skin. When he shut his eyes he saw her face, the wonderful eyes filled with love and longing. Sometimes he dreamed she was there, bending over him, speaking softly and bathing his forehead with cool cloths. But he knew it was a dream because she was lost to him, given in marriage to the rajah of a neighbouring state, a man old enough to be her grandfather.

'Lakshmi.'

And then his brother was there, shaking his head.

'Why the devil didn't you take her away while you had the chance, you fool?'

And he was right. Greville was always right. But the chance was gone now. Why had he not acted? He had broken his promise.

'I'll find a way, my love.'

He had believed it too, then. They could have found a place somewhere; they could have carved out a future together. What matter if others looked askance; what matter if there was a scandal? He was no stranger to it. But the thought of what it might mean for her had stayed him for the news would have swept like fire through the length and breadth of the Indian continent. News travelled fast there. And while he hesitated, she was lost.

'Lakshmi!'

Claire wrung out the cloth in cool water and laid it on Eden's forehead. His flesh so pale before was now flushed and hot to touch. Though his eyes were open they did not register her presence and when she spoke to him he did not hear her, but tossed in feverish dreams, speaking the names of people and places she had never heard of. Sometimes he spoke in a strange foreign language whose origin she could only guess at. Her own helplessness tormented her. What if he were to die? She owed him so much and yet knew so little about him. How had he come to be involved in that dreadful business on the moors? She had gleaned a little from the men who brought him to the house, but many questions remained unanswered.

From the beginning she had insisted on doing her share of the nursing care, taking turns with Ellen when the doctor was from home dealing with his other patients. It was the least she could do and precious little at that. It was shocking to see so strong a man laid low. Yet half a dozen others had been hurt in this affair and seven killed. Five were Harlston's men, the rest were wreckers. Yet death made no such distinctions. It mattered little whose hand fired the shot. She shivered. She knew it was illogical, but the uneasy feeling persisted that she was somehow to blame.

Lifting the cloth from his brow again, she replaced it with a
cooler one and rinsed out the first, using it to wipe the sweat from
his face and neck and the hollow above the collarbone. For a brief
moment her hand brushed the skin of his breast. Claire drew in a
sharp breath. His flesh was fiery to the touch. Hastily she poured
more cold water into the basin and rinsed the cloth again. Then
she bathed his chest as far as the line of the bandage would permit,
her gaze taking in each visible detail of the powerful torso. She
had not thought a man's body could be beautiful until now.
Beautiful and disturbing, too, for it engendered other thoughts.

She had fled her uncle's house to avoid being married to a lech-
erous old man, but what of being married to a younger one, a man
like this? If her suitor had looked and behaved like Eden, would
she have fled? Would the thought of sharing his bed repel her? Her
own flesh grew warmer then for it took but a second to know the
answer. Yet what mattered most was the freedom to choose. She
had always thought that somewhere there existed the man for her,
though she had no idea of the circumstances in which she might
meet him. What had not occurred to her was the idea that someone
else might wish to do the choosing for her. How could one find
love through another's eyes? Only the very deepest love would
ever tempt her into matrimony, the kind of love her parents had
shared. It was that or nothing and on this she knew there could be
no compromise.

Shocked by the tenor of her thoughts she tried to dismiss them,
but it proved impossible while that powerful physique was before
her demanding consideration. Her eyes returned to his breast, her
hand travelling thence to his good shoulder, moving with smooth
and gentle strokes down his arm. Beneath the fine-veined skin she
could see every detail of the curved musculature beneath, the
strong bone at elbow and wrist, the dark hair along his forearms,
the sinews in his hands. She took his hand in hers and drew the
damp cloth down his palm to the fingertips, then turned it over and

repeated the process. His hands were big yet finely shaped with long tapering fingers; hands capable of knocking a man down, or supporting a woman in need. The recollection sent a *frisson* along her spine. Disturbed by the memory for all sorts of reasons she forced it to the back of her mind. Mark Eden was a stranger who had once come to her aid. She knew nothing more about him. Perhaps she never would.

The thought was abruptly broken off by a hand closing round hers. Claire's gaze returned at once to her patient's face. His eyes were open now and apparently directed at her, though they shone with a strange inner fire.

'Mr Eden?'

He made no reply save to carry her hand to his lips. Feeling their hot imprint on her skin, she tried to extricate herself from his hold. It tightened instead and pulled her down towards the bed. She fell across him and suddenly his lips were on her neck and cheek, seeking her mouth. Claire turned her head aside, feeling the rasp of stubble and hot breath on her skin.

'Mr Eden, please!'

The words had no effect. His lips sought her ear instead and found it, his tongue exploring its curves. The touch sent a shiver through her whole body, awakening new and unexpected sensations.

'Lakshmi,' he murmured. 'Lakshmi, my love.'

Claire stiffened and pulled away, heart thumping, but Eden was no longer looking at her, his head tossing on the pillow, the grey eyes feverish and unfocussed. She realised then that he had not seen her at all, in all likelihood had no idea of her presence. In his disordered mind he was with a very different woman.

The knowledge hit her with force. It was a timely reminder of how little she knew of this man or the events that had shaped him. Detaching herself from his slackened hold, she walked a little way from the bed and took several deep breaths to try and recover her composure, her thoughts awhirl with what she had heard. It raised so many questions. Questions she knew she would never dare to ask nor had any right to. Looking at her patient now, she thought he was an enigma in every way. She would swear he was not from the labouring class whatever his dress proclaimed. His speech, his whole manner, precluded it. And yet the men in Gartside obviously knew him and he them. However, he was as unlike them as fine wine was from vinegar. On the other hand many ex-soldiers, even of the educated officer class, were forced to look for alternative employment now that hostilities with France had ceased. No doubt Eden too had had to adapt to the circumstances in which he had found himself. Those circumstances would remove him from her sphere soon enough. It was a disagreeable thought, for she could not forget how his touch had made her feel, if only for a moment. Yet it was no use to dwell on it; another woman had his heart. She could only pray that when he was recovered he would recall nothing of what had just passed.

Marcus had no idea how long he was unconscious, but the next time he came round it was still light and he was lying in a large comfortable bed between clean white sheets. For a moment his mind was blank. Then memory began to return. Turning his head, he saw a familiar figure at the bedside.

'George?'

'Welcome back.'

'How long have I been here?'

'Almost two weeks.'

'Two weeks!' He started up, only to feel a painful twinge in his shoulder.

'Have a care. It's mending, thanks to the efforts of my sister and Miss Davenport, but you're not there yet.'

Marcus lowered himself onto the pillows again. His friend was right; the savage pain was gone to be replaced with a dull ache. Clean bandages covered his injured shoulder and breast.

'Could you manage a little broth?' George inquired.

'Yes, I think I could.'

In fact, with his friend's help he managed half a bowlful.

'Excellent. Your appetite is returning. You'll soon be up and about.' The doctor replaced the dish on the side table and smiled.

For a moment neither man spoke. Then Marcus met his friend's eye.

'Thank you for all you've done, George. That's two I owe you now.'

'You owe me nothing.'

'Not so. I only hope I can repay you one day.'

'My hope is that the men responsible for the outrage are found and brought to justice.'

'You're not alone in that.'

'You were lucky, Marcus. It was a bad business. Seven men dead and six others injured. Those are the ones I know about. The wreckers took their wounded with them.'

'They had no choice. Arrest would mean a death sentence.'

'Aye, desperate men will do anything it seems.'

'Including murder.' Marcus's jaw tightened. 'They knew we were coming, George, and they knew our route. They chose a perfect spot for the ambush.'

'So it would seem.'

Seeing the other man's quizzical gaze, Marcus smiled faintly. 'You want to know how the devil I got mixed up in it, but are too polite to ask.'

His friend laughed. 'Is it that obvious?'

'You were never good at hiding your thoughts. But I do owe you an explanation.'

'I admit to curiosity.'

'When I returned from India two months ago I was summoned to Whitehall.'

'Whitehall?'

'Yes. The government is keen to break the Luddite rebellion.

That's why the rewards for information are so generous. Intelligence gathering is dangerous, though, so they knew whoever they chose would have to be experienced.' He paused. 'They sent one of their finest operatives up to Yorkshire, a man born and bred in the county who, suitably disguised, would blend in.'

'What happened?'

'He was betrayed and murdered. Shot in the back.'

'Good Lord!' George shook his head in disgust. 'But betrayed by whom?'

'That's what I mean to find out. I am his replacement.'

'You?'

'Who better? I've done this kind of work before, for the Company in India. It seems word of that got back to London.'

'But you could have refused.'

'They knew I wouldn't, though.'

'How so?'

'Because the murdered man was my brother.'

Chapter Three

For a moment George stared at him dumbfounded before the implications of the words struck home.

'Greville?'

'Yes.'

'Dear Lord, Marcus, I'm sorry. I had no idea. I read about his death in *The Times*, but the piece said he'd had a riding accident.'

'The matter was hushed up and the story fabricated. The authorities didn't want the truth made public. Greville was a government agent working under the alias of David Gifford.'

'Ye gods.' George sat down while he tried to marshal his scattered wits. 'The news of his death made quite an impact in these parts, what with Netherclough Hall being virtually on the doorstep.'

'I can imagine. It rocked London, too. Greville was well known in diplomatic circles. Besides which he left no male heir, only a young daughter.'

'Then the title and the estate pass to you.'

'Yes. Behold the new Viscount Destermere.' Marcus accompanied the words with a humourless smile. 'It is a role I never thought to have.'

'But one you will perform well nevertheless.'

'Thank you for that vote of confidence. I'll do my best, though

I never wanted to step into my brother's shoes. He was always welcome to them, for it seemed to me that my destiny lay elsewhere.'

'Circumstances have a habit of changing our plans, do they not?' said George.

'As you say.'

'So what now?'

'Officially I'm not back from India yet, but I shall have to put in an appearance soon.'

'And what of your niece?'

'Lucy is now my ward. At present she is being cared for by an elderly aunt in Essex. Hardly a suitable state of affairs. I shall bring the child to live here in Yorkshire. After all, Netherclough is her ancestral home.'

'I see.'

'After that I shall pursue my investigations.' He paused. 'The house is ideally situated for the purpose, being right in the heart of things.'

'You can't be serious. These men are dangerous, Marcus. They've murdered Greville and tried to kill you. I know they had no idea of your true identity but, even so, if they got wind of your real purpose here…'

'Let's hope they don't. But come what may I shall find out who killed my brother. It is a matter of family honour that the culprit be brought to justice. That is the very least I can do for his daughter.' He paused. 'Besides, I owe it to his memory.'

George nodded reluctantly. 'I can't blame you for wanting to discover the truth, but have a care, I beg you.'

'I'll be careful. As soon as I'm able I shall leave for London and Mark Eden can disappear for a while. Give it out that he went back to his family to convalesce.'

'Very well.'

'How much have you told your sister and Miss Davenport?'

'They don't know your real identity. Apart from that I stuck as close to the truth as possible.'

'Good. I regret the necessity for deception.'

'So do I. Ellen and I are very close and I should not like to impose on Miss Davenport.'

'When the time is right they will be informed. I owe them that much at least. In the meantime I take it I can rely on your discretion.'

'Need you ask?'

'I'm sorry.' Marcus sighed. 'That was unpardonably rude after all you've done.'

'Just promise me you won't leave until you're strong enough.'

'You have my word. Besides, at this moment the thought of a journey to London fills me with dread.' He ran a hand over his chin. 'In the meantime I need to bathe and shave. I'm beginning to feel like a pirate.'

Having spent over two weeks abed, Marcus was determined to get up and, as George provided no opposition to the idea, he did so the very next day. Though still weaker than he would have wished, the pain of the wound had almost gone and provided he made no sudden movement it felt almost normal. Somewhat reluctantly he submitted to wearing a sling for a few days, but felt it a small price to pay, all things considered. A message had been sent to his lodgings and his things were duly sent round. Looking at his reflection in the mirror, Marcus smiled wryly. The best that could be said was that the clothes were clean and serviceable and they fitted. They were hardly in the first stare of fashion. Just for a moment he saw his brother's face in the glass and it wore a pained expression. Almost he could hear his voice:

'Good Lord! What ragbag did you get those out of, Bro?'

Marcus grinned. A ragbag indeed, by Greville's standards anyway. His brother had always been both extravagant and elegant in his dress. They hadn't met since Marcus had been packed off to India ten years before. Now they would never meet again, or not in this life anyway. His jaw tightened. If it was the last thing he ever did, he would find the men responsible for that.

He finished dressing and made his way downstairs to the parlour. When he entered he discovered he was not the first there. A girl was sitting by the window, bent over the open sketchbook in her lap. For a moment he checked in surprise, sweeping her with a comprehensive gaze from the dusky curls to the toe of a small slipper peeping from beneath the hem of a primrose yellow morning gown. She looked familiar somehow. Then he remembered.

'Ah, Miss Davenport. Good morning.'

The pencil hovered in mid-air as she looked up. Claire had been so absorbed in her task that she had not heard him come in. For a moment she was rooted to the spot and could only stare. She had forgotten just how imposing a presence he was. In addition to that she was only too aware of the scene that had taken place in the sickroom earlier. Did he remember any of it?

If he was discomposed by her scrutiny it was not evident. Indeed, the cool grey eyes met and held her gaze. His expression gave nothing away. Recollecting herself quickly, she returned the greeting.

'Mr Eden, I am glad to see you so far recovered.'

'If I am, it is in no small part due to you.'

'I did very little, sir.'

'George tells me you have been a most excellent nurse. An unusual role for a young lady.'

'I…it was the least I could do.'

'It is my profound regret that I have no recollection of it.'

Claire's spirits rose in an instant. 'I'm so glad.' Then, seeing his eyebrow lift, 'I mean, so glad that I was able to help—in some small way.' Knowing herself to be on dangerous ground, and growing warm besides, she changed the subject. 'Please, won't you sit? You should avoid tiring yourself unduly.'

His lips curved in a satirical smile. Ordinarily he would have treated such advice as presumption and responded with a pithy set down, but on this occasion he said nothing. Having taken the suggestion, he watched her resume her seat. As she did so he let his gaze rest on her, quietly appraising. The sprigged muslin gown was a simple and elegant garment, but it revealed her figure to perfection. A most becoming figure, he noted. Moreover the primrose yellow colour suited her, enhancing her warm colouring and dark curls.

'What are you drawing?'

'It's just a sketch that I wanted to finish.'

'May I see it?'

'If you like, but I wouldn't want to excite your anticipation.'

She rose and handed him the book, watching as he leafed through it, wishing she were not so aware of his nearness, wishing she could divine the thoughts behind that impassive expression.

'You are too modest, Miss Davenport. These landscapes are very fine. You have a real eye for line and form.'

'You are kind, sir.'

'I speak as I find.' He glanced up at her. 'Who taught you to draw?'

'My mother, mostly. She was a talented artist. And Miss Greystoke taught me a great deal.'

'Miss Greystoke?'

Claire was silent for a moment, conscious of having given away more than she had intended. Then she upbraided herself silently. It was a trivial detail and could make no possible difference.

'Yes. She was once my governess.'

'I see.'

Marcus was intrigued, for suddenly another piece of the puzzle had fallen into place. However, he had not missed her earlier hesitation either. Why should she wish to hide the fact? Unwilling to antagonise her, but not wishing for the conversation to finish just yet, he continued to leaf casually through the book.

'These are all local views, are they not?'

'That's right. The countryside hereabouts is an artist's dream. It's so wild and beautiful.'

'And dangerous,' he replied.

Claire's cheeks grew hot as the recollections of their first encounter returned with force. It angered her that he should allude to it again for he must know it was painful in every way. However, it seemed she was wide of the mark for Eden gestured to the newspaper lying on the occasional table beside him.

'Another mill has been attacked by a mob and another loom destroyed, and all in the space of a fortnight.'

'Oh, yes.' Recovering her composure, she followed his gaze to the paper. 'Men fear for their livelihoods. So many have been laid off and those who are still in work have seen their wages cut.'

'Does that excuse murder?'

'No, of course not, but it does explain why people are so angry. It is well nigh impossible to feed a family on eight shillings a week.'

'You say that with some authority.'

'I have been with Miss Greystoke to visit several families in the town. She and her brother do what they can to help, but…' The hazel eyes met and held his. 'It is no pleasant thing to see children starving.'

'No, it is not.'

'You must have seen much poverty in India.'

'Yes.'

'Ironic, is it not, that it should exist in England too, a country we think more civilised in every way?'

There could be no mistaking the earnest tone or the sincerity in her face and he was surprised by both. In his experience young ladies of good family were usually preoccupied with balls and pretty dresses, not the problems of the poor. Would she prove to be one of those worthy but tiresome females eternally devoted to good causes?

'True,' he replied, 'but the war with France has been much to blame. Until trade can be resumed at its normal levels the situation is unlikely to change.'

'And in the meantime the mill owners lay off more men. The introduction of the steam looms only exacerbates the situation.'

'Progress cannot be resisted for ever. The wreckers will be brought to a strict accounting eventually.'

She heard the harsh note in his voice and met it with a sympathetic look. After his recent experience it was not surprising that he should be angry.

'Have you any idea who was responsible for shooting you?' she asked.

'No, but I do intend to find out.'

'You will put yourself in great danger.'

'So I apprehend.'

'I wish you would not.'

'Why?'

Again the grey gaze met hers and it was she who looked away first.

'Because I would not see you killed. There has been enough bloodshed of late.'

'I am grateful for your concern, but if bloodshed is to be prevented in future the men responsible must be brought to justice. I mean to see that they are.'

The tone, though quiet, was implacable, and for a moment there was an expression in the grey eyes that sent a shiver along her spine. Then it was gone.

'But these are disagreeable subjects,' he said. 'Let us speak of other things.'

'Such as?'

'Tell me about yourself.'

'It would hardly make for interesting conversation.'

'On the contrary,' he replied. 'I find myself curious.'

Her heart missed a beat. 'About what?'

'About why a young lady like yourself should bury herself in a place like this.'

'I am not buried here.'

'No?'

Ignoring the provocative tone, she lifted her chin.

'Certainly not. I have good friends and am kept busy enough.'

'And what do you do for your own amusement? When you are not about your good works?'

'I sketch, Mr Eden.'

'Touché!'

Claire's cheeks flushed a little, not least because she suspected he was the one in control of this situation. It was too dangerous to let it continue so, before he could question her further, she seized the initiative.

'And what of you, sir?'

In spite of himself he was amused. 'What of me?'

'Doctor Greystoke said that you and he are old friends. From your days in India.'

'That's right.'

He was glad George had told a partial truth even if he could not divulge his friend's real name. It made things easier. Anyway, he didn't want to lie to her.

'He said you were based in the same barracks at Mandrapore.'

'Did he also tell you he saved my life?'

The hazel eyes widened. 'No, he did not.' She paused. 'Won't you tell me how?'

'My men and I were ambushed by bandits and there was a fierce fight. Many of the force were killed and the rest of us left for dead. Fortunately, another contingent of soldiers happened along and took the survivors to the company barracks at Mandrapore. George Greystoke was the doctor in residence. It was thanks to his efforts that I pulled through. While I was convalescing we played a lot of chess and the friendship developed from there.'

'He said only that you and he met as a result of his work.'

'True enough, but also far too modest. Typical of George.'

She smiled. 'Yes, I believe it is. He is a good and kind man in every way. You must have been glad to see him again after so many years.'

'It was a welcome surprise, believe me. I had no idea he was here. Last time we spoke of such things his family was living in Richmond.'

'Miss Greystoke told me that he removed here after their father died.'

'I remember George left India to take care of the family's affairs at that time.'

'He was subsequently offered a position in Helmshaw,' she explained. 'When the previous doctor retired.'

'And you, Miss Davenport?' he asked. 'How came you to be in Yorkshire?'

'I told you, I came to visit Miss Greystoke.'

'Your parents permitted you to travel alone?'

The pink colour deepened in her face, but she forced herself to meet his gaze.

'My parents had no say in the matter since they are both dead.'

'I'm sorry.'

'Yes, so am I.'

He heard the note of bitterness beneath the words and was surprised since it was at variance with her normally cheerful demeanour.

'Then whom do you live with now?'

'With my father's relations.'

'And when do you return to them?'

'I…I have no set plans.'

For a moment there was a heart-thumping silence. She had told as much of the truth as possible and hoped now that he would let the subject drop. Much to her relief he seemed to accept it and merely nodded. Then he handed her the sketchbook.

'I look forward to seeing the finished picture, Miss Davenport.' She took it thankfully and retired to her seat by the window to continue the task. For a moment or two he watched and Claire, conscious of that penetrating gaze, had to force herself to ignore it. It was with relief that she heard the rustle of paper as he picked up the news sheets and began to read.

In fact, Marcus barely scanned the page in front of him. His mind was otherwise engaged. Far from accepting her words at face value he found his curiosity roused to a degree she would have found alarming. For all that she tried to pretend that there was nothing unusual in journeying alone to so remote a place as Helmshaw, he was quite undeceived. Ordinarily no respectable young woman would do so. And yet there was nothing in her that he found disreputable. Everything in her manners and appearance spoke of a gentle upbringing. She was no minx; naïve perhaps, but not of doubtful virtue. God knew, he'd had enough experience to judge. And she had spirit, enough anyway to stand up to Jed Stone. Recalling the incident and the perpetrators, Marcus felt only contempt. It was fortunate that he'd been there to intervene. She would have had no chance against such scum as those and he could no more stand by and see a woman assaulted than he could fly. Her self-control had been impressive. Most young women would have been reduced to hysterics by what had happened. Though much shaken, she had not treated him to a fit of the vapours nor even cried, though he could see she had wanted to. It was unexpected and oddly touching, serving to underline her vulnerability. At least he hadn't come too late that time.

Disturbed by his own train of thought, Marcus laid aside the paper and glanced once more at Claire who, apparently, was engrossed in her drawing. Then he rose and, having excused himself politely, left the room. Claire watched him go, feeling a strange mixture of relief and disappointment. With a conscious effort she forced her attention back to what she was doing.

* * *

Marcus stood by the garden wall, looking out at the view. The scenery was beautiful and it was pleasant to feel the sun on his face once more. The enjoyment of the moment was enhanced by the knowledge that but for good fortune and expert doctoring he might never have done so again. His health was improving daily and he would soon be able to dispense with the sling. The inaction of the past few days was beginning to chafe now. Besides, there were several matters requiring his attention. Foremost of these was the need to return to Netherclough and take up the reins of government there.

When he had left it all those years ago he had little thought to see the place again. Who could have foreseen the circumstances that would demand his return? His father would be turning in his grave if he knew that his scapegrace son was now Viscount Destermere. Not without reason either. Thinking of the wild days of his youth and the reckless pranks he had embarked upon, he knew his father had had much to bear. Perhaps if they had been closer… Marcus grimaced inwardly. After their mother's death, he and Greville were left to a succession of tutors before being packed off to school. They had seen little of their parent. It was Greville that he looked to for advice and guidance, not his father. Their last words together had been spoken in anger and yet, paradoxically, the old man might have been pleased with his son's performance since. India suited Marcus down to the ground; it provided a disciplined environment but also enough scope for an adventurous spirit. He had loved its diversity, its colour, its vibrant life. Once he had thought to see out his days there. Now fate had decreed otherwise. He had responsibilities and he must fulfil them. It was time to face down the ghosts of the past and go home.

Having come to that decision, he imparted it to his friend when they met a little later. Greystoke heard him in silence and then nodded.

'If that is what you wish to do then I will support you in any way I can.'

'Thank you. There is one more thing, George. Before I go, your sister and Miss Davenport must be told of my real identity.'

'If that is what you want.'

'I owe them that much.'

'Ellen will never breathe a word, and I believe that Miss Davenport is both sensible and discreet.'

Marcus nodded. 'It has sat ill with me to dissemble to those who have done so much towards my recovery. It's time they knew the truth.'

'Do you wish me to speak to Ellen?'

'Yes, as soon as may be. I will see Miss Davenport myself.'

He was waiting by the garden gate when Claire returned from her afternoon walk. At first she did not notice him, her attention on the steep track that led down off the hill, and her heart leapt to see the tall figure standing there. Suddenly she was conscious of her rumpled gown and windblown hair and of the fact that she was carrying her bonnet, not wearing it.

However, if he found anything amiss it was not apparent in his expression. He opened the gate to let her pass and then, offering her his arm, led her across the garden.

'Will you spare me five minutes of your time?' he asked. 'I should like to speak to you.'

'Of course.'

He found a convenient bench for them to sit on and, having seen her comfortably ensconced, favoured her with an explanation of recent events and of his identity. Claire heard him without inter-ruption. More than anything else she was conscious of things falling into place: so many questions about this man had just been answered. Listening now, she wondered how she could have mistaken Marcus Edenbridge for anything other than the aristo-

crat he was. Everything about that tall commanding presence proclaimed it, from his physical appearance to his gentlemanly behaviour in championing her cause against Jed Stone and his cronies.
It came as no surprise that he should seek out the men who killed
his brother, even at the risk of his own life.

'I apologise for the deception,' he went on, 'and I ask for your
discretion now. The true identity of Mark Eden must not become
generally known.'

'You may be assured of my silence, sir.'

'Thank you.'

She paused, dreading to ask the next question, but needing to
know the answer. 'May I ask when you intend to leave for
London?'

'In three days' time.'

'I see.' Her spirits sank. It was hard to visualise this place
without him somehow and she knew that his absence would leave
a yawning gap.

'It is a necessary stage in my plans.'

'So you can announce the return of Viscount Destermere?'

'Exactly. London will be thin of company at present, but word
will get round all the same.'

'Will you remain there, sir?'

'No. I shall travel into Essex and collect my ward before returning to Yorkshire.'

Her hand clenched around the ribbons of her bonnet. He was
coming back! Then she registered the remainder of what he had
just said.

'Your ward?'

'Yes, my brother's child, Lucy. She is six or thereabouts.'

'Have you never seen her before, then?'

'No, though, of course, I knew of her existence from
Greville's letters.'

'Of course.'

'Her mother died when Lucy was born.'

'Poor little girl. She has lost a great deal in her short life. Six is too young to be orphaned.'

For a moment he regarded her shrewdly. 'Yes, you are right.'

'There is never a right time to lose one's parents, but children are so vulnerable.'

'Indeed they are.'

'I am sure she will welcome some stability after all the disruption she has endured.'

'In any event, I shall give her a home for as long as she needs it.' He smiled and for a moment the grey eyes warmed. 'When I return to Netherclough Hall I hope to have the honour of receiving you there, Miss Davenport, along with Dr and Miss Greystoke.'

At those words, Claire felt her heart miss a beat. She would see him again after all. Almost immediately she told herself not to be so foolish as to refine upon it. He was merely being polite. He owed the Greystokes such an invitation. If she was included, it was because good manners demanded that he did not slight their friend. Once honour was satisfied they would have nothing more to do with each other. The man she had known as Mark Eden was gone, replaced by Viscount Destermere, one who was so far her social superior as to make even the thought of such a connection truly laughable. That was reality. He belonged to another world, a world of wealth, position and power. One day in the not-too-distant future he would marry—a young woman of his own class who would provide the heirs to continue his line. That too was reality and she acknowledged it. All that had happened here would one day be relegated to the back of his memory and she with it. It was an oddly dispiriting thought.

Chapter Four

Lying in bed later that night, Claire found herself unable to sleep for her mind was racing, turning over all she had learnt. It turned too on her situation. This interlude with the Greystokes had been a welcome respite from trouble but, having been here nearly a month, she did not deceive herself that it could continue. They had been more than kind, but she could not impose on them much longer. Besides which, the uneasy thought persisted that her aunt might have kept Ellen's letters and might remember them now. Her uncle had been made to look a fool, a situation that would not long endure if he so much as suspected there was a remedy. She must find a secure position and soon, a place her uncle would never think of looking.

And then the germ of an idea occurred to her. An idea that was both wild and wonderful together. Could it work? Would she dare suggest it? And if she did, what would be the response? Almost she could see the Viscount's expression, the cold reserve returning to those grey eyes. He could be an intimidating figure when he chose. Would he consider it the greatest piece of presumption? Would he even listen? Claire bit her lip. There was only one way to find out: she must seek an opportunity to speak with him alone and then ask him.

The first part of her plan proved quite easy; the following morning Dr Greystoke went out on his rounds at ten and Ellen left to call on someone in the town. Their noble guest was ensconced in the parlour, perusing the newspaper. Hearing the door open, he glanced up and, perceiving Claire, rose from his chair and made her an elegant bow.

'Miss Davenport.' His gaze swept her from head to toe. 'No need to ask if you are well.'

'Thank you, sir.'

Not knowing what else to say, she sat down on the edge of the couch and watched him resume his seat. She swallowed hard. It had all seemed so easy when she was lying in bed last night, but now that the moment had come it was a different matter. There was a knot in her stomach and her mouth felt dry. For all his polished manners he seemed so commanding a presence, so remote from her in every way. How could she have presumed to think he would agree to her request? And yet… She closed her eyes a moment and saw her uncle's face. Could she risk his finding her because she had lacked the resolution even to try to put her plan into action? Claire lifted her chin.

'May I speak to you, sir?'

He laid aside the paper. 'Of course.'

She had his attention. It was now or never. She took a deep breath.

'I would like a position in your household…as governess to your ward.' Before he could say a word she hurried on. 'My education is good. I can speak French and Italian and write a fine hand. I know about arithmetic and the use of the globes. I can play the pianoforte and sing and sew and draw. Miss Greystoke can attest to my family background and character. And I like children. I used to teach my younger cousins.'

It was out. She had said it. With thumping heart Claire waited. For a moment he did not move or speak though the grey gaze never left her face, and under their cool, appraising stare she felt her cheeks grow warm.

'I confess I am surprised, Miss Davenport,' he said then. 'Not by the quality of your education, but by your desire to become a governess.'

'As I told you, my parents are dead and I must earn my living, sir.'

'And what of your other relations? The ones with whom you live.'

'They cannot provide for me indefinitely. I always knew that I should have to find a suitable position one day.'

'And why do you think this suitable?'

'Your ward is of excellent family, she is motherless and she needs someone who will look after her.'

'Do you think that I will not look after her?'

'No, of course not. I never meant to imply any such thing.' She paused. 'But a young girl also needs a woman's presence.'

'True. How old are you, Miss Davenport?'

Her colour deepened but she met his eye. 'I am almost one and twenty.'

'Are you not a little young for the role?'

'By no means. I know how it feels to lose one's parents and how important it is for a child to feel secure, to know that there will always be a sympathetic female presence she can turn to for guidance, someone who will always have her best interests at heart, someone who will really care.'

It came out with quiet passion. In fact, it was not just the tone but the words that took him aback for he could not doubt the sincerity of either. He knew she was speaking from experience. Had her own life been unhappy after the death of her parents? Had that anything to do with the relatives she spoke of? His curiosity mounted and with it the feeling that there was something he wasn't being told.

'My estate at Netherclough is remote. Apart from the local village there is no society for miles around. How would you bear the solitariness of the place?'

'I should bear it very well, sir. I was born in the country and spent the first thirteen years of my life there. Thirteen happy years.'

He heard the wistful note and was unexpectedly touched by it. Even so he felt the need to probe a bit further.

'And when your parents died you went to live with your father's relations.'

'Yes.' Her heart began to beat a little faster.

'And your uncle resides in…?'

'Northamptonshire.'

'You *are* a long way from home, aren't you?'

Not far enough, she thought. Aloud she replied, 'Oh, not so far. Stage coach travel is improving all the time, is it not?'

'Is it?'

Claire could have kicked herself. Of course, a man like this would never use stage coaches. Why would he, with a stable of fine horses and numerous carriages at his beck and call?

'Surely your uncle would be most alarmed by your failure to return home,' he continued.

'Not at all, sir, since I should write and inform him of the altered circumstances.' It was a blatant lie but it couldn't be helped. She went on, 'Besides, he would be the last person to stand in my way. He told me so himself.' That part was true at any rate.

'I see. And what sort of salary would you require?'

This was something she had not considered and for a moment was thrown. What did governesses earn? Knowing a response was required of her she plucked a figure out of thin air.

'Thirty pounds per annum.'

'You set a high price on your skills, Miss Davenport.'

Her cheeks went scarlet. However, if he expected her to retract he was mistaken. Instead her chin lifted.

'My services are worth the money, sir.'

'That has yet to be determined.'

'Then you will employ me?'

If she had hoped not to betray too much eagerness she was wide of the mark. He could see it in her face. Moreover, it was underlain by something akin to desperation. She really wanted this job. Thinking carefully, he weighed up the possibility. His ward was certainly going to need a governess and that was a serious responsibility since whoever filled the role must fit the child to take her place in society one day. Such a person must be intellectually capable and of unimpeachable reputation. Miss Davenport, though young, was well educated and evidently of good family. George and his sister spoke well of her. Though he sensed a mystery somewhere, what did he actually know against her? Nothing, he decided. In spite of the somewhat unusual manner of her arrival in Yorkshire, he believed her reputation to be good. She was courageous; she had come to his aid when he needed it. It was clear that she needed the situation and he was in a position to help.

He remembered all too clearly how it felt when one could do nothing. For a second Lakshmi's face swam into his mind. Could he abandon another young woman to her fate? The world was a hard place when one did not have the protection of wealth. Claire Davenport was not asking for money; she was asking for the means to earn it and he respected that. Did she not deserve a chance? He threw her a cool, appraising look and made up his mind.

'Very well,' he said. 'Consider yourself hired—for a probationary period of three months. If we are both satisfied with the situation at the end of that time, the post will become permanent.'

For a second she wasn't sure that she had heard him correctly. Then it sank in and fierce joy swept through her.

'Thank you, sir. You won't regret it, I promise you.'

'See to it that I don't, Miss Davenport.' The grey eyes locked with hers. 'I give you fair warning that I expect the highest standards in every respect. If they are not met the arrangement will be terminated immediately. Is that clear?'

'Very clear, sir.'

'As long as we understand each other.'

Claire left him shortly afterwards and, unable to contain her elation, went into the garden. Once there she let out a whoop of joy. Three months! Three months to prove herself. And she would prove herself! She would try by every means in her power to make a success of this. Her uncle would never think of looking for her at Netherclough, and by the time her probation was complete she would have reached her majority. She would be free.

Alone in the parlour the Viscount stood awhile, gazing down into the fire. He was committed now. Time would tell whether the decision was the right one. Yet there was something about Claire Davenport that he found hard to dismiss: beneath that outward show of spirit was an underlying vulnerability. Moreover, he acknowledged that she was a very pretty girl. No doubt his ward would prefer someone young and attractive as a governess. What really mattered, of course, was competence. That would become evident soon enough. Three months would demonstrate whether his decision had been the right one or not.

Two days later he prepared to leave for London, having first taken his leave of his hosts and of Claire.

'We shall meet again very soon, Miss Davenport. In the meantime is there anything I can bring you from the capital?'

It had never occurred to her that he would even ask and the question threw her.

'I thank you, no, sir.'

'You must be the first woman ever to say so,' he replied, regarding her with the familiar cool appraisal that caused a fluttering sensation in her stomach. 'I half expected a lengthy shopping list.'

'Then you have been spared it.'

'So it would seem. I suppose I should be grateful.'

Thinking of the little money remaining to her, she knew there was no possibility of indulging herself, even if she had thought of it.

'I expect to be gone for two weeks or so,' he went on. 'I shall inform the housekeeper at Netherclough when to expect me. At that time I shall arrange for a carriage to collect you.'

It was an attention she had not expected.

'Thank you, sir.'

'It is my wish that you should be there when I return so that you can become acquainted with my ward from the outset. I think we should start as we mean to go on.'

'As you wish, sir.'

'Until then, Miss Davenport.'

He favoured her with a bow and then was gone. Watching his departing figure, she was conscious of a strange sense of loss.

The feeling stayed with her in the days that followed. He was such a charismatic figure that when he was absent the house felt different, not less friendly or less welcoming exactly and yet still lacking. Although she made every attempt to keep busy, Claire found herself counting the days until she should be able to take up her new position. It represented a first step into a larger world, one that only a few short weeks ago she could never have thought of entering.

Eventually the day came, a fortnight later, when a carriage arrived to transport her to Netherclough Hall. With very real regret she said farewell to Ellen and George Greystoke and thanked them for their kindness. Like his sister, George seemed genuinely affected to see her go.

'I wish you all good fortune in your new life, Miss Davenport,' he said as they stood together by the gate.

Ellen smiled. 'I hope you will be very happy, my dear.'

'I'm sure I shall be,' Claire replied. 'I'll write as soon as I can and tell you how I go on.'

'I shall look forward to that.' She took Claire's hand for a moment and gazed very earnestly into her face. 'You know that you can always come to me if you need to, my dear.'

'Thank you.'

Claire gave her friend a last hug and climbed into the carriage. A liveried footman put up the steps and closed the door. As the vehicle pulled away she leaned from the window to wave. Only when her friends were out of sight did she settle back into her seat and look around her. The carriage was larger and more opulent than anything she had ever seen. Furthermore it was so well sprung that even the worst bumps in the road went almost unnoticed. The four bays that pulled it were spirited and swift, as different as could be from her uncle's carriage horses. He could never have afforded any as fine as these. Never would she have expected to ride in such style or comfort.

Glancing at the valise beside her, she was forcefully reminded that it contained all her worldly possessions. If the footman had been surprised by the lack of baggage, he was too well trained to betray it. Perhaps he had assumed her trunks would be following later. She smiled ruefully. A governess had no need of fine gowns. As long as her appearance was clean and neat it would suffice. A new chapter of her life was beginning and for the first time she had a measure of control over how it would unfold.

For a while she was so wrapped in thought that she paid no heed to the country through which they were passing, but eventually it impinged on her consciousness again and she found herself curious to see Netherclough Hall. By repute it was a very grand old house and set in a large attractive park. That at least would afford long walks in the fresh air and some pleasant scenes to sketch. For all the Viscount's doubts she had no fear of solitude and had never minded her own company.

The thought brought her employer to mind again. It seemed strange to think of him in those terms but she knew she must accustom herself to it. Mark Eden was gone. She was entering the service of Viscount Destermere. There could be no hint of earlier familiarity. That had belonged to a set of extraordinary circumstances—circumstances that must never be alluded to in any way. It was not to be supposed that she would see very much of her employer anyway. Probably their paths would cross but rarely. The knowledge gave her a strange pang.

She was drawn from her thoughts when, at length, the carriage turned in through large wrought-iron gates that gave onto a long driveway between mature chestnut trees. Beyond it, rolling green parkland stretched away to wooded hillsides. With excitement and trepidation Claire craned eagerly for a view of the house. When it came into view round a bend in the drive she drew in a sharp breath. Netherclough Hall was an imposing residence built of grey stone, nestled in a fold of the hills. From its numerous chimneys and crenellated walls to the stone mullions and ancient porch it was in every way a nobleman's residence. Beneath its sloping grounds a river ran through trees among the water meadows.

The Viscount had not lied when he said his estate was remote, but far from feeling concerned Claire knew only a sense of satisfaction at the location. It was definitely the last place her uncle would ever think of looking for her.

Presently the carriage drew up outside the stone porch beyond which was a great iron-clamped door. Another footman admitted her to a flagged hallway hung with racks of antlers and ancient weapons. A great carved-oak staircase led to the upper floors. Claire looked round, trying to take it in, but just then footsteps announced the arrival of the housekeeper, a plump middle-aged woman in a neat grey gown and lace cap who introduced herself as Mrs Hughes. When the courtesies had been observed she offered to show Claire to her room.

This proved to be a light and pleasant chamber at the rear of the house, overlooking the gardens and the park. Comfortably furnished, it appeared to have been newly decorated. Elegant blue-and-gold hangings and thick rugs added a feeling of cosiness and luxury. A cheerful fire burned in the grate.

'I hope everything is satisfactory,' said Mrs Hughes.

'It's beautiful.'

The housekeeper smiled, clearly pleased by the reaction. 'I hope you will be happy here, Miss Davenport.'

'I'm sure I shall. Thank you.'

'Is the rest of your luggage to follow, miss?'

Claire knew a moment of acute embarrassment. 'No. Everything is here.'

The only indication of the older woman's surprise was a brief silence. Then she smiled again.

'Well, then, perhaps you would care to take some refreshment after your journey?'

'That would be most kind.'

Having removed her bonnet and spencer, Claire followed the housekeeper to a small parlour. A footman appeared a short time later with a tray. Mrs Hughes poured the tea and offered her guest a slice of seed cake. Thus fortified, Claire began to relax.

'This is a beautiful house,' she observed. 'Have you been here long, Mrs Hughes?'

'Thirty-five years. I took up my post in Lord Destermere's time. The older Viscount Destermere, I mean.'

'I see.'

'His sons were mere children then, of course. Who could have foreseen what tragedy would follow?' She shook her head. 'It will be good to have this house inhabited again.'

'I imagine it will.'

'The estate needs attention too, after all these months. Lord Destermere will find himself busy enough, I have no doubt.'

'Yes, I'm sure he will.'

'Not that anyone expected to see him again after he was packed off to India.'

'Packed off?'

'There was some scandal involving a young woman, I believe.

Someone his father considered unsuitable. I never really knew the details.' She leaned forward confidentially. 'Master Marcus and his brother were rather wild in their youth. I put it down to them losing their mother when they were boys. Their father took her death hard and became very withdrawn. Just between ourselves, Miss Davenport, he didn't take the interest in his sons that he might have.'

Claire listened with close attention for the words stripped away some of the mystery surrounding her new employer. The story saddened her, too. Children were so vulnerable, as she had good cause to know. It could be no wonder that two bewildered little boys should look to their father for support and guidance. When their parent failed to provide it or show any interest they must have sought to get his attention in the only way they knew how.

'They got up to enough mischief as boys, but that was nothing compared to what happened once they came down from Cambridge and went to London. They got in with a very fast set indeed. Gaming, drinking, horse racing, opera dancers. You name it.'

'That must have grieved their father.'

'There were some terrible rows, believe me,' replied Mrs Hughes. 'However, Master Greville calmed down a great deal when he married. In fact, it was the making of him.'

'Was his wife very beautiful?'

'Oh, yes, and so accomplished. The toast of London. He was very much in love with her.'

'How sad that she should have died so young.'

'Yes, indeed. He was almost distracted by her loss. For some time he couldn't even bear to look at his infant daughter.'

Hearing those words, Claire felt a sudden chill. Had history repeated itself? Her heart went out to Lucy, and for the first time the burden of her new responsibility was brought home to her.

'I really thought all would be well again after he inherited the title, but first there was the business of his wife's untimely demise and then the dreadful news of his own death.'

'But now Lord Destermere is returned. Perhaps all may yet be well,' replied Claire.

'I truly hope so.' Mrs Hughes set down her cup and saucer. 'And now perhaps you would like me to show you around the house?'

'Indeed I should, if it is no trouble.'

'No trouble at all, miss. Besides, it's such a rambling old place that it's easy to get lost.'

And so there followed a guided tour. The reception rooms were beautiful, and there was a library, which Claire made a mental note to revisit as soon as possible, as well as the private apartments and a long gallery lined with family portraits. The last room they visited was the schoolroom. It was spacious and light and it too had been recently redecorated. Moreover, it was supplied with rugs, table and chairs, two small desks and a blackboard and easel. A shelf held a selection of old books and toys and an ancient rocking horse stood in one corner. There was also a fireplace with logs ready laid. Claire saw it with some relief, recalling the chilly room where she and her cousins had taken their lessons under Miss Hardcastle's exacting eye. This was cosy in comparison, though a glance at the books revealed they were too advanced, and thus unsuitable for a young child.

'We expect His Lordship tomorrow,' said Mrs Hughes.

Claire's heart gave a peculiar lurch. Tomorrow. She regarded the prospect with mingled excitement and trepidation. When she had told the Viscount that she liked children it had been the truth, but her experience of them was limited. Could she do the job? Could she give an orphaned child the care needed? Then she thought back to her own childhood and the benevolent influence of Ellen Greystoke. Surely those precepts would be good ones to follow, comprised as they were of firmness and kindness, always backed by sincere interest. Please God, she thought, let me get it right.

Chapter Five

It was therefore with mixed feelings that Claire awaited the Viscount's return the following day. In the event, it was late afternoon when a large and handsome carriage drew up before the house. From the resulting bustle among the servants it was clear who had arrived. Hastily smoothing her skirts she hurried to the hallway where Mrs Hughes was already waiting. Uncertain of what to expect and unwilling to push herself forward Claire remained in the background. And then he was there, a tall elegant figure in a travelling cape and high-crowned beaver hat. At the sight of him her heart began to beat a little faster. His presence seemed to fill the room somehow as though the house had been waiting only for his arrival to seem complete. In that moment she knew how much she had missed him. The realisation was disturbing, the sentiment inappropriate. Forcing her expression into what she hoped was a becoming calm she drew in a deep breath. Marcus, looking round the hallway, perceived her at once, the grey eyes missing no detail of her appearance from the dark curls to the simple sprigged muslin gown. She looked as neat as wax, he thought, favouring her with a bow.

'Well met, Miss Davenport. May I introduce your new charge?' He glanced down at the small figure at his side. 'This is my ward, the Honourable Lucy Edenbridge. Lucy, this is Miss Davenport who is to be your new governess.'

The child dropped a polite curtsy and stared at Claire with big blue eyes. She was clad in a blue cloak, and a straw bonnet partially concealed light brown curls. In one small hand she was clutching a toy. She looked lost somehow, and a little timid.

Claire smiled at her. 'Hello, Lucy. What a lovely doll.'

The child made no reply and lowered her eyes. Marcus glanced down and surveyed her keenly.

'You should answer, child, when you are spoken to.'

Lucy's cheeks reddened, but still she remained silent. Marcus raised an eyebrow. Fearing that the scene would escalate, Claire cut in.

'It's all right. This has been a big change and it will take her a while to find her feet and grow accustomed to all the new faces around her.'

'You may be right,' he replied.

Claire bent down so that she was on Lucy's level. 'What do you call your doll?'

There followed another silence. Then, very quietly, 'Susan.'

'That's a good name. It suits her very well. Shall we take Susan upstairs and show her where her room is? She must be feeling tired after such a long journey.'

After a moment the child nodded. Claire held out her hand.

'Come, then.'

Lucy looked up at her uncle and he nodded.

'That's right. You go along with Miss Davenport.'

A small hand stole tentatively into Claire's. The Viscount caught her eye.

'I will speak with you later, Miss Davenport. There are various points we need to discuss.' He paused. 'In the meantime, Mrs Hughes will send up a tray for Lucy. It has indeed been a long journey and she is tired. An early night is in order, I think.'

'Yes, sir.'

As Claire led the child away she was conscious of the penetrating gaze that followed them to the stairs.

In fact, he had been quite right. By the time Lucy was ensconced in her room and had eaten some supper she was pale with fatigue so Claire undressed her and put her to bed. As she tucked the sheet in she was aware that the child watched her with solemn, sleepy eyes.

Claire smiled. 'Would you like to have Susan with you?'

This elicited a nod. Retrieving the doll from a nearby chair, Claire handed it over and watched as it was tucked carefully under the covers. Then she gently brushed the child's face with her hand.

'Goodnight, dear. Sleep well.'

Within a very short time Lucy was asleep, clearly worn out by the journey and perhaps too by the anxiety of altered circumstances. As she looked at the forlorn little figure in the big bed her heart went out to Lucy. How lonely and frightened the child must be. She knew how it felt to be alone in the world and cast on the mercy of others, and that was at thirteen, not six years of age.

She remained in the room until she was quite certain that Lucy was fast asleep, and instructed the maid to leave a night light burning. If by some chance the child did wake up, at least she wouldn't be on her own in a strange place in the dark.

Having seen to her charge's immediate needs, Claire made her way to the drawing room, mindful that her employer had asked to speak to her. When she entered he was standing by the hearth. He had been leaning on the mantel, staring down into the flames, but hearing her come in he glanced up and then straightened.

'Ah, Miss Davenport. How is my ward?'

'Asleep, sir. As you suspected, she really was very tired.'

'Yes, I imagine she was. It was a long journey and there has been all the upheaval attendant on her removal. What she needs now is some stability.' He regarded her keenly. 'I take it that you have seen the nursery.'

'Yes, sir.'

He smiled faintly. 'It has been some years since I was there, and is no doubt lacking in some essentials. You may have whatever you need for the discharge of your duties. Money is no object. Just tell me what you want and I'll see that you get it.'

Somewhat taken aback, she thanked him. 'There are a few things missing,' she admitted, 'chiefly books suitable for a child of Lucy's age.'

'That will be rectified as soon as possible. In the interim she needs some time to grow accustomed to her new surroundings. It will all be very strange and frightening. Let her have plenty of fresh air and exercise, Miss Davenport. Then introduce her lessons gradually.'

'As you wish, sir.'

'This is her home now and I want her to feel at ease here.'

For the second time Claire was taken aback for there could be no mistaking the sincerity with which he spoke. There was, besides, real compassion in the orders he had given and she was touched.

'I will do my best to see that she does, sir.'

'I am sure you will.' He paused, surveying her keenly. 'And what of you, Miss Davenport? Does your room meet with your approval?'

'Oh, yes. It is beautiful.'

Again she found herself caught unawares. She knew enough of life to realise that employers usually gave little thought to the comfort of their servants.

'Good. If you find you need anything else, tell Mrs Hughes and she will arrange it.'

'Thank you. That is most kind.'

For a moment there was silence and she felt acutely aware of that disconcerting grey gaze. Then he smiled.

'Then if there is nothing else I will not detain you.'

She dropped a graceful curtsy and retraced her steps to the door, pausing briefly to look over her shoulder. However, he had turned back towards the fire and seemed to have dismissed her from his mind. Claire opened the door quietly and slipped away. On returning to her room she sat down and began to write the promised letter to Ellen.

* * *

In the days that followed she heeded her instructions. The early autumn weather was pleasant, so it was no hardship to take her young charge out of doors. Besides which it gave Claire a chance to talk to her and find out more about her. Although she was shy and her education had been somewhat disrupted due to circumstances, Lucy was not unintelligent and had an enquiring mind. She was quick to learn the names of the flowers and trees and living creatures they encountered on these walks. When told a story she was an avid listener. Little by little Claire added to their activities, always taking care to vary them and to try to make them interesting.

She had not expected to see much of her employer at all, but he occasionally came to the nursery. One day, when teaching Lucy her letters, she looked up to see the tall figure in the doorway. Realising who it was, she felt her heartbeat quicken. Following her gaze, Lucy saw him too and paused in her task, regarding him uncertainly.

He smiled down at her. 'How are you today, Lucy?'

She reddened and lowered her eyes. 'Very well, thank you, Uncle Marcus.'

'What have you been doing?'

Lucy moved her hand so that he could see the copybook in which she had been working. He surveyed it closely and the letters written in large childish script.

'Well done,' he said then. 'You're making good progress, I see.'

Lucy's blush deepened. Over her head he exchanged glances with Claire.

'Well done, Miss Davenport.'

She had half expected to hear irony in the tone, but there was none and her own face grew a little warmer.

'She is quick to learn,' she replied.

'I'm pleased to hear it. I should not like my niece to be an ignoramus.'

'I can assure you, sir, she is far from being anything of the sort.'

'Good.' Marcus looked down at his niece. 'Now, Lucy, copy out all those letters again. I wish to speak to Miss Davenport.'

Obediently the child returned to her task. Seeing her once again employed, he drew Claire aside.

'The books and materials you asked for have been ordered,' he said. 'They should be here within the week. Is there anything else you require?'

'Not at present, thank you.'

'If you think of anything later, be sure to let me know.' He paused. 'Has the child's appetite returned? Is she sleeping properly?'

'Yes, sir, on both counts.'

'Does she seem to be settling down?'

'I think she is beginning to, yes, but it is likely to take a while before she really feels at home.'

'Yes, I suppose it will.' For a moment he surveyed her in silence. 'Well, then, I won't detain you further.' Throwing another glance towards his niece, he took his leave of them.

She watched the departing figure a moment and then went back to see what Lucy was doing. The child looked up, regarding her quizzically.

'What's a nigneraymus, Miss Davenport?'

Claire bit back a smile. 'A very stupid person. Not like you at all.'

'Oh.' Lucy digested the information thoughtfully. 'If I learn all my letters, will Uncle Marcus like me better?'

'He likes you now.'

'Does he?'

'Of course. Did he not bring you here to live with him?'

'Yes.'

'Well, then.'

'It's just that I don't see him very much.'

'Your uncle is very busy,' Claire replied. 'Netherclough is a big estate and it takes up a lot of his time.'

Lucy nodded slowly. 'Papa was always busy, too.'

'Gentlemen often are, but it doesn't mean they don't care for you.' She put a reassuring hand on the child's shoulder and smiled, hoping that what she said was true.

As she and Lucy went for their afternoon walk Claire pondered the matter. She knew that after months without a master, Netherclough really did need Marcus's close attention. Very often she would see him ride out with Mr Fisk, the land agent, or else he would be closeted in the study with piles of paperwork. So far as the physical welfare of his niece was concerned he had shown a great deal of consideration and compliance. She lacked for nothing. The same was true of her education: the list of books and schoolroom materials Claire had submitted had not been questioned. It seemed he trusted her judgement and was prepared to back it financially. Of course, as he had intimated, money was no object. If Mrs Hughes was to be believed, the Edenbridge family was among the wealthiest in the country. However, when it came to the child's emotional needs the case was rather different. Marcus spent very little time with her, most of it comprising short visits to the nursery, as today. Although his manner showed interest, he seemed to hold himself aloof somehow as though, having seen to all the material aspects of his guardianship, he was absolved from deeper involvement. She hoped that, as time went on and matters fell into a routine, he might be able to spend more time with Lucy.

She had been so absorbed in thought that she hadn't paid much attention to the direction of their steps that afternoon, but realised now that once again Lucy had brought them to the paddock where several horses were grazing. It was clear at a glance that they were hunters, huge, powerful beasts all sixteen hands or more at the shoulder. Unperturbed by its size, Lucy was feeding one of them through the fence with handfuls of grass. It was clear that the child knew to hold her hand out flat and that she had no fear of the great teeth or the long tongue that whisked the grass away. As the horse munched she stroked its nose gently.

'You like the horses, don't you?' said Claire then.

Lucy nodded.

'Shall we find the head groom and ask if we can have a look around the stables?'

Lucy turned round, her expression animated. 'Oh, yes, please, Miss Davenport.'

And so they spent a delightful hour walking along the row of stalls and loose boxes and admiring the beautiful animals they encountered there. It was immediately clear to Claire that the Viscount and his late brother had a good eye for horseflesh. The head groom was Mr Trubshaw, a stocky, grey-haired individual with a weathered face and a thick Yorkshire accent, and he possessed a fund of knowledge about his charges. He told Lucy the name of each horse and a little of its history. She listened avidly, committing all the details to memory, and asked questions in her turn. Seeing her interest was genuine, he warmed to her very quickly and soon the two were chatting like old friends. Claire watched thoughtfully. Trubshaw had accomplished more in an hour with the child than Marcus had managed in weeks. Lucy was in seventh heaven here and that knowledge gave her an idea.

Later that evening, when Lucy was in bed, Claire inquired of Mather where His Lordship was to be found. The butler directed her to the small salon. It was the same room he had interviewed her in before, when they had spoken about books and teaching equipment.

Marcus was seated in a chair by the fire, but he rose as she entered. Claire caught her breath. He was dressed in cream-coloured breeches and a coat of claret velvet over immaculate linen. A single fob hung from his waistcoat. His hands were innocent of adornment save for one gold signet ring. It was a simple costume, but she thought it would have been hard to find one more elegant or better suited to such a powerful physique.

'Good evening, Miss Davenport.'

She replied to the greeting and took the offered chair.

'How may I help you?'

'I wish to speak to you about Lucy?'

The dark brows twitched together. 'Is something wrong? Is she ill? Has she been misbehaving?'

'No, nothing like that. I wanted to ask if there is a pony in your stables that she might ride.'

'A pony?'

'Yes, the horses are all too big, you see.'

Undeceived by the innocent tone, he threw her an eloquent look. 'Is the child keen to ride?'

'Yes. I believe she has a real affinity with horses.'

She told him about the visit to the stables. He heard her in silence, thinking carefully as he did so. It was not an outlandish request. Horsemanship was one of the accomplishments expected of a young lady of Lucy's station, and it was healthy exercise besides.

'There is nothing in the stable that is suitable at present,' he replied, 'but I am sure that a pony could be found.'

'I know that Lucy would be delighted.'

'I'll speak to Trubshaw in the morning. He knows every horse within a twenty-mile radius of Netherclough.'

'He is most knowledgeable,' she replied.

'Yes, he is. It was he who taught me and Greville to ride. He'll be an ideal teacher for Lucy, too.'

'I have no doubt he will.' Claire took a deep breath. 'However, I was hoping that perhaps you might go out with her sometimes, sir.'

The grey gaze came to rest on her face while his own assumed an expression of hauteur. Feeling her cheeks grow warmer, Claire hurried on before her courage failed her.

'I know you have been very busy since your return, but this would provide a good opportunity for you to spend some time with the child.'

'What are you implying, Miss Davenport?'

'Nothing. It's just…'

'Just what?'

'It's just that I thought it might bring you together more.'

'Did you indeed?'

'I do not mean to criticise,' she said, 'but it is true that you have seen very little of the child so far and, well, she notices, sir.'

The grey eyes grew as cool as his tone. 'You think I neglect her?'

'No, of course not. Well, not deliberately anyway.'

'So you do think so.'

She swallowed hard. 'The only reason I said anything is because Lucy asked me if you liked her.'

'And what did you say, may I ask?'

'That I was sure you did.'

'How very reassuring to have your support,' he replied. 'However, it is not your place to discuss me with my niece.'

'She asked the question, sir, and I answered it. I intended no disrespect in doing so.'

For a moment he was silent. Almost she could feel the anger radiating off him and her heart sank. She had spoken too frankly and antagonised him. Perhaps now she had made the situation worse.

'If I have caused offence, I beg your pardon, sir.'

'As well you should. In future you will confine yourself to your duties, Miss Davenport, instead of interfering in matters that do not concern you.' He got to his feet. 'That will be all.'

Uncomfortably aware of having made a false step, she rose from her chair and dropped a curtsy before beating a retreat, aware as she did so of the fierce hawk-like gaze that followed her every step of the way. Only when she was safely in the hall did she let out the breath she had been holding. Her cheeks burned. How angry he had been. Yet in spite of that she could not regret having said it, even if he did ignore the words.

After she left him Marcus poured himself a glass of brandy and took a deep swig. Claire's assessment had been quite correct: he was angry. Angry with her for presuming to tell him his duty and angry with himself because he knew the words were merited. It was true he had been very busy since his return; Greville's death had left a vacuum and there were numerous matters requiring his attention. However, he realised now that in part they had been an excuse for avoiding his young niece. Having spent the last ten years soldiering, he was unused to children and unfamiliar with their needs. The journey from Essex had been more difficult than he had anticipated, for the child was withdrawn and shy of him. Though he spoke to her with the utmost gentleness he had hardly been able to get half a dozen words out of her. He had tried telling her stories about the animals in India that he thought she might enjoy but, though she heard him quietly, she had offered no response. Moreover, she ate very little and slept badly. Clearly the disruption of recent months was taking its toll on her. More than once he had been overwhelmed with a sense of inadequacy.

Claire had known what to say, he recalled. From the first she had instinctively known how to get past the barrier that Lucy had been protecting herself with. He sighed. He had spoken more harshly than he should have done, but her words had touched a nerve. At the same time, he acknowledged, she was offering him an opportunity. Could it work?

After the unfortunate interview in the salon, Claire had seen Marcus only twice in the following week, and that was when he had come to the schoolroom. As usual he had stayed only a short time, just long enough to see what his niece was doing and to ask about her progress. When he had spoken to the child it was always in a tone of quiet encouragement, but this had never elicited more than a few shy words from Lucy. Seeing it, Claire had been saddened. Were the two of them destined to remain polite strangers?

She had said nothing at all to Lucy about the matter of a pony. Marcus had promised to speak to Trubshaw, but would he remember? He *was* very busy. She wouldn't raise the child's hopes only to see them dashed. Nor would she raise the subject again with Marcus himself. It was too loaded a topic now. He had made no reference to their conversation and his manner to her was one of polite aloofness. It seemed that she and Lucy were both to be relegated to the periphery of his affairs.

It came as a surprise, therefore, when a footman came to the nursery to say that His Lordship desired Miss Davenport and Miss Lucy to attend him in the stable yard after luncheon. Hearing the summons, Claire felt the first faint stirrings of hope. Had he kept his promise?

'Why does Uncle Marcus want us to go to the stables, Miss Davenport?'

'I don't know, dear. We must go and find out.'

When they arrived, the Viscount was already there, talking to Trubshaw. Seeing their approach, he greeted them both and then nodded to the groom. The man promptly disappeared into the stable and emerged a few minutes later leading a grey pony. Understanding the implication, Claire felt her heart soar even as her critical eye took in the details of the new arrival. A sturdy, shaggy little creature, the pony stood approximately twelve hands high. He had a bushy mane and tail and gentle brown eyes. A perfect choice, she thought, and her face lit with a smile for she could not but remember when she had been given her first pony. The memory was bittersweet.

Beside her Lucy's eyes widened.

'He's wonderful, isn't he, Miss Davenport?'

'Yes, he is.'

'May I ride him one day, do you think?'

'You had better ask your uncle,' she replied.

For a moment her gaze met his. Then Marcus looked down at the child and smiled. 'Of course you can ride him. He's yours.'

'Mine? To keep? Really?'

'Yes, really.'

Too overcome for speech just then, she flung her arms round him and hugged him. Taken totally by surprise, Marcus felt himself redden and then somehow, rather awkwardly, his arms were round the child and he was hugging her back. Then together they walked over to the pony.

'His name's Misty,' he said.

Lucy looked up at him. 'I like his name. It suits him.'

'Yes, I think it does.'

'How old is he?'

'Er…' Marcus looked at Trubshaw for help.

'Ten, my lord,' replied the other.

'He's older than me,' said Lucy.

'That's so he can teach you how to ride, miss,' replied the groom.

She nodded thoughtfully, then looked at her uncle. 'Can I ride him now?'

'Why not?' He lifted her up and sat her on the pony's back. 'Hold on to his mane. That's it.' He looked at the groom. 'Take her for a walk around the yard so she can get used to him.'

As they set off he watched for a moment or two and then glanced back at Claire only to see that she was already looking at him, her face lit with a dazzling smile. His heart missed a beat and for the second time that afternoon he was taken totally by surprise. She was more than a pretty girl, he realised then. Furthermore, the expression in those glorious eyes was joyful and tender and its warmth was directed at him. The effect was to take his breath away.

'Thank you,' she said.

Marcus collected himself quickly. 'He's hardly bloodstock,' he replied, 'but he's quiet and steady enough for the child to learn on.'

She nodded. 'Lucy adores him already.'

He followed her gaze back to the child and the pony, and then he smiled, too. 'I believe she does.'

'It will be hard to keep her away from him now, but he will be so good for her, I know it. He'll build her confidence like nothing else could.'

'Yes, I think he will, and for that I owe you my thanks. If you had not mentioned the idea, it might not have occurred to me.'

'I'm very glad I did.'

'So am I.'

The sincerity in his voice was unmistakable, and the grey eyes looking into her face held an expression she had never seen there before. It disturbed and excited in equal measure, like the memory of his lips on her neck and throat. The recollection sent a shiver along her skin and she was more than ever glad he had known nothing of it. Besides, she reflected, in his fevered dream he had been kissing someone else.

Just then Lucy returned, bright-eyed and smiling, from her short excursion. Marcus lifted her down.

'Can I ride him again tomorrow?' she begged.

'Yes, I don't see why not,' he replied. 'If Miss Davenport doesn't mind.'

He looked over the child's head and met Claire's eye. Lucy looked up anxiously.

Claire laughed. 'No, I don't mind.'

'Will you teach me how to ride properly, Uncle Marcus?'

'If you wish.'

'Oh, yes, please.'

'Very well, but I warn you now. I shall expect you to try hard.'

'I will try hard, I promise.'

She tucked her small hand into his and gave the other to Claire. Then they walked back to the house together.

'Will Miss Davenport come riding with us too, Uncle Marcus?'

'If she wishes to,' he replied.

The grey eyes rested on Claire. Her heart leapt. It would be wonderful to ride again. She had always loved it, but the opportunities had been few and far between in recent years for it was a pursuit that found little favour with her aunt. Equally quickly she knew it would not be possible to take up the invitation. She had no riding clothes and no means of getting any either with the few meagre shillings remaining to her.

'I'm afraid I cannot,' she replied.

'Why not?'

'I regret that I have no suitable costume.'

'I see.'

Much to her relief he didn't pursue it. In any case, she realised, he must have understood how the case was. He had seen every gown she possessed many times. Her salary would be paid quarterly and wasn't due for weeks yet. Besides, if he went out alone with Lucy it would strengthen the relationship between the two of them and that could only be to the good.

Chapter Six

Having tucked Lucy into bed that night Claire took herself off to the library to find a new novel. It was her favourite room, a warm, comfortable place with wonderful old chairs in which it was possible to curl up and lose oneself in a good book. She was perusing the shelves when a footman entered with the intelligence that His Lordship desired her presence in the study.

Wondering what it could possibly be about, Claire made her way there. The Viscount was seated behind a large desk. He had apparently been reading some papers, but looked up as she entered and smiled faintly. After inviting her to sit, he opened a drawer in the desk and took out a small box.

'It occurs to me that if Lucy is to learn to ride she will require a riding habit and some boots. I would like you to attend to it.' Opening the box, he took out a pouch of coins and laid it on the desk. 'That should cover the expense.'

'Yes, sir.'

'It also occurs to me that you might require an advance on your salary.' He laid another pouch beside the first. 'Shall we say ten pounds, to cover immediate expenses?'

Claire felt warmth rise to her face. Ten pounds! It was more money than she could ever recall seeing at one time in her whole life.

'I should have thought of it earlier,' he continued, 'but there have been many matters requiring my attention. I apologise for the oversight.'

'I…not at all.' She sought for the right words, feeling oddly tongue-tied. 'Thank you.'

'I have some business in Harrogate tomorrow. I thought perhaps you and Lucy might like to come along. I understand from Mrs Hughes that there are some good drapers in the town and an excellent seamstress. You can get Lucy's riding habit made up there. Order one for yourself at the same time. There is enough there to cover the cost.'

Claire felt her face grow very warm and the hazel eyes that met his were bright with indignation. Somehow she controlled her voice. 'I thank you, sir, but I cannot accept such a gift. It would be most improper to do so.'

He raised one eyebrow. 'Miss Davenport, when my ward has learned to ride it will be necessary for you to accompany her when I cannot. That being so, you will require the appropriate costume to do it in. It is a vital part of the equipment you require to do your job—like the horse and the saddle.' He paused. 'I take it there will be no difficulty attached to my providing *those?*'

Hearing the ironic tone, she lifted her chin. 'It is not at all the same thing.'

'I beg to differ. I can see very little difference.'

'Perhaps not, but I assure you, sir, that I can.'

'Your opinion in this matter is of no moment, Miss Davenport, since it is my wish as your employer that you should ride with my ward. And as your employer I expect my wishes to be obeyed.'

The tone, though perfectly level, was implacable. She knew it would be fruitless to argue, but only suppressed the desire with great difficulty. Had it been Mark Eden she would have yielded to the impulse—with Marcus Edenbridge she could not. It was infuriating, like the suave expression on that handsome face. How arrogant he could be at times and how determined to get his own way.

Though he guessed quite accurately at the thoughts behind the hazel eyes, he remained undeterred. Following up his advantage, he continued, 'Should you see anything else that Lucy might need, you should feel free to make the purchase.'

'As you wish, sir.'

'Quite so, Miss Davenport.'

Her hands clenched in her lap as she wrestled with a strong desire to hit him. She mastered it and tried to focus on what he was saying.

'The carriage will leave at nine o'clock.'

'We will be ready, sir.'

'Until tomorrow, then.'

It was clearly dismissal. Claire retrieved the purses from the desk and rose from her chair. She was halfway to the door when he recalled something else.

'Incidentally, I have asked Dr and Miss Greystoke to honour me with their company for dinner next Thursday. I would be pleased if you would join us.'

Taken unawares, she heard him with surprise and then with pleasure. It would be wonderful to see her friends again. Gathering her wits, she nodded.

'I should be delighted.'

'Good.' He favoured her with a charming smile. 'That's settled, then.'

After she had left him Claire returned to her room. Laying the two purses on the table, she regarded them thoughtfully. With that one casual gesture he had rescued her from financial embarrassment. Moreover, he didn't have to do it. She could not have asked him for money, particularly since she was essentially here on a trial basis. It was within his rights to withhold any payment until that period was over. Yet he had given it anyway. It was an act of kindness and one she had not looked for. But then there was the matter of the riding habit. He must have guessed what her response would be and had met it most adroitly, leaving no possibility of refusal. The knowledge of her defeat still rankled. For a moment his face returned to her mind.

'Impossible man!' she said aloud.

Attempting to dismiss that provoking image, she turned her thoughts to the morrow. With a trip to town in the offing, she would be able to rectify some of the deficiencies in her wardrobe. It occurred to her that, having seen every gown she possessed, he must have realised how the matter stood. The thought that he had assessed her wardrobe and found it wanting was mortifying. Worse, he was right. It was inadequate and unsuited to her present role. It had been foolish of her to think otherwise. By suggesting this trip he had saved her from some potentially embarrassing situations, damn him!

As she had anticipated Lucy was eager for the forthcoming treat and both of them were ready at the appointed time. The carriage stood waiting, a liveried footman by the open door. The Viscount was already in the hallway. Looking at that tall elegant figure, Claire knew a moment's misgiving. However, nothing of their earlier encounter was apparent in his manner. On the contrary he glanced at the clock and smiled.

'You are punctual, Miss Davenport.'

Unable to think of a reply, she merely inclined her head.

He gestured toward the door. 'Shall we?'

Having lifted Lucy into the vehicle, he held out a hand to Claire. For a few brief seconds she could feel the firm clasp of his fingers. His touch seemed to burn through her glove. Then, having spoken to the coachman, he climbed in after her and seated himself opposite as the carriage moved forwards. Aware of his presence to the last fibre of her being, she arranged her skirts and hoped that nothing of her feeling showed in her face.

Fortunately Lucy diverted his attention with a question. He answered her with his customary patience and showed no sign of irritation when it was followed by two more. Now that the barriers were starting to come down, he clearly wanted to encourage the child to talk to him. As she watched the scene it occurred to Claire that he would be a good father as well as an indulgent uncle for there could be no doubt he would have children of his own one day. The thought was pleasing and unwelcome together. Before she could ask herself why, Lucy broke in.

'Uncle Marcus used to live in India, Miss Davenport.'

'So I believe,' replied Claire.

'When we were travelling from Essex he told me stories about it.'

'Oh?'

'Yes, all about hunting tigers and riding on elephants.'

'How exciting!' Then, recalling her defeat the previous evening, she smiled. 'Perhaps he'll tell you another story now. I'm sure you'd like that, wouldn't you?'

'Yes, I would, if you please, Uncle Marcus.'

Torn between disbelief and amusement the Viscount threw Claire a most eloquent look. It was met with an innocent expression that did not deceive him for a moment and he was strongly tempted to deliver a severe set down. Then he saw Lucy's eager face and knew he could not. After making a mental note to deal with Miss Davenport later, he favoured them with a tale about crossing a river on an elephant which had chosen to take a cooling shower while its passengers, of whom he was one, were still aboard. Lucy laughed in delight.

'Was anyone watching, Uncle Marcus?'

'Roughly half the population of the local village, as I recall.'

'What did you do?'

'The only thing I could do. I adopted a stiff upper lip and pretended to be quite unconcerned.'

Lucy giggled and, unable to help herself, Claire laughed, too. He regarded his audience with a pained expression.

'This really is most unkind of you both.'

That had the effect of sending Lucy into fresh peals of laughter, as he had known it would. Claire was both impressed and touched by the way he engaged with the child, and by his ability to take a joke; his expression now was far removed from the haughty individual she had spoken to the previous evening.

Sensing her regard, he looked up and for a moment met her gaze. Then the light of humour faded a little and was replaced by a different kind of warmth altogether. Conscious of that look, Claire felt her heart miss a beat and she quickly looked away.

Seeing her unease, Marcus was annoyed with himself. He had been caught off guard when he should have been prepared, for he had already felt the effect that her laughter could have. Once again it lit her face and made her look beautiful. She laughed sincerely, from the heart, without any trace of affectation. He realised too that it pleased him to see her laugh like that. Hitherto her demeanour, though pleasant and courteous, had always seemed a little reserved, but in unguarded moments she had revealed another side to her personality, one that was fun-loving and light-hearted. It suited her. More, he found it intriguing. Almost at once he brought himself up short. As Lucy's governess and a member of his staff she was strictly off limits. He had appointed her to the post because it suited him; it was convenient and she was eligible and he wanted to help. Now he realised, somewhat belatedly, that he had not been completely impervious to her charms either.

Claire, sensitive to the atmosphere, felt the change in his manner and upbraided herself for being too forward. It must not happen again. She had not failed to recognise the expression in his eyes when he looked at her and was appalled. Her security depended on keeping this post and she would only do that if her behaviour was above reproach. There could be no familiarity between them. Besides, their social positions made it quite impossible that he would consider her as anything more than a diversion. That kind of liaison could have only one end. It was a lowering thought.

Worse was the knowledge that she would forfeit all respect if she was ever to be so foolish as to encourage such attentions. Besides, as she knew full well, there was already a woman in his heart.

In many ways it was a relief when the carriage reached its destination and drew up in the main thoroughfare. The Viscount turned to Claire.

'I shall leave you here for the time being,' he said. 'Wakely will accompany you and carry your packages. I shall return in two hours' time.'

'Very well, sir.'

'In the meantime I trust that you will have a productive shopping expedition.'

'I am sure we shall, sir.'

The footman opened the door and, having let down the steps, handed Claire and Lucy out onto the street. The Viscount nodded farewell and the vehicle moved on. For a moment or two Claire watched it depart and then took Lucy by the hand.

'Come. Let us see what this place has to offer.'

In fact, their investigation of the town's shops was enjoyable and rewarding. Moreover, she and Lucy were the objects of almost fawning attention by the traders they met for the mode of their arrival had been noted. Such a handsome equipage could only belong to a wealthy man and the crest on the door left people in no doubt as to his identity. Two elegantly dressed females attended by a footman were certain of the warmest welcome everywhere they went. Claire was torn between amusement and alarm. It had not occurred to her that they would attract such notice. On the other hand, it was a novelty to be afforded the undivided attention of every shopkeeper they encountered. The latter almost fell over themselves to offer help and advice.

The first stop was the draper's shop recommended by Mrs Hughes, where bolt after bolt of fine cloth was displayed for her inspection. Eventually she settled on two lengths of figured muslin, in blue and jonquil respectively. They were totally unexceptionable, perfect for her newfound role. Along with them she chose a soft lilac mull. It was simple and plain, but it would make an elegant dress for the forthcoming dinner party with the Greystokes. The fabrics were relatively inexpensive, too, which meant that she could save the remainder of her money in case of need.

When it came to the matter of riding habits Lucy had decided ideas of her own. Rejecting the draper's suggestion of a dependable brown serge, she chose a deep blue velvet instead. Claire didn't argue. It was a pretty colour and it enhanced the child's blue eyes. She chose the brown fabric for herself.

Having purchased the cloth, they went next to the seamstress where they were ushered into an immaculate parlour and served tea while dress patterns were discussed at length. Delighted to have the custom of such exalted clients, the seamstress went into raptures over their chosen materials and assured them both of her ability to contrive the most stylish and elegant gowns imaginable. The conversation about styles and trimmings and measurements went on at such length that eventually Lucy grew bored and plumped herself down in a chair to play with her doll.

At last all the arrangements were complete and they escaped from that establishment to move on to the milliner and thence to the bootmaker. After two hours they had spent what seemed to Claire to be a truly prodigal sum of money. At the same time she had to acknowledge that it was very pleasant to have the means to do it and to be free to choose what she liked rather than what her aunt considered suitable for a young lady. That thought produced others less welcome and, as they walked along the street, she prayed that her uncle would never think to look for her in Yorkshire. In a momentary fit of panic she wished she were safely at Netherclough again, concealed from the public gaze. Then she took a deep breath and told herself not to be so foolish. It couldn't possibly hurt to enjoy one simple shopping trip.

While Claire and Lucy were thus engaged, Marcus had gone to call upon Sir Alan Weatherby, the local magistrate. He had sent a letter some days earlier, announcing his intention. The missive aroused both curiosity and surprise in the recipient, but he received the visitor with considerable pleasure. The news of Marcus Edenbridge's return from India had aroused considerable interest in the town, and, with his assumption of the Destermere title, made him a personage of some importance in the neighbourhood. However, in this case the matter was more personal: Weatherby had been a friend of the late Lord Richard Destermere, and had stood as godfather to his sons.

'Welcome back, Marcus,' he said, taking the other's hand in a hearty grip.

'Thank you, sir. It's good to be back.'

For a moment the two men were silent, regarding each other in mutual appraisal. Then Weatherby smiled.

'I see that India agreed with you, my boy.' He clapped him on the shoulder. 'Come, let us go into the study and celebrate your return with a glass of wine.'

Once the niceties had been observed, the older man set down his glass and regarded the other with a shrewd gaze.

'I sense there is more to this than just a social call.'

'Yes, good though it is to see you.' Marcus paused. 'It is about my brother I would speak.'

'A sad business, Marcus. A bad business in every way.'

'You saw Greville before he died.'

'Yes, he paid me an unofficial visit in the guise of David Gifford. He told me about his mission here—as a magistrate it was my job to lend him whatever assistance I could. I was glad to do it, too.

The Luddite crew have stopped at nothing in the pursuit of their evil ends.' Weatherby paused. 'Your brother paid a heavy price for trying to stop them.'

'Yes, he did, but I intend to bring his killers to justice.'

'You can count on my full support.'

'Thank you, sir.'

'Someone found out what he was doing and silenced him. The killing had all the hallmarks of an execution.'

'You saw his body?'

'Yes.' Weatherby's hand clenched on the arm of his chair. 'As soon as I heard the name David Gifford I knew who it was. Later I visited the scene of the crime—a deserted barn on the edge of the moor. My guess is he was somehow lured to the spot and then killed.'

'Have you any idea whom he might have met that evening?'

'No, but he must have thought it important to be there.'

'Was he following a lead, perhaps?'

'Who knows? At any rate he must have been getting close if someone felt the need to silence him.'

'Who else knew about his mission here?'

'Only Sir James Wraxall. He's also a magistrate and he owns several mills.'

'So he would also have an interest in helping to catch the wreckers.'

'Absolutely. He was most keen to help. It was he who provided Greville's cover by hiring him as a wagon driver at the Gartside mill.'

'Did he know David Gifford's real identity?'

'No, only that his task was to find and destroy the Luddite group.'

'I see.' Marcus drank the rest of his wine and set down the glass. 'Well, this has been a most helpful conversation, sir.'

'What are you going to do?'

'I don't know yet. First I need to find out who my brother's associates were, and who he was due to meet the night he died.'

'I'll make some discreet inquiries. If I find out anything at all, I'll send word.'

'I'd appreciate it.'

'In the meantime I trust you're settling back to life in England.'

'Yes, though I little thought I'd ever return.' Marcus smiled. 'It has been good to see Netherclough again. And it's not just my home now—my niece lives there, too.'

'Ah, yes, Greville's child. I have not seen her since she was a baby.'

'Lucy is six now.'

'Good Lord! Is she really? At all events, it's too young to be cast adrift in the world. Lucky for her she has you, my boy.'

'I'll try to live up to expectation.'

'I'm sure you will.' The older man eyed him keenly. 'Meanwhile, you need to think about the future. As Viscount Destermere it is incumbent on you to marry and get heirs to carry on the family name. Find a good woman, my boy. I did and I've never regretted it.'

Marcus grinned. 'I'll keep it in mind.'

Having taken his leave, he returned to town to collect Claire and Lucy. Both looked to be in good spirits so he assumed the shopping expedition had been a success. On enquiry he was proved right.

'It was most satisfactory, sir,' replied Claire. 'I hope your business was concluded equally well.'

'Indeed it was, Miss Davenport.'

His expression was enigmatic and not for the first time she found herself wondering at the thoughts behind those cool grey eyes. However, he seemed disinclined to talk after that and, as Lucy was busy with her doll, Claire occupied herself agreeably by admiring the view from the window. Thus the rest of the return journey passed in companionable silence.

* * *

In the days following, Claire's time was spent in the schoolroom or in the grounds where she and Lucy walked when the weather was fine. The estate was beautiful, for some of the trees were changing colour and the rolling green acres of park and woodland were tinted with gold and russet hues. Sometimes they walked along the banks of the river and looked for a kingfisher or watched the brown trout finning against the current. At others they walked in the woods and collected handfuls of burnished conkers from the horse chestnut trees, and listened to the songs of the wild birds.

When it rained and they were compelled to remain indoors, Claire used the long gallery for exercise, thinking up games to play. It was during one of these that Lucy's gaze came to rest on one of the portraits.

'Papa,' she said then.

Claire came to stand beside her. 'Your papa?'

'Yes. Aunt Margaret said he's with the angels now, like Mama.'

'I'm sure she's right.'

'She said he wasn't coming back.'

'Do you miss him, Lucy?'

'I suppose so. Only I never saw him much. He was always very busy, you see.'

Claire did see, all too well. She put her arm round the child's shoulders and drew her closer.

'You have your Uncle Marcus, though, and you have me.'

Lucy nodded. 'I like Uncle Marcus. He makes me laugh.' She paused. 'I like you too, much better than Great-Aunt Margaret. She was old and cross.'

'Was she?'

'Yes. I was glad when Uncle Marcus came for me.'

Although the words were said matter-of-factly, Claire felt her heart go out to the little girl who had never known what it meant to be part of a loving family.

'Are you happy here, Lucy?'

The child looked up at her with solemn eyes that were somehow much older than their six years. Then she nodded. Claire breathed a sigh of relief. It was often hard to know whether children were happy, but at last Lucy seemed to be adjusting to her new environment and to the people in it. She pointed toward the next picture. It was of two young men in sporting costume. Both carried guns under their arms and were accompanied by several dogs. A brace of pheasant lay at their feet.

'See, there's your papa with Uncle Marcus.'

'How old were they?'

'About seventeen, I'd say.'

'That's quite old, isn't it?'

Claire supposed it was when you were six. She smiled. 'Yes, quite old.'

Pleased to have the thought confirmed, Lucy turned back to the portraits.

'Who is that lady there?'

'I'm not sure.'

'That is your mother,' said a voice behind them.

They turned in surprise to see Marcus there. Neither of them had heard him approach. Claire wondered how long he had been there and how much of the conversation he might have overheard. He came to join them in front of the painting.

'She's very pretty,' said Lucy.

'Yes, she is,' he replied. 'You look like her.'

'Do I?'

'I think so.'

Lucy surveyed the portrait with wistful eyes. 'I wish she was here.'

'If she were, I think she would be very proud of you.'

That drew a faint smile. Claire, looking over the child's head, met his eye and smiled, too. Then she turned back to the pictures and by tacit consent they strolled on a little way, eventually coming to a halt before another canvas. This time a haughty nobleman stared down at them out of the frame.

'My father,' said Marcus, by way of explanation.

Looking at the cold, aloof expression on that face, Claire remembered what the housekeeper had told her earlier.

'I can see the family likeness,' she observed.

'There is a physical likeness,' he acknowledged. 'Otherwise we were chalk and cheese, and it wasn't a case of opposites attracting.'

'I'm sorry to hear it.'

'He did have a lot to put up with admittedly. Greville and I were no saints. We sowed some wild oats between us. The old man was glad to see the back of me in the end.'

'Was that why you went to India?'

'I was sent to India in consequence of a scandal,' he replied. 'At the time I fancied myself in love with a most ineligible young lady. We planned an elopement to Gretna Green, but my father found out and scotched the scheme just in time.'

'Just in time?'

'Yes. He was right in that instance. The marriage would have been an unmitigated disaster. Of course, I only realised that with the wisdom of hindsight.'

'And so you found solace with the East India Company.'

'Very much so. The place suited me very well and the Company offered the possibility of an exciting and varied career.'

'And you never looked back?'

'At first, but less and less as time went on. Eventually I came to see that what I'd believed to be love was merely boyish infatuation.'

'I see.'

'Do you think me fickle?'

She shook her head. 'No, just young—and perhaps a little foolish.'

'I was certainly young, and very foolish. However, India changed that. You might say I grew up there.'

'It must have been exciting.'

'It was, some of the time.'

'I should like to hear about it.'

'Some time perhaps,' he replied.

The tone was courteous enough and the words accompanied with a smile, yet she knew that there had been an indefinable shift, as if an invisible barrier had come down between them. Clearly there were things about those years in India that he did not wish to discuss, and she had no right to trespass there. Was the mysterious Lakshmi among them? What had happened? Clearly he had been very deeply in love with her. In that case, why had he returned to England without her? Surely a man like Marcus Edenbridge wouldn't give a snap of his fingers for social convention. In his position he didn't need to. Perhaps the boot was on the other foot and the lady had not cared enough for him. Perhaps she had loved someone else and jilted him.

Before further contemplation was possible a maidservant arrived to inform them that some parcels had arrived. Marcus excused himself and she and Lucy took themselves off to investigate. The parcels in question proved to be from the seamstress. The next hour was spent trying on the finished garments. Claire could not but admire the workmanship. It was very fine indeed and far better than she could have done herself. The new muslin dresses were neat and functional, but the lilac evening gown was a more elegant creation, fitting close at the bust and then falling in graceful folds to her feet. The bodice, though modest, revealed her figure to advantage. In comparison to London fashion she supposed it to be unremarkable, but it was, nevertheless, a more fashionable gown than any she had owned before and she knew full well she would enjoy wearing it. The riding habit was neat and elegant, the severe lines of the military-style jacket relieved by gold frog fastenings. It fitted like a glove to the waist before falling away into the full skirt. A jaunty little hat trimmed with ostrich feathers completed the ensemble. The shade and style were well suited to her figure and colouring, and at a stroke transformed her from girl to woman of fashion. The thought was both welcome and disturbing. It occurred to her to wonder what her employer would think of the transformation. Then she told herself not to be foolish. He probably wouldn't even notice. Uncle Hector never seemed to notice such things. At the very most a new gown had called forth a grunt from that quarter. Fortunately no one else was likely to see it, so it would not attract undue attention.

Meanwhile, Lucy had been parading up and down in front of the mirror, admiring her new riding habit from every possible angle. The colour was a perfect foil for her brown curls and blue eyes. Lifting the hem of her skirt, she stuck out a toe to see the effect of the fabric against the polished leather of a new boot. Then she smiled as her gaze met Claire's in the glass.

'Now Uncle Marcus can teach me to ride,' she announced.

Chapter Seven

The first lesson was duly arranged for the following afternoon. Claire accompanied her young charge to the stable yard where Marcus was already waiting. He smiled to see Lucy's new costume and bade her turn around so he could view it from every angle.

'Very pretty,' he said then.

'I chose the material,' she confided.

'You chose well.' He tweaked one of her curls and then turned to Claire. 'I'll take her out for an hour or so and let her get used to the saddle.' He glanced at her muslin frock. 'I take it you're not accompanying us today.'

'No, sir. I thought it best if I did not.' Seeing him raise an eyebrow, she hurried on. 'This being the first time Lucy has ridden. The fewer distractions she has the better.'

The grey gaze met and held hers in a long and level stare. Recalling an earlier conversation, she felt her heart begin to beat a little faster. Was he annoyed? However, to her relief he merely nodded.

'Well, you may be right on this occasion. However, in future I shall expect you to come along, Miss Davenport.'

'As you wish, sir.'

'I do wish it.'

Conscious of that penetrating gaze, Claire tried to appear unconcerned. However, it wasn't easy when he was standing so close.

With no little relief she watched him turn his attention to his niece, lifting her easily onto the pony's back. She listened as he showed the child how to sit and how to hold her reins. Lucy hung on his every word.

Once she was ready he swung onto his own horse. He looked as if he belonged there, she thought, a born horseman. There was an elegance about the tall, lithe figure, and a suggestion of contained strength. She watched him take the pony's leading rein and touch his horse with his heels. Then they set off, followed at a respectful distance by Trubshaw. Claire watched until they were out of sight and then retraced her steps to the house.

Lucy took to the experience of riding like a duck to water and the following day saw her and Claire in the stable yard again. This time, both were dressed to ride. The Viscount made no comment on Claire's appearance and merely greeted her with his customary courtesy.

In fact, he had noted the habit with approval, his critical gaze taking in every detail. It was elegant and quietly stylish and, he thought, it became her very well indeed, showing off her figure to perfection. And what a figure! A man could span that waist with his hands. Even the sober colour looked good on her too, he thought, complementing her dark curls and enhancing those wonderful hazel eyes. He smiled wryly. It remained to be seen whether she could ride. He had selected a pretty bay mare for her, a willing creature but well mannered withal.

Whatever doubts he might have had on that score were soon allayed. She had an excellent seat and a light hand on the reins. Moreover, she looked very much at home in the saddle. He found himself wishing they were alone so that she might really put the mare through her paces. For some time they rode at Lucy's pace, but then, feeling the need for something more challenging, he reined in and told Trubshaw to go on ahead.

'We'll catch up in a minute.' He looked across at Claire. 'These horses need to stretch their legs.'

At the thought of a gallop her eyes brightened. Part of her suspected he was also testing her, but she didn't care. Once again she was aware of his regard and felt rising warmth along her neck and face. To hide her confusion she kept her eyes on the departing figures. When she judged they were far enough away she threw him a quizzical glance. He met and held it.

'Well, Miss Davenport?'

For answer she touched the mare with her heel. The horse sprang forwards into a canter. Out of the corner of her eye Claire saw the Viscount's chestnut drawing level. She grinned. So he wanted to test her, did he? She leaned forwards a little and gave the horse its head. The mare accelerated into a gallop, her neat hooves flying across the turf. Exhilarated by the pace and the rushing air Claire laughed out loud. Behind her she could hear the thudding hoofbeats of the other horse and then a moment later saw it draw level. A sideways glance revealed a grin on its rider's face. In that second she knew he was deliberately keeping pace and had no intention of being outrun. The two horses swept on up the slope to where Lucy and Trubshaw were waiting. Claire reined in and then leaned down to pat the mare's neck. Lucy was agog.

'It was a draw, Miss Davenport. I was watching.'

Claire laughed. 'I think you're right.'

'I'm going to ride like that one day,' the child continued.

'Yes, but not just yet,' said Claire.

'Certainly not,' agreed the Viscount. Then, seeing Lucy's crestfallen expression, he softened the blow. 'You'll learn soon enough.'

As they set off again he reined his mount alongside Claire.

'How do you like the mare?'

'I like her very well.'

'I thought you might. She was a lady's horse before, and is of a sweet temperament.'

'Her owner must have been sad to part with her.'

'I imagine so. However, I could hardly have mounted you on one of my hunters.'

Claire threw him a swift sideways glance in which dismay was clearly registered. Surely he hadn't bought the horse on her account? That was ridiculous. He must have had the animal for some time. Yet she couldn't recall having seen her when she and Lucy visited the stables before. Furthermore, the mare was no more than fifteen hands and finely made, certainly not up to a man's weight. As the implications dawned she felt a strange sensation in her breast. It was a feeling compounded of gratitude and alarm. He had already shown her a great deal of consideration. More than she had any right to expect.

Although he could not follow her train of thought he could not mistake the expression of dismay on her face and he mentally rebuked himself for his clumsiness. He had meant to let her think the horse had been part of his stable.

'I purchased her along with Lucy's pony,' he said. 'As I told you, I shall require you to accompany my niece when I cannot.'

The tone was cool and firm and precluded argument. Claire avoided his eye and kept her gaze straight ahead between the horse's ears.

'Yes, sir.'

It was the only reply she felt able to give. He was her employer and his wishes prevailed. More than that, she had enjoyed herself too much today to want to forfeit the chance of riding in future. Now that she was on a horse again she realised how much she had missed it.

Somewhat to her disappointment, business occupied him for the next few days so she and Lucy had to go out without him. Trubshaw was in attendance as usual but the Viscount was conspicuous by his absence. Claire tried hard not to miss him but, though it was undoubtedly a pleasure to ride, it wasn't the same somehow. She was annoyed with herself for feeling the lack. For goodness' sake, she was too old for what amounted to a schoolgirl crush! He certainly wouldn't be giving her a moment's thought. Why should he? He had hired her to do a job. If he showed her any additional courtesy it was on account of what had gone before and, perhaps, because of her connection with the Greystokes.

That last proved a calming thought. The Viscount valued Dr Greystoke's friendship very highly and was also beholden to Ellen for her previous care of him. He would not risk offending either by his treatment of Claire. Having got a new perspective on the situation, she cringed inwardly when she remembered her response to his kindness. What a vain little fool she must appear. As if a man like Marcus Edenbridge would look twice at a governess! Why should he? He could have his pick of all the eligible young women in the land. Mortified now, Claire resolved to demonstrate a different kind of behaviour when next they met.

That proved to be on Thursday when the Greystokes came to dine at Netherclough. Claire was relieved to learn that they were to be the only company that evening. It meant there was no one else to note her presence and perhaps mention it to others later. Her whereabouts would remain secret. She dressed with care, selecting her new lilac gown. It was simple and elegant without being ostentatious, and the colour suited her. As she had no other jewellery her only adornment was her locket. Nevertheless she was not displeased by her appearance when she looked in the glass. It should at least pass muster. Affording her reflection a last wry smile, she left her chamber and made her way to the drawing room.

She arrived to find the guests talking to their host, but at her entrance they greeted her with expressions of pleasure, which she returned with equal sincerity.

George gave her a beaming smile.

'Good to see you, Miss Davenport, and how very well you look.'

Ellen echoed the sentiment. 'Indeed you do, my dear. And what a delightful gown.'

The Viscount, listening, knew the words for truth. As he hadn't seen the frock before he gathered it must be a new purchase. Clearly the trip to Harrogate had been productive. The colour of the fabric became her well, suiting her dark curls and fresh complexion, and his critical eye could find no fault with the cut or the style. It epitomised simple, understated elegance. She seemed to have an instinct for it. He noted that she was wearing the silver locket again. It was a pretty trinket, but amethysts would go better with that gown. Even so it showed off her figure well and, he reflected, a figure like hers should be shown off. It was beautiful. His imagination stripped away the dress and contemplated what lay beneath. He caught his breath. With an effort of will he forced the image away and his attention back to his guests.

A short time later dinner was announced. He offered his arm to Miss Greystoke while her brother led Claire in. Throughout the meal, though he kept up his part in the general conversation, Marcus found his attention repeatedly returning to Claire. Yet his critical eye could discern not the least hint of awkwardness in her demeanour, and her manners were impeccable. Far from seeming out of place, she looked as though she belonged.

Once the meal was over the two ladies withdrew to the drawing room, leaving the men to talk over their brandy and cigars. Claire had been looking forward to having the opportunity for private speech with Ellen, and when at last the two of them were alone she seated herself on the sofa beside her friend.

'Now tell me all,' Ellen said. 'And especially about your young charge.'

She listened avidly as Claire supplied the details.

'I am so glad that all is well. I gathered as much from your letter, but it's always reassuring to hear it from your own lips.'

'I have nothing to complain of,' said Claire. 'The Viscount takes a great interest in Lucy's education and provides whatever I ask for in that regard.'

'Excellent.'

'He is most solicitous about the child and seems anxious to ensure her happiness.'

'So it would seem.' Ellen paused. 'Has he said any more about finding the men responsible for his brother's death?'

'No, but that does not mean he has abandoned the scheme.'

'At least he can use his position to enlist the help of the authorities. That must be far safer than adopting a false identity.'

'I cannot think he will do so again, not now he has Lucy to consider.'

Had they known it, the conversation in the dining room was turning on a similar theme.

'Have you taken further action?' asked George.

'I called upon Sir Alan Weatherby in Harrogate last week. He is my godfather—was Greville's too—and is a local magistrate besides. He is most anxious to have information about the wreckers. Rest assured, if he learns anything I shall know of it soon after.'

'Then he knows the truth?'

'Yes. Sir James Wraxall also knew of Greville's mission here, though not his true identity. He knew my brother by the pseudonym of David Gifford.'

'Wraxall knew?'

'Yes, and lent his full support to the scheme.'

'I suppose he would, being a local magistrate. All the same he is not a popular man in the district.'

'Magistrates rarely are popular,' said Marcus.

'Wraxall is a mill owner, too. He was the first to cut wages.'

'Ah, I see.'

'I am glad you have chosen this way to find your brother's killers.'

'I hope the disappearance of Mark Eden didn't cause you any difficulties?'

'None at all. As you asked, I gave it out that he had gone to stay with relatives further north. I left the destination suitably vague.'

'I am much obliged to you, George.'

'No offence, but I rather hope Eden does not return.'

The Viscount smiled wryly. 'Really? I rather liked him.'

'Seriously, Marcus.'

'Seriously, George, so do I.'

A short time later they rejoined the ladies in the drawing room and the conversation was directed into other channels for a while. Then George suggested some music. The Viscount's grey eyes gleamed. Recalling the story-telling episode on the way to Harrogate, he looked straight at Claire and seized his opportunity for revenge.

'Perhaps Miss Davenport will oblige us with a song.'

As he had foreseen, Claire could hardly refuse. He watched as she got up and moved to the pianoforte. When her back was to the others she threw him a most eloquent look. His grin widened. Enjoying himself enormously, he followed her to the instrument and riffled through the sheet music until he found the piece he was looking for. Then he handed it to her.

Torn between annoyance and amusement Claire took it from him, scanning it quickly. In fact it was neither difficult nor unfamiliar as she had suspected it might be. He wasn't that unkind, she decided. All the same she would have preferred not to be the centre of attention. Thank goodness it wasn't a large company.

'I'll turn the pages for you,' he said.

Undeceived by that courteous offer she nevertheless returned him a sweet smile.

'How very kind.'

The grey eyes held a decidedly mischievous glint, but he vouch-safed no reply and merely stationed himself beside her. Supremely conscious of his proximity but unable to do anything about it, she turned her attention to the music. Then, taking a deep breath, she settled down to play.

After hearing the opening bars Marcus's amusement faded and was replaced by pleasure and surprise; she played and sang beautifully, more so than he could ever have supposed. He had expected competence, but not the pure liquid notes that filled the room. Her voice was clear and true and had besides a haunting quality that sent a shiver down his spine and seemed to thrill to the core of his being. He had heard the song countless times, but never so movingly rendered. When at last it came to an end he was quite still for some moments before he recollected himself enough to join in the applause. He wasn't alone in thinking the performance good. Greystoke too had been much struck by it.

'Wonderful!' he said at last. 'First class, Miss Davenport.'

'I had a first-class teacher,' she replied, looking at Ellen.

'There can be no doubt about that,' Marcus replied. 'You are both to be congratulated.' This time there was no trace of mischief in his face when he looked at Claire. 'Please, won't you play something else?'

Her heart beat a little faster for he had never used quite that tone before. It was unwontedly humble. Controlling her surprise, she could only acquiesce.

'Yes, of course.'

Turning to the pile of music, she drew out a piece at random. It was much more difficult and she was glad of it for it meant she wouldn't be tempted to look at him instead. However, she soon became conscious that he felt no such constraint. Her skin seemed to burn beneath that penetrating gaze and only with a real effort of will could she keep her expression impassive and her concentration on the music. Soon enough the melody claimed her and filled her soul. Marcus saw her surrender to it and felt all the passion of that skilled performance as he too was transported. He knew then that he was listening to something quite out of the ordinary, something that both awed and delighted, and he didn't want it to end.

When it did he was first to lead the applause. However, the others were not far behind him. George Greystoke got to his feet.

'Bravo, Miss Davenport!'

She received their praise with a gracious smile and then rose from the piano stool, insisting that Ellen be allowed her turn. When her friend bowed to the pressure Claire retired to a seat across the room. Marcus's gaze followed her, but he remained by the pianoforte and presently turned his attention to his guest, consulting with her about the choice of music and then waiting to turn the pages as she played. He was, thought Claire, a most courteous host, and, seeing him now, his attentions to herself did not seem so marked at all, but rather the good manners of one accustomed to moving in the first circles. It was foolish to refine on a look or a gesture. He would treat any female guest with the same polished courtesy.

The remainder of the time passed agreeably enough until, soon after the tea tray had been brought in, the Greystokes took their leave.

'It has been a most delightful evening,' said Ellen as they stood together in the hallway.

'I hope to have the pleasure of seeing it soon repeated,' Marcus replied.

He shook hands with George and then came to stand by Claire to wave the guests off.

'Miss Greystoke is right,' he observed as the carriage pulled away. 'It has been a most delightful evening.'

Claire glanced up at him and smiled. 'Yes, it has.'

They remained there together until the vehicle was lost to view round a bend in the drive, and then turned and walked back into the hallway. For a moment they paused, neither one speaking. Aware of him to her very fingertips, wanting to linger and knowing she must not, she forced herself to a polite curtsy.

'I'll bid you a goodnight, sir.'

Marcus wanted to detain her, but could think of no valid reason for doing so. Instead he took her hand and carried it to his lips.

'Goodnight then, Miss Davenport.'

Reluctantly he watched her walk away and then returned to the drawing room and poured himself a large brandy from the decanter on the table. He tossed it back in one go and poured another. As he did so he glanced across the room to the pianoforte and, in his imagination, heard Claire singing and knew again the *frisson* along his spine. He also knew that what he felt was a damn sight more than admiration for fine musical skill. When they had been alone together after the guests had gone he had wanted to take her in his arms. No, he corrected himself, what he had really wanted to do was carry her up the stairs to his bedchamber and make love to her all night.

Almost immediately he felt self-contempt. Claire Davenport was not some trollop to be used for an idle hour's amusement. She was a respectable young woman. She was Lucy's governess, for heaven's sake. A role he had appointed her to. Any liaison between them would make that position untenable and he would be responsible for ruining her reputation and then for causing her to leave. Only a real cur would do that. Only a cur put his own desire before the welfare of the woman he claimed to care for. For both their sakes there could be no familiarity between them. It was not only his feelings and hers that were involved here, but Lucy's, too. She was beginning to settle into her new home, to trust him. It was obvious that she was also growing attached to her new governess. Could he be responsible for the loss of yet another person she cared for? Could he put her through that? It needed but a moment's thought to know the answer. There must be no advances to Claire, no matter what it cost him. Had she been living with the Greystokes it might have been different, but the minute he hired her he had put her out of reach. The irony did not escape him.

Claire returned to her room and retired to bed, but sleep would not come. Her thoughts were troubled and her mind raced. Every time her eyelids closed Marcus's face was there. His words echoed in her memory. She could still feel the warmth of his hand on hers. The memory set her pulse racing, like that other memory of his lips on her skin. When he was near it was hard to think of anything else. His presence drew her as a moth to a flame and, just as surely, she knew that yielding to temptation would mean getting badly burnt. Men of rank might dally with their servants, but they did not marry them.

The knowledge brought with it a feeling of overwhelming sadness. If things had been different…if they had met under other circumstances…but she could not imagine any circumstances under which they would have met. Her uncle, though a gentleman, did not move in such exalted circles. He was flattered by the notice of a man like Sir Charles Mortimer. What would he have said to the notice of a viscount? What would have been his reaction if such a man had offered for her hand? She knew the answer too well: the offer would have been accepted immediately and she would have been expected to comply. Her heart beat a little quicker at the thought. If she had been promised to a man like Marcus Edenbridge would she have sought to escape the match? The answer brought another wave of warmth to her neck and face. Just as quickly she realised how ridiculous it was even to consider the possibility. Ridiculous and dangerous. She was not safe yet. This post was her refuge, her protection. She would do nothing to jeopardise it, no matter what her personal inclination.

In the morning she would resume her duties as though nothing had happened. When she and Marcus Edenbridge happened to meet, she would behave with the utmost propriety. Never by word or sign would she let him suspect what she felt for him. This evening, delightful as it had been, was a one-off occasion, a favour perhaps for past aid. It would not happen again. He had discharged his obligation and in future his socialising would be done among his social equals. The knowledge gave her a pang; she had enjoyed herself this evening. It had given her a glimpse of another world, one to which she would never belong. It served to reinforce how very different were their social positions.

In the days that followed the Viscount behaved with the utmost propriety when their paths crossed. He visited the nursery each day and took a keen interest in what Lucy did, but he never lingered or tried to interfere in any way. To Claire he was unfailingly civil, but never more than that. Just occasionally the grey eyes betrayed a stronger emotion, but it was never given further expression.

He also rode with them less frequently, having many other matters requiring his attention. Although she missed him, Claire was grateful for the distance between them. Sometimes she would look from her window and see him ride out across the estate, sometimes alone, but more usually with the land agent. Then she would know that she and Lucy would be riding with Trubshaw that day. Her young charge made good progress and gained in confidence. Soon she was clamouring to be let off the leading rein. The next time that Marcus appeared in the nursery she petitioned him on that score.

'I've been riding for three weeks now, Uncle Marcus. Can't I please ride Misty without being led?'

He dropped to one knee so that they were face to face and then he smiled. 'I don't see why not.'

Lucy flung her arms round his neck. 'Thank you, Uncle Marcus.'

He returned the hug and looked over the child's shoulder to Claire.

'The pony is quiet enough. I think she'll come to little harm,' he said. 'In any case, one learns by doing. Is that not so, Miss Davenport?'

'Indeed it is, sir.'

Lucy looked at him solemnly. 'Will you come with us, Uncle Marcus?'

He grinned and ruffled her hair. 'I have a lot of things to do today.'

She threw a conspiratorial glance at Claire. 'But I might fall off.'

'Well, you might,' he agreed. 'But then you'll just have to get back on, won't you?'

'Yes.'

The tone and facial expression were so forlorn that Claire was unable to restrain a grin. Her young charge was clearly not above using feminine wiles to get her own way. Even so she didn't expect him to succumb. His expression said very plainly that he knew what she was about, but to her surprise she saw him smile.

'Oh, all right, then, you ghastly brat. I'll come.'

Undismayed by this mode of address, Lucy smiled up at him.

'But only if you have completed all of your lessons first,' he added, with belated severity.

Desperately wanting to laugh, Claire turned away and fixed her attention on the view from the window. The Viscount stood up, regarding her with a speculative expression.

'You will inform me later, Miss Davenport, if Lucy has not done everything she ought.'

'Yes, sir.'

He looked at his ward and jerked his head towards the desk. With the sweetest of smiles Lucy returned to work. Seeing her once more bent over her copybook, he turned back to Claire. Though she had assumed an expression of becoming gravity she was unable to hide the laughter in her eyes. It was fascinating, all the more so because she was quite unconscious of the effect it had on the beholder. If they had been alone, he would have taught her about the dangers of exerting fascination. As it was he could not permit himself that very attractive luxury so, reluctantly, he made her a polite bow instead and then took his leave.

Claire didn't set eyes on him again until they met in the stable yard that afternoon. However, apart from a brief, polite acknowledgement of her presence he focused his attention on his ward. Claire was glad of it. It also afforded an opportunity of watching them together. He was, she thought, a good teacher, for he was quiet and firm in delivering instruction, but always ready to praise. As always, Lucy hung on his every word, clearly eager to please him. She learned quickly. He had only to tell her something once and she remembered it.

As she was off the leading rein a groom and not Trubshaw attended them. And as it was Lucy's first solo outing the pace was necessarily gentle, but Claire didn't mind. It was just pleasant to be out of doors on so fine a day and in so beautiful a place. All the trees were turning now, the foliage a glorious display of red and russet and gold, and the autumnal air was rich with the scent of leaf mould and damp earth. It was good to be alive on such a day. She glanced at her companions. It was good to be in such agreeable company. Even if it could not last for ever she would enjoy it now.

Lulled by the easy pace and the beauty of her surroundings, Claire was totally unprepared for the sudden violent eruption of a pheasant from the long grass at her horse's feet. For one heartbeat she had an impression of beating wings and a squawking cry and then her startled mount shied violently, throwing her hard. Earth and sky and trees spun crazily for some moments afterwards, so she lay quite still until the scenery had stopped moving and she could get her bearings again. Then she was aware of someone beside her and of anxious grey eyes looking down into hers.

'Claire, are you hurt?'

For a second she did not reply, being aware only that he had used her Christian name, a mode of address that he had never employed before. Then she shook her head.

'I…I don't think so. Just a little dazed, that's all.'

'Can you sit up?'

A strong arm brought her to a sitting position and supported her there. She managed a wan smile. 'Nothing broken, I think,' she said. 'Only my pride is a little bruised.'

'That will mend. Can you stand?'

'Yes, I think so.'

She made to rise, but was saved the trouble for his arm was round her waist, lifting her onto her feet. It stayed there while the groom was despatched to retrieve her horse. Feeling somewhat foolish and not a little self-conscious, she disengaged herself from his hold and took a tentative step away. Without warning the ground shifted under her feet and she swayed. If he had not caught her she would have fallen.

'I think that's the end of your ride for today,' he said. 'We must get you back to the house.'

'There's really no need. I'll be all right in a minute or two.'

'Nonsense! Your cheeks are the colour of paper. You need to go and lie down for a while.'

'Really, I…'

'Don't be a little fool. If you get back on that horse now you'll be off again within a minute.'

He guided her to his own horse and without further consultation she was lifted in a pair of powerful arms and transferred with consummate ease onto the front of his saddle. As the implications dawned Claire paled further. Surely he could not be intending to… It seemed that he was for, having given orders to the groom to lead the mare back, Marcus swung up behind her. Then, taking the reins in one hand, he locked the other arm around her waist. Claire tensed, her heart racing.

'I can ride home,' she protested. 'There's really no need…'

In mild panic she tried to resist the arm. For answer it tightened a little, pulling her closer.

'I think otherwise,' he replied, 'and for once you're going to do as you're told, my girl.'

With that he turned the horse for home. Seeing there was no help for it, Claire capitulated, lapsing into warm-cheeked silence. As he glanced down at her his lips twitched.

'What, no furious counter-argument?'

'Would it do any good?'

'Devil a bit,' he replied.

It drew a wry smile in return. She might have known how it would be. Being used to a life of command, this man had an expectation of getting his own way, and an infuriating habit of succeeding, too. In any case she didn't feel much like arguing. Her head was beginning to throb now and, in spite of her assertion to the contrary, she was no longer convinced that she could have ridden back by herself. Moreover, there was something comforting about having the responsibility removed and she felt grateful for that solid and reassuring presence.

Lucy regarded her somewhat anxiously. 'Are you all right, Miss Davenport?'

'Not quite right,' she replied, 'but I shall be better soon.'

'It was a naughty pheasant, wasn't it?'

'Very naughty.'

Marcus grinned. 'If I see it again I'll shoot it.'

Satisfied with this, Lucy nodded and trotted along beside the groom.

Claire sighed. 'I should have been better prepared. Then I would not have fallen off.'

'You could scarcely have avoided it,' Marcus replied. 'The bird was well concealed and there is nothing like a pheasant for putting a rider on the ground.'

The tone was both humorous and kind and not what she had been expecting. There was also an unusually gentle expression in the grey eyes. Seeing it, Claire felt her pulse quicken. Not knowing quite what to say, she lapsed into silence.

'It's all right,' he said. 'You don't have to talk if you don't want to. Lean your head on my shoulder and rest.'

Claire reclined against him and closed her eyes. The gentle motion of the horse and the warmth of the man were soothing and gradually she began to relax. There would probably be some bruises tomorrow, but all things considered she'd got off lightly.

They returned to the stables some twenty minutes later. Marcus instructed the groom to see to Lucy and then dismounted, lifting Claire down after. Just for a moment she had a sensation of weightlessness before he sat her down gently on the cobbled yard, surveying her with a critical eye. She still looked a little pale though not quite as much as before.

'Can you walk?'

She replied hurriedly in the affirmative, dreading that if she did not he would carry her. The idea of presenting such a spectacle to the watching servants filled her with horror. Much to her relief he did not gainsay her this time, but merely offered her his arm, and his free hand to Lucy.

'Come then, let us go in.'

He escorted them in and sent Lucy to change before escorting Claire to the door of her room.

'I will have Mrs Hughes send up some water,' he said. 'You must have a hot tub at once. If not you'll be as stiff as a board tomorrow.'

Claire's cheeks turned a deep shade of pink. Gentlemen did not commonly refer to such things in front of ladies, yet he seemed quite unembarrassed. He was also right. A hot bath would help enormously. Lowering her gaze from his, she nodded.

'Thank you.'

'After that you must lie down for a while until you feel better.'

'But Lucy…'

'I will see to Lucy. You just concern yourself with getting well again.'

With that he left her. Claire slipped thankfully into her room and closed the door, leaning upon it in relief.

In fact, Marcus was right. A hot tub and a lie down did much to restore her. She was right though about incurring some bruises, but Mrs Hughes had come to the rescue with tincture of arnica so the discomfort was considerably lessened. It was from the housekeeper that she learned about the Viscount's plans to host a soirée.

'It is to be a fairly small gathering,' said Mrs Hughes, 'but it will be so pleasant to see company at Netherclough again.'

Claire felt the first stirrings of apprehension. Company posed a possible threat to her anonymity here. However, she forced a smile. 'Yes, I'm sure.'

'His Lordship wishes to establish his return in the neighbourhood,' the housekeeper continued, 'and that can only be to the good, can't it?'

'Oh, yes. When is the event to be?'

'On Tuesday next. There's a deal of work to do before we can pass muster, of course, but I doubt not we'll pull it off.'

'I'm sure you will.'

'Perhaps he'll ask you and Miss Lucy to come down for a while.'

Claire's stomach lurched. The possibility had not occurred to her and now occasioned real alarm. She had no desire for anyone to see her here. It wasn't that she thought they'd find a governess of any interest at all, but gossip spread and a careless word in the wrong place might mean her uncle somehow got to hear of it. Then she would be lost. When she had asked for this job it was in part because Netherclough was remote. It had not occurred to her that her employer would entertain. Too late she realised it had been a foolish oversight on her part.

In the days that followed this conversation she waited in trepidation lest the Viscount should approach her to solicit Lucy's presence in the drawing room. If he did she would be obliged to accompany her charge. She could not risk arousing suspicion by refusing or making difficulties. As he hadn't mentioned the occasion to her at all, perhaps it was because he had no intention of having either of them there.

But on his next visit to the nursery, he explained, 'I would have asked you to bring Lucy down tomorrow evening,' he said, 'but the affair is not due to start until eight, which is really too late for her.'

Claire seized her chance. 'Yes, sir, you are quite right.'

'It's a pity but, on this occasion, it can't be helped.'

'She is also shy and might feel daunted at the prospect of so many strange faces.'

He looked thoughtful. 'I had not thought of that.'

Claire felt flooding relief. He seemed to have accepted what she said. She was off the hook and, perhaps, when she and Lucy did eventually appear in company, all need for circumspection would have passed.

On the evening of the soirée he came to say goodnight to his ward. He had got into the habit now and Lucy clearly derived pleasure from seeing him.

'You look very nice, Uncle Marcus,' she said, surveying the tall figure clad in impeccable evening dress.

Claire silently agreed with the assessment. He wore a dark coat with cream-coloured breeches and waistcoat and immaculate linen. It was simple, almost severe, but it enhanced every line of that lean, athletic form. She thought it would be hard to find a more elegant figure, or a more striking one. He was, she acknowledged, a very handsome man.

He smiled down at the child. 'I hope the rest of the ladies will be so easily pleased.'

Hearing the words, Claire experienced an unexpected pang. Of course there would be ladies present. Moreover, they would be ladies of his social class. Some, no doubt, would be single and on the lookout for a husband. He was, she knew, a most eligible bachelor. Annoyed with herself for thinking such thoughts, she tried to dismiss them. A man like Marcus Edenbridge could set his sights as high as he liked. Not only would he never look her way, but, once married, the secluded rural idyll she had enjoyed would be shattered for good.

They bade goodnight to Lucy and then withdrew to the passage outside the door. Marcus paused a moment, surveying Claire keenly.

'Are you all right, Miss Davenport? You look a little pale.'

'I am quite well, thank you, sir. Just a little tired, that's all.'

'Perhaps an early night, then?' he suggested.

'Yes,' she replied. 'That was my intention.'

He bade her a goodnight, favoured her with a polite bow, and then was gone. Claire waited until he reached the end of the passage and headed down the stairs. Then very quietly she followed, stopping in the shadows on the landing, watching him descend to the hallway. The sound of horses' hooves and wheels on gravel announced the arrival of the first guests. She saw them enter, heard him greet them, speaking and smiling with the polished assurance that so characterised him.

Looking at the beautiful clothes of the arriving guests, Claire became painfully conscious of her plain muslin frock. It soon became clear too that several of the ladies were young and very attractive. From their smiles it seemed that their host was making quite an impression. But then he was the kind of man that women did notice. She sighed. When she had come to Netherclough she had wanted to preserve her anonymity. Now she had got her wish. Marcus wouldn't give her another thought. Why should he? He had plenty of other distractions now. She was merely the governess and could be nothing more. For just one moment she wished she could be down there too, wished she could be one of that elegant gathering. Then he might glance across the room and, seeing her there, might smile and come across and solicit her hand for a dance. How would it be to dance with him? She would never know. Sadly she turned away and went to seek solace in the library.

It was gone eleven before the last of the guests departed and Marcus had waved them off. The evening had been a success in that it had fulfilled its aim of reacquainting him with the wealthy and aristocratic neighbours he had not seen for over ten years. On the other hand, having re-established the connection, he was reminded why he hadn't missed them. With a wry smile he acknowledged that he had been scrutinised and weighed and measured, mostly by the matrons with unmarried daughters. Their fawning attentions left him in no doubt they considered him a good catch. Yet for all their undoubted accomplishments the young women present were lacking somehow. They were either too diffident or too conscious of their own social consequence. At some point he knew he would have to marry and get heirs to continue the family name, but he had seen nothing tonight that remotely tempted him. The thought of a London Season held little appeal either.

Unlike Greville, he suspected he would not find his soul mate among the society beauties. The woman he loved was lost to him for ever and he had never found her like again. He wondered now if he ever would. The past ten years had not been without female companionship, of course, but now he found it hard to remember their faces. They had given their bodies willingly and he had satisfied a need with them, but his heart had remained untouched. Having experienced the grand passion, he found it hard to settle for less.

Recalling the simpering smiles and downcast eyes that had been his lot for much of the evening, he found himself wishing Claire had been there. She would not have looked out of place in such a gathering. On the contrary, her appearance there would have put a few noses out of joint. Moreover, there was nothing diffident or arrogant about her and she was invariably agreeable company. He realised then that he had missed her. A glance at the clock revealed the advancing hour. It was probable that she had retired long since. Conscious of disappointment, he made his way upstairs.

As he passed along the corridor he saw that the library door was slightly ajar. The gleam of light beyond suggested that the room wasn't empty. Curious, he pushed the door further open and glanced in. The pool of candlelight revealed another presence and he smiled in recognition. Claire was curled up on the sofa by the fire, clearly engrossed in the book she was reading. For a moment or two he watched her, his gaze taking in every detail from the dark curls to the small foot peeping out from the hem of her dress, then he pushed the door to behind him and crossed the room to join her.

Hearing a footstep, she looked up and perceived him there. Her heart skipped a beat as she saw who it was. Then, belatedly aware of her informal pose, she straightened quickly.

'No, don't get up,' he said. 'I didn't mean to disturb you. In truth, I didn't think anyone was in here till I saw the light.'

She glanced at the clock and with a start of surprise noticed the late hour. Surely it had been only eight-thirty the last time she looked? Before she could say anything Marcus disposed himself casually on the sofa beside her. Then he glanced at her book.

'What are you reading?'

Very much aware of that charismatic presence and trying not to show it, she replied, *'Sense and Sensibility.'*

'I see you find it absorbing.'

'Very much so. The author is both perceptive and witty.'

'Indeed she is.' He smiled faintly. 'You enjoy reading novels, then?'

'Of course.'

'You do not subscribe to the view that they are unsuitable reading matter for young females?'

'Certainly not. That is the kind of nonsense my uncle used to spout.' Then she stopped, suddenly aware that she had no idea of where he might stand on the issue.

Seeing her expression, Marcus interpreted it correctly. 'No, I do not share that view. Losing oneself in a good story must rank as one of life's great pleasures.'

'Why, so I think.'

'Your uncle is of a conservative disposition, I take it.'

'Yes, sir.' She might also have added, *and humourless, joyless and cold,* but bit the words back, having no wish to allude further to her background. It might prompt more awkward questions. Instead she changed the subject. 'Did you have an enjoyable evening, sir?'

'Tolerably so,' he replied.

Her unwillingness to talk about her relatives had not escaped him, but he knew better than to try to force her confidence.

'I have thought on what you said earlier about Lucy's shyness,' he continued, 'and I am determined that she must be helped to conquer it. As opportunity permits I would like you to bring her down to the drawing room. With you to support her she will soon grow accustomed to company.'

Claire heard him with sinking heart, but knew she couldn't refuse. 'As you wish, sir.'

'She must learn to take her place in society, and if anyone can help her it will be you, I think.'

'You underplay your own role, sir.'

He smiled faintly. 'I am not skilled with young children as some are, but I'm learning.' He took her hand and carried it to his lips. 'But then I have a good example to follow, do I not?'

Claire felt her face grow hot, not only on account of the words but the warmth of the fingers pressing hers and the unmistakable expression in his eyes.

'You are kind, sir.' She made to rise. The hold on her hand tightened a fraction.

'You are not leaving?'

'I think I must.'

'What are you afraid of?'

'I…nothing.'

'Then why are you trembling?'

'I'm not trembling,' she lied.

'Are you afraid of me?'

'No, sir.' That much was true, she thought. It was not him she feared now.

'Good. I would not have you so.' He smiled. 'Therefore will you not stay awhile?'

Claire fought down the temptation to say yes. 'It is late, sir.'

For a moment she thought he would insist, but to her relief he sighed and let go of her hand. 'Yes, I suppose you are right.' He rose with her. For a moment or two they faced each other in silence. 'Goodnight, then, Miss Davenport.'

'Goodnight, sir.'

Dropping a polite curtsy, Claire walked away, conscious of the grey eyes watching her retreat. Her heart was thumping, her hand burning from his touch. More than anything she would have liked to remain and more than anything she knew she must not. Marcus Edenbridge was forbidden fruit and she dared not forget it.

Chapter Eight

The day after the soirée Claire was returning from a walk with Lucy when they met the Viscount in the hall. With him was Dr Greystoke, who was clearly on the point of departure. He looked round and, seeing Claire, smiled.

'Miss Davenport, how very good to see you again.'

'I am happy to see you too, sir.'

'I hoped I might see you for my sister entrusted me with a message. She begs you will do her the favour of visiting next time you are free.'

'I should be delighted. I am free on Friday afternoon.'

'Excellent. I'll send the carriage over for you.'

Before she could answer, Marcus interrupted. 'There is not the least occasion to do so. Miss Davenport is welcome to have the use of one of my carriages.'

She looked up quickly, but his expression revealed nothing. 'Thank you, sir, if you are sure it will not be inconvenient.'

'Not the least bit,' he replied.

'That's settled, then,' replied Greystoke, beaming. 'I'll tell my sister to expect you on Friday.'

With that he bowed and then he and his host moved away to the door. As she and Lucy continued on towards the nursery Claire reflected on the pleasure of the forthcoming visit to Ellen. It would be good to see her friend again, though she had not expected to be able to do so in such ease and style. It had been kind of Marcus to offer the carriage, though by doing so he spared the Greystokes' coachman an additional journey. That must have been the reason, she decided.

When she returned to her room later it was to find a long, narrow box on the table beside her bed. For a moment she frowned, wondering what it was, knowing it certainly didn't belong to her. Then she saw the note underneath. Rather apprehensively she opened it and read:

Please accept this as a small token of my appreciation for your help in settling Lucy into her new home.

Claire opened the box with trembling hands and then gasped to see the necklace that lay on the satin lining within. Made of silver and set with amethyst flowers, it was quite the prettiest thing she had ever seen. The stones would complement her lilac gown to a nicety. That realisation, and the implication that followed hard on its heels, brought a rush of colour to her face. Then her hand stole to her cheek in dismay. There was no possibility of her accepting this. It would be utterly wrong to do so. No single lady could accept such a gift from a man unless he was a close relative or perhaps her fiancé. To take it would be a gross breach of etiquette and, worse, would be morally compromising. She must return it at once.

For fully five minutes she paced the floor, turning over in her mind various schemes for doing so. She could wait until she knew he was out of the house and then leave it on the desk in his study. But that would mean writing a note to go with it. How to phrase such a note, though, so that it would be firm and courteous together? Perhaps she could leave the box without a note. She sighed. That would look rude and cowardly, too. There was only one way and that was to talk to him face to face. It wasn't a solution she greeted with enthusiasm.

Summoning her courage, she went in search of him and was informed by Mather that His Lordship was in the study. Seeing her come in, the Viscount rose from his chair and greeted her with a smile.

'Miss Davenport. What a pleasant surprise.' He gestured to a chair. 'Won't you sit down?'

'I'll stand if you don't mind, sir.'

One arched brow lifted a little. 'As you wish. How may I be of service?'

Claire laid the box containing the necklace on the desk in front of him.

'By taking this back.' Drawing a deep breath, she hurried on before her courage failed her. 'It was a most generous thought and I am grateful for it, but you must see it is absolutely impossible for me to accept this gift.'

'Why?' he asked.

She had half expected wrath or indignation, but this left her staring in disbelief. 'Why?' she echoed. 'You know why.'

'I don't think I am obtuse, but in this instance I fail to see why at all.' He favoured her with a quizzical look. 'Do explain it to me.'

'Well, because I…because it's inappropriate.'

'Ah, you don't like it.'

'Yes, I do like it. It's beautiful, but…'

'But?'

'You must know that a lady may not receive such gifts from a gentleman.' Claire paused, feeling the room growing hotter. 'Particularly not from a gentleman who is also her employer.'

'Who says so?'

'I say so.'

'But I wish you to have it, and as your employer I have the final word on the matter, I think.'

'Not this time,' she replied.

'I beg your pardon?'

Her gaze met and held his. 'I think you heard me perfectly well, sir.'

'You know, arguing with your employer is a bad habit, Miss Davenport.'

'I have no wish to argue with you.'

'You are arguing now.'

'No, sir, I'm *telling* you that I cannot accept this gift.'

For a moment there was a tense silence as she waited for his anger. What came instead was a penetrating stare.

'You suspect an ulterior motive perhaps?'

'I suspect nothing, but I cannot take it.'

'You have earned it.'

'You pay me well enough already, sir. I do not require any additional remuneration.'

'But I wish to give it.'

She shook her head. 'The matter is closed.' Seeing him about to interrupt, she pre-empted him. 'Please.'

There was an appeal in her eyes that would not be resisted. He made a vague gesture with his hand.

'Very well, since you feel so strongly about it let us say no more on the subject.'

Feeling immeasurably relieved, Claire dropped a polite curtsy and left quickly before he could change his mind. Marcus made no attempt to stop her, merely looked thoughtfully at the box on his desk. Then he sighed.

For the next two days Claire avoided him but when they did meet he made no reference to their earlier discussion. Nor did he seem in any way displeased. It was almost as though the incident had never happened.

On Friday, the day appointed for her visit to Helmshaw, the Viscount's barouche duly appeared at the door. She had wondered if he would forget, but it seemed his memory was good. Once again Claire was conscious of being beholden to him. At the same time she was grateful, too. As always where Marcus Edenbridge was concerned she seemed to experience contradictory feelings.

On her arrival at the Greystokes' house she was greeted at the door by Eliza. Seeing who it was, the maid smiled and then stared wide-eyed at the carriage standing at the gate. Recovering herself quickly, she bobbed into a respectful curtsy.

'Miss Greystoke is expecting you, ma'am.'

She showed the guest into the parlour. Ellen looked up and smiled.

'Claire, I am so glad you are come.' She looked at the maid. 'Eliza, bring us some tea, please.'

As the maid departed the two women sat down on the sofa.

'It is so good to have you back here,' said Ellen then, 'if only for a short time. I have missed you very much.'

'And I you.'

'I suppose I should be thankful that you are only ten miles off and not a hundred. You are treated well?'

'I have no cause for complaint.'

'I am glad.' She paused. 'I confess I did feel anxious when first you took the post. It is good to know that the anxiety was unfounded.'

Claire's heartbeat quickened a little. 'But why should you be concerned?'

'It was because I wondered about Lord Destermere's motives in hiring you and on such a handsome salary.' Ellen coloured faintly. 'I am quite ashamed—I see now that my suspicions were unworthy.'

Listening to this and recalling the recent past, Claire felt her own face grow pink. 'Lord Destermere is many things, but he is not dishonourable.'

'No, I truly believe he is not.' Ellen paused. 'It's just that when one has seen a little of the world such thoughts inevitably occur. You are a very attractive young woman after all.'

'You have no reason to be concerned, though I thank you for it all the same.'

Her companion smiled and then changed the subject and they chatted agreeably until Eliza came in with the tea.

'I am sorry that George is not here,' said Ellen. 'He had hoped to be, but at the last minute he had to attend a birth in Gartside.'

'Your brother is an excellent physician. The people here are fortunate.'

'Goodness knows there is need.' She paused. 'I wonder, when we have had our tea, if would you walk with me into Helmshaw? There is something I should like you to see.'

'I'd be glad to come with you, but let us take the carriage. It is at our disposal after all and it will be better than keeping the horses standing too long.'

'As you wish.'

Thus it was that half an hour later they embarked on the short journey to Helmshaw.

'We must tell the coachman to wait in the square. The carriage will not be able to negotiate the narrow lanes.'

Claire was puzzled now, but made no demur, trusting to her friend's judgement. They alighted in the square and turned off it along a narrower thoroughfare. Having followed this for perhaps a hundred yards, Ellen turned off again, this time along a narrow muddy lane with mean houses on either side. Ragged children played nearby. Presently she stopped outside a door halfway down the row, and knocked. A girl of about eight opened it.

'Who is it, Meg?' said a voice from within.

'Miss Greystoke, Ma.'

On hearing the name a woman looked up from the stool by the hearth. She was probably in her early thirties, but looked ten years older. In her arms she held a baby. With them were five other children, ranging in age from two to about twelve years. They eyed the newcomers with solemn-eyed curiosity.

'Come in, Miss Greystoke,' she said.

As they stepped over the threshold Claire saw with a sense of shock that the house had just one room. Apart from the table and two rough benches, the only other furniture was a bed in the far corner and a wooden dresser. A small fire burned in the hearth and a meagre pile of wood lay in a box nearby. The room was clean but cold, for the heat reached only a few feet beyond the hearth. The younger children were huddled together on the bed for warmth. The air smelled of damp. By the look of things the small heap of potatoes on the table was dinner for all of them.

'Mrs Dobson, I have brought a friend today. This is Miss Davenport.'

'Pleased to meet you, ma'am. Any friend of Miss Greystoke's is welcome here.'

'I came to see how little Sarah is doing,' Ellen continued. 'Is her cough improving?'

Mrs Dobson glanced down at the baby. 'Aye, ma'am, a little, thank you.'

Her voice shook as she spoke and now that her eyes had become accustomed to the dim light Claire could see she had been crying.

'Has something happened, Mrs Dobson?' she asked.

To her horror the woman burst into tears. Then, clearly overcome with embarrassment, she began to apologise.

'I'm so sorry, ma'am. It's just that I don't know which way to turn.' She took a deep, shuddering breath. 'Since my Jack died things have gone from bad to worse. The landlord came for his rent yesterday. 'Tis already weeks in arrears. If we don't pay up by the end of the month, he'll evict us.'

Claire stared at her, appalled. 'But where will you go? What will you do?'

'I have no more idea of that than you do, ma'am. My oldest boys have tried to get work, but there's none to be had.' She glanced across the room to the two in question. 'In the meantime there's seven mouths to feed and the baby ill. If it hadn't been for Miss Greystoke's kindness, we'd have starved by now.'

'What happened to your husband?'

'He died the night Harlston's loom was destroyed by the wreckers.' She dashed away fresh tears with the sleeve of her shabby gown. 'He'd volunteered for the work to try to earn a bit more money. They shot him through the heart.'

Listening to her story, Claire turned cold. That had been the night Marcus had been wounded. She recalled with dreadful clarity the morning she'd found him on the moors, and the wagon bringing the dead back for burial. Unbeknown to her one of those men had been Jack Dobson. The tragedy of it struck her with force.

'I am so very sorry to hear of your loss.' Even as she spoke, the words sounded woefully inadequate. Worse, she hadn't even brought any money with her that day. There was no practical help she could offer.

'Thank you, ma'am.'

Ellen took a small bottle from her reticule. 'I have brought some more medicine for the baby.' She put it on the table and, unobtrusively, a small knotted handkerchief alongside. Claire guessed that it contained coin.

'God bless you, ma'am, for your kindness, and Dr Greystoke, too. Pray thank him for us.'

'No thanks are necessary,' Ellen replied.

They left shortly afterwards, retracing their steps along the lane. For a while they did not speak, each of them lost in thought. Claire was more than ever conscious that, but for fortune, she too might have been reduced to destitution and worse. She knew very well how it felt to be alone and penniless and frightened.

They reached the corner of the lane and turned into the wider thoroughfare beyond. Two men were standing by a doorway opposite, engaged in quiet conversation. One then went inside. The other turned to leave. As he did so he looked round and stopped in his tracks. Claire found herself looking straight at Jed Stone. She paled. His expression changed too and a wolfish smile played about his lips as the predatory gaze hardened. In an instant all the details of their encounter in Gartside returned with force. Sickened, she turned away, but not before Ellen had seen the look on her face. She shot a swift glance at the man opposite and then back at Claire.

'Is anything wrong, my dear?'

'No, nothing.'

Claire took her friend's arm and hurried on, terrified that Stone might try to bar their way. However, he made no move in their direction at all. Rather he remained where he was, staring after them with the same lupine smile on his lips.

'Who was that man?' asked Ellen. 'He seemed to know you.'

'I don't know. Perhaps he has seen me before in town.'

'Yes, that must be it.'

To Claire's relief Ellen did not pursue the matter and five minutes later they reached the waiting carriage without further incident. However, as the vehicle pulled away Claire saw Stone again, this time watching them from the corner of the road that led off the square. She knew that he must have followed them and the thought made her distinctly uneasy. Then she became aware that Ellen was speaking to her.

'I hope you will forgive me, my dear, but I must confess to an ulterior motive in taking you to meet the Dobsons today.'

Claire regarded her quizzically. 'Motive?'

'Yes. I was wondering...' She hesitated. 'I was wondering, do you think that some sort of employment might be found for them on the Netherclough estate?'

Claire stared at her in surprise for a moment but, now the words were out, it seemed an obvious solution. She wondered that she had not thought of it herself.

'I don't know,' she replied, 'but I could certainly ask.'

'Would you?'

'I'd be glad to.'

'The family has a good reputation in the town. Mr Dobson was known for being a hard-working man and his wife is a good woman. I have done what I can, but it is precious little. If they do not get real help soon, I fear the worst, especially for the baby.'

Claire nodded. 'When I return to Netherclough I shall speak to Mar...Lord Destermere at the earliest opportunity.'

'Bless you. It would mean so much if—' She broke off. 'But I must not get ahead of myself here. There may be no position for them after all.'

'They shall not be allowed to starve. Netherclough is a large estate. There must be something they could do.'

'I hope it may be so. These times have brought so much hardship to the people hereabouts. Old Mrs Grundy told me yesterday that Sir James Wraxall has cut his workers' wages to seven shillings a week.'

'Seven shillings! Are you sure?'

'Quite sure. Mrs Grundy's son works in one of Wraxall's mills.'

'But people could scarcely manage on eight shillings,' Claire replied.

'I know, but that is of no concern to men like Wraxall. He alone seems to prosper in these hard times. Only six months ago he was able to buy Beardsall's mill when its owner went bankrupt.'

Claire was sickened. How could such a wealthy man behave with such callous unconcern for those who depended on him? Indignation rose like a tide and along with it the knowledge of her own impotence.

Ellen's words stayed with her, even after she had taken her

leave. As the carriage began the return journey, Claire was doubly determined to try and do something for the Dobsons. She was realist enough to know that she couldn't save everybody caught up in the economic depression, but it might be possible to help one family at least.

Mindful of her promise to Ellen she sought an interview with her employer the very same evening. On learning from Mather that His Lordship was in the study, she presented herself at the door. The Viscount was reading through some paperwork but, on seeing her there, looked up in surprise. Then he rose and smiled.

'Miss Davenport, what an unexpected pleasure. Won't you sit down?'

Claire sank into the offered chair and folded her hands in her lap to stop them trembling. Now that they were face to face it was suddenly less easy to broach the subject. The affairs of people like the Dobsons were hardly his concern. Would he consider her request the grossest piece of presumption?

'I hope you enjoyed your visit to Miss Greystoke,' he said.

'Yes, thank you.'

'Good. I'm glad to hear it.'

Claire bit her lip, knowing she must speak and not quite knowing how to begin. The silence stretched.

'Was there something you wished to discuss?' he prompted.

'Yes.' She took a deep breath. This was her chance. 'I was wondering…well, hoping that you could offer employment to the Dobson boys.'

He raised one arched brow. 'And who, pray, are the Dobson boys?'

'Their father was killed when Harlston's machines were attacked. He was one of the escort. Do you remember? The night you were shot?'

'I could hardly forget it,' he observed.

'No, I suppose not. Well, the thing is that Mr Dobson's death has meant that his family is destitute. He left a wife and six children. The oldest boys have tried to find work, but there is none to be had. If they don't get help soon, the whole family will be evicted and left to starve.'

'May I ask how you know all this?'

'Ellen took me to visit the family this afternoon. Mrs Dobson is a good woman and does the best she can, but their plight is pitiful indeed. Ellen tries to help, and Dr Greystoke too with medicine for the baby, but there is only so much they can do, sir.'

'Ah, yes. Miss Greystoke is known for her charitable works, is she not?' He paused, regarding her keenly. 'Is she behind this request, by any chance?'

Claire felt her cheeks grow warm. 'She asked if I would speak to you.'

'I see.'

'She understands perfectly that there may be nothing for them here. Only…'

'Only?'

'Netherclough is such a large estate and it requires so many staff. She…we wondered if places might be found for two more. In the gardens, or the stables perhaps?'

'I do not run a charitable institution, Miss Davenport. While I can sympathise with the plight of people like the Dobsons, I cannot change the times we live in.'

'No, but you can help to make things a little better.'

The grey eyes met and held hers. 'I do not need you to tell me what I can and cannot do.'

'I'm sorry. I did not mean to be presumptuous. It's just that I'd hoped…'

'Hoped what?'

'That you might at least consider it.'

'If such aid is offered to one family, it sets a precedent for others.'

'It could be done discreetly.'

'Perhaps. If there was work available. As it is, Netherclough is fully staffed. I'm sorry.'

The tone expressed finality and Claire knew it was useless to pursue the matter and stupid of her to have assumed he would help. Rich men stayed rich because they didn't give money away unless they had to. For a split second Ellen's words about Wraxall leapt to mind and with them a surge of indignation and impotent anger. She had thought Marcus was of a different stamp. Trying to force the lid down on her temper, she rose from her chair and faced him.

'I quite understand, sir. I'm sorry to have bothered you with this. After all, the Dobsons can always go to the workhouse.'

With that she swept out of the room, leaving Marcus staring after her in slack-jawed astonishment. A moment later he was on his feet.

'Claire! Claire, come back here!'

The only reply was swiftly retreating footsteps. He swore softly. For a second he was sorely tempted to go after her but resisted it, knowing that if he did he might do something he'd regret. Like giving her a good shaking perhaps. Had he not treated her with consideration? And was he to be treated to such a display of scorn just because he had refused this one request? A totally unreasonable request at that?

'Damn!'

He flung out of the chair and went to stand by the hearth, glowering down into the flames. No one had ever spoken to him like that. Certainly not a governess. Miss Davenport needed to learn her place—or lose it. That thought gave him pause. He drew in a deep breath. By rights the vixen should be given her marching orders, but he knew perfectly well he wasn't going to dismiss her. Lucy would be upset by it. He couldn't do that to the child, even though such a step would have the advantage of ridding him of an argumentative, troublesome little jade.

* * *

After she left him Claire marched straight to her room there to pace the floor, fists clenched. Her face still burned and the memory of the recent interview did nothing to cool it. He could have intervened! He was the richest man in the county! With a shaking hand she dashed away the tears that started in her eyes. She had expected so much more than a flat refusal to help.

For some minutes she paced, until her anger cooled a little. Moving to the window, she stared out at the beautiful gardens and rolling parkland beyond. How was it that some people had so much and others so little? And should not the rich help the poor when they could? She did not grudge the wealthy their good fortune. There had always been social inequality and always would be, but what about fair treatment? The labourer was worthy of his hire. How could men like Wraxall justify paying seven shillings a week and causing families to starve? How could honest employment be withheld by those who had the power to give it?

Claire sighed and sat down disconsolately on the edge of her bed. Gradually as her anger cooled it gave way to more rational thought. She should have realised that the Viscount would be more likely to refuse than to accede to her request. A house like Netherclough was always properly staffed. It ran like a well-oiled machine. It occurred to her then that most of its employees were drawn from the local area. Indeed, its owner was a key employer in his way. And he paid fair wages. The admission brought her back to earth with a jolt.

Claire knew then that she had absolutely no right to criticise or to tell him what he ought to do. Had he not shown her kindness up to now? Recalling the attentions she had received, she began to feel guilty. Mingled with it was shame for losing her temper. She had spoken to him as she might have done to an intimate. Yet this man was among the foremost in the land. Not only that, he was her employer, the being who held her fate in his hands. The realisation of the true extent of her folly acted like a bucket of cold water. How could she have been so stupid? He had made it clear at the outset that continued employment was dependent on satisfactory completion of the probationary period. The latter still had well over a month left to run. Instead of getting on with her job she had allowed her feelings to run away with her and behaved like an idiot. If he gave her notice to quit, it would be no more than she deserved. Truly appalled now, she knew that she owed him an apology—and soon.

For a while she deliberated. Should she go now or wait, hoping his anger might have cooled by the morrow? But then she had her duties to perform and likely would not see the Viscount at all. She certainly couldn't imagine him visiting the nursery and even if he did it was not the right place to say what needed to be said. No, it must be now. Pausing only to bathe her face and tidy her appearance, she retraced her steps to the study and knocked on the door.

'Come!'

Claire swallowed hard and, summoning all her courage, went in.

At first he didn't look up from the desk, seemingly absorbed in the papers before him. She had leisure to observe the sharp crease between his brows. Heart thumping, she took a tentative pace forward and stopped again. Then he did look up. For just a split second the grey eyes registered surprise. Then it was gone. She could detect no sign of outward anger, but the steely expression was infinitely worse.

'Well?'

It was hardly a promising beginning, but she knew there was no possibility of leaving before she had atoned for her behaviour. As he waited, Marcus knew a moment of intense and gloating satisfaction. So she had thought better of it, had she? As well she might. He leaned back in his chair, relishing the moment.

'I wish to apologise, sir, for what I said earlier. It was quite uncalled for and unpardonably rude.' She took a deep breath. 'I beg your pardon.'

For the second time he knew surprise, though now his expression gave no hint of it. He could not mistake the note of sincerity in her words either. Indeed, she looked abject. The hazel eyes met his in mute appeal. As they did so every vestige of his former satisfaction vanished and was replaced with quite a different feeling.

Mistaking his silence, Claire felt sick inside. She had failed. He had not forgiven her. His anger was still very much alive. And why would it not be? She made a vague, despairing gesture with her hand.

'That's all I came to say, sir.'

With that she turned away and walked towards the door. She never reached it for Marcus was out of his chair and across the room in three strides. Seizing her by the wrist, he pulled her round to face him. For just one second, grey eyes burned into hazel before he drew her close and brought his mouth down hard across hers in a searing kiss. He felt her tense and try to resist him. It availed her nothing. His mouth demanded her response, to acknowledge what was in her heart. Crushed in that powerful embrace, Claire felt her blood race, every part of her alive to the touch and taste and scent of him. Unable to escape, or to ignore the sudden igniting of that inner fire, she abandoned herself to his kiss.

When at last he drew back a little and looked into her eyes, it was to see an answering recognition and his heart leapt.

'I suppose it's my turn to apologise now,' he said, 'but for the life of me I cannot. I've wanted to do that for weeks.'

She shut her eyes as the enormity of the situation dawned. He shook her gently.

'Look at me, Claire.'

Unable to resist the appeal in his voice, she obeyed.

'Now tell me you feel nothing for me.'

'I cannot tell you that for it would be false. But this cannot be.'

'Why not?'

'Because it's wrong. Surely you see that?'

'No, I don't. How can this feeling be wrong?'

'Because of who we are. Because of our different situations. I will not be a rich man's plaything, Marcus.'

'Is that what you think this is about?' he demanded, stung.

'Isn't it?'

'I have never thought of you in those terms.'

'Then why did you kiss me like that?'

'Because I couldn't help myself.'

'Was this why you gave me the governess post here?' she asked.

'No, of course not.' His hold slackened. 'Do you really think me capable of such a calculating act?'

She shook her head. 'I'm sorry.'

'Besides, it was you who sought the post, remember?'

'Yes, I remember.'

For a moment there was a tense silence. Then the grey eyes narrowed.

'Why? Why did you want this place so much?'

She swallowed hard. 'I told you—I had to earn my living.'

'No, there's more to it than that, isn't there?' She tried to turn away but his hands on her shoulders prevented it. 'Tell me why, Claire.'

'I...it's something I should have told you long since. Only I did not know how.'

Marcus waited. Unable to withstand that scorching gaze, Claire averted her eyes and for several seconds was silent. Suddenly she wanted to tell him everything and yet part of her feared his response. Would he be angry with her for withholding the truth? There was only one way to find out.

'It concerns my uncle.'

That certainly wasn't what he had been expecting. 'Your uncle? How so?'

'He became my legal guardian after my parents died. He was…*is* a man of stern principles and not given to demonstrating affection, even to those nearest to him. In consequence we were never close.'

'That is hardly to be wondered at.'

'Although he provided for my material needs in childhood, I always knew that one day I should have to earn my living. That much had been made clear. In any case the thought of leaving did not distress me greatly. I expected that he would find me a situation.'

'And did he?'

'Yes, as the intended wife of one of his friends. A man old enough to be my father.'

'Good God! But of course you refused the offer.'

'Yes, I refused.' She took a deep breath. 'My uncle was furious. He said he would not be forsworn and that the marriage would take place no matter what.'

'But he could not compel you to wed against your will.'

'You have never met my uncle, sir. He would not hesitate to use force and told me as much. I knew him well enough to understand it was no idle threat.'

Marcus's jaw tightened. 'Did he hurt you, Claire?'

'No. I pretended compliance. He is so used to being obeyed he could not conceive of disobedience in any member of the family. Having lulled him into believing he had won, I packed a bag and escaped out of the bedroom window one night.'

Torn between indignation and amusement he shook his head. 'And then?'

'After that I knew I had to get as far away as possible and to the one person in the world I knew would help me.'

'You refer to Miss Greystoke, I collect. You had kept in touch then?'

'I received a letter from her not long after I arrived at my uncle's house, and I was permitted to reply—under my aunt's direction. That was all. None of Ellen's subsequent letters ever reached me, though she told me she wrote several times.'

The grey eyes hardened. 'They were kept from you?'

'I believe so. But in spite of that I never forgot her. She had always been so kind to me, you see. I just prayed that when I reached Helmshaw she would still be there.'

As he listened to the tale it seemed to Marcus that many pieces of a puzzle had just dropped into place.

'It was fortunate for you that she was,' he replied, grim-faced.

'Yes, and fortunate for me that you came along when you did.'

Remembering the incident in Gartside, he felt a surge of unwonted anger. The idea of any man laying hands on her was intolerable. He had let Jed Stone off far too lightly. And yet was he much better? Had he too not forced his attentions on her, a vulnerable young woman who was under his protection? He should keep her from harm, not be the cause of it. *I will not be a rich man's plaything.* The words smote his conscience hard.

'I did what any self-respecting man would have done.'

'No, not just any man.' The hazel eyes met and held his and, seeing the expression there, he felt his heart miss a beat. 'And then you gave me this situation and with it the means to support myself,' she went on. 'It was like the answer to a prayer.'

For a moment he was silent, regarding her with a level gaze. 'You need have no fear that I shall divulge your whereabouts to your uncle.'

'Thank you.'

'I think it unlikely he would trace you this far in any case but, even if he did, he will not remove you from this house.'

'I'm sorry. This might still put you in a difficult position with the law.'

'But you cannot now be far off your majority.'

'In a few more weeks I shall be one and twenty. Then his authority over me will be at an end.'

Marcus knew a moment of inner relief. He had not the least fear of meeting her uncle—indeed, would rather have relished doing so—but the legal aspect of the matter was trickier. Technically the brute did have the right to remove her from the house and compel her return. In the same instant he knew he would never permit that to happen. The idea of any young woman being forced into such a marriage was repugnant, but when that woman was Claire it became unthinkable.

He looked down into her face. 'Why didn't you tell me, Claire? Did you not trust me enough?'

She met his gaze and, interpreting it correctly, her heart thumped harder. 'I'm so sorry. I know it was wrong of me, but I was afraid you might turn me away.'

'I would never turn you away. Nor would I ever let harm come to you.'

He drew her closer and kissed her mouth, gently this time, and just for a moment. Then he drew her against him, holding her close, breathing in the fragrance of her hair. It felt right to hold her in his arms; she belonged there. He had known that feeling only once before, and had never thought to feel it again. He wanted her now with every fibre of his being, wanted to carry her to the couch and continue this to its delightful conclusion. But he knew he could not. He could not take advantage of her innocence or her vulnerability.

Claire heard him sigh and felt his hold slacken.

'Forgive me,' he said then.

It took every ounce of her willpower not to reach out for him, not to surrender to the heat in her blood. The memory of his kiss burned still. She could feel yet the warmth of his hands, the lean hardness of the body pressed against hers. It was like being on the brink of a lake of fire and wanting nothing more than to plunge in and be consumed. The expression in his eyes left her in no doubt he felt it, too, that he wanted her just as much. Was this what her parents had felt for each other?

The memory jolted her back to reality. What they had felt was love, not passion merely; the kind of love that finds expression in a lifetime's commitment, not in a dishonourable and furtive liaison. Marcus might want her, but his heart was given elsewhere. She knew beyond all doubt that she cared for him, that she had always cared for him, but she could never be his mistress. While she was not fool enough to think he would ever marry her, she could at least retain his respect and his regard. It was all she had.

'I should go,' she said.

Unable to follow all the thoughts behind the hazel eyes, he recognized the resolution in her expression. He knew also that she was right.

'Go then, Claire, if you must. I'll not prevent you.'

With unconcealed relief she saw him stand aside. Before he could change his mind she slipped past him and out of the door, fleeing for her room and not daring to look back.

Grim-faced he stood on the threshold, watching her retreating figure. Part of him was tempted to go after her and to bring her back, but he knew he must not. His fists clenched at his sides and slowly he turned away, shutting the door behind him. Then he let out the breath he had unconsciously been holding. As he calmed a little and more rational thought intervened he could only regard his behaviour with abhorrence. There could be no repetition of what had happened today. Somehow he must find the self-discipline to live in the same house with her, to see her every day, and behave as though they were merely polite acquaintances brought together by circumstance. In the meantime he could only hope that she would forgive him.

True to his intention he avoided her for several days, deciding that they both needed space and time to try to put the incident behind them. In any case there were many matters requiring his attention and he spent hours closeted with Fisk, discussing estate business. Sometimes, when he looked out of the study window, he caught a glimpse of her walking in the gardens with Lucy. Once he heard them laughing together and wondered what had caused their amusement. It was good to hear a child's laugher around the place. He wondered suddenly if Lucy was ever lonely. While she had her governess there were no children of her own age to play with. Recalling his own childhood adventures with Greville, he knew that his brother had been an important part of his life. It came to Marcus then that he would very much like to have children of his own.

A sound at the door brought him back to the present. Mather was there to say that John Harlston had called.

'Ah, yes. Show him in, Mather.'

'Yes, my lord.'

A few moments later Harlston appeared. The Viscount smiled and held out his hand.

'Thank you for coming, Mr Harlston.'

'My pleasure, sir.'

Having invited his guest to sit and plied him with a glass of sherry, Marcus got straight to the point.

'I have asked you here in order to enlist your help in catching the Luddite wreckers.'

The other regarded him with some surprise. 'I will certainly do all in my power.' He paused. 'You have a plan?'

'Yes. I intend to set a trap.'

'A trap? How?'

'If you are in agreement, word will get out about the delivery of a replacement power loom to your mill. There will be a wagon and a suitable escort, but no loom—only a contingent of militia concealed beneath the tarpaulin, and another riding behind the convoy just out of sight.'

Harlston considered it and then nodded slowly. 'By heaven, it might just work.'

'I believe it might.' The Viscount paused. 'However, secrecy is essential if the wreckers are to take the bait. The fewer people who know about it, the better. The escort need not know until the last minute. As for the militia, only Major Barstow needs to be told initially. I believe we may rely on his discretion.'

'What about the other mill owners?'

Marcus met and held his gaze. 'I would prefer to say nothing for the time being.'

'Very well, sir. I'm sure you have your reasons.'

'I do, and they are good ones.'

'Will you apprise Major Barstow or shall I?'

'I will speak to him. I intend to be one of those in the convoy.'

'You, sir?' Harlston's astonishment was plain. 'Forgive me, but have you considered? It is most dangerous work.'

'I am fully aware of that, Mr Harlston, but I have special reasons for undertaking it. I am also well able to defend myself should the need arise.'

'Of course you are, but…'

'It is pointless to try to dissuade me on this point. My mind is made up.'

'As you will. May I ask when you are proposing to put the plan into action?'

'At the end of the month. That will afford us plenty of time to see that everything is in place.'

'If it works, and there is no reason to suppose it will not, the area will be rid of that murderous crew once and for all.'

'That is my intention.'

Harlston regarded him steadily for a moment. 'May I ask why you take such a keen interest in the matter, sir?'

'I cannot answer that at present. Suffice it to say that the business of catching these men is important to me for several reasons.' Marcus paused. 'I must ask you to trust me.'

'Very well, sir.'

'Thank you.'

The two men shook hands and Harlston left a short time later. For some minutes after his visitor had gone Marcus remained alone in the study, turning over the details of the plan in his mind. It was simple but, in his experience, the simplest ideas were often the best. When Harlston said it was dangerous he had spoken the truth, but Marcus would not ask other men to do what he wasn't prepared to do himself. Besides, this was also personal. One way or another he intended to bring Greville's killers to justice.

He tossed back the remainder of his sherry and rang the bell for Mather. When the butler appeared shortly afterwards he was directed to send for Mr Fisk. The land agent duly arrived a few minutes later.

'You wished to speak with me, my lord?'

'Yes. Am I right in thinking that one of the estate cottages is currently standing empty?'

'That is correct, my lord. It has been vacant since old Ramsbottom died. He had no surviving family.'

'Quite so. As it has been uninhabited for several months, the place may possibly need some renovation to make it habitable. You will put matters in train immediately.'

'Certainly, my lord.' Fisk paused. 'Am I to understand that the cottage is about to be tenanted again?'

'Yes.'

'Very good, my lord.'

'That will be all, Mr Fisk.'

Having dismissed his agent, the Viscount sat down at his desk and began to pen a letter to Ellen Greystoke.

Chapter Nine

Claire strolled along the river bank while Lucy ran on ahead collecting brightly coloured leaves. From time to time she would run back and show Claire a particularly prized specimen, which was duly admired. The afternoon was cool but fine and, feeling the need to escape the confines of the house, Claire had not hesitated to take her young charge out for a walk. Besides, the place was peaceful and pleasant, affording plenty of opportunity for private reflection.

After that last momentous encounter with Marcus she had not set eyes on him, and correctly surmised it was deliberate policy. In many ways she was glad of it. He had the good sense to avoid temptation. She smiled sadly. The temptation was not all one-sided as she knew full well. She had come to care for him more deeply than she could ever have dreamed possible. It was a passion that could never be realised for to do so would render her position here untenable. She must not jeopardise that. It wasn't going to be easy to keep a cool head. In spite of good intentions they would be thrown together, and each time would make it harder for both of them. Somehow she must find the strength of mind to resist the attraction he represented, even though every part of her longed to succumb. He could never be for her. Eventually, he would marry a lady from among the *ton* and bring her here to be mistress of Netherclough. His wife would be a fortunate woman, she thought.

Claire's twenty-first birthday was drawing near. In a little over four weeks she would be a free agent. Uncle Hector would have no authority over her and it wouldn't matter if he did find out where she was. No doubt there would still be an unpleasant scene in which he would castigate her for ingratitude, but she could bear it. Besides, she was under the Viscount's protection. Even her uncle would think twice before crossing such a powerful man. She just hoped that Ellen would not be subjected to any disagreeable scenes for her part in all of this.

By a strange coincidence it seemed that her friend had also been thinking of her, for the following morning brought an unexpected communication:

My Dearest Claire,
    Forgive the brevity of this letter but I have so little time to write at present. Even so, it would be most remiss of me if I did not apprise you of the most recent developments regarding the Dobson family. Yesterday I received a letter from Lord Destermere to say that he had lately been informed of their attempts to find employment following Mr Dobson's untimely demise. His Lordship informs me that a vacancy exists in his household for a kitchen maid, and wonders if the situation would suit Mrs Dobson. The position is offered along with a vacant cottage on the Netherclough estate. Furthermore, he undertakes to find suitable situations for the eldest Dobson boys.
    I lost no time in imparting all this to Mrs Dobson, and you can well imagine the family's joyful response on receiving the news. My own gratitude towards Lord Destermere can scarcely be expressed, but I have written to thank him for his great kindness. However, I also know that sincere thanks are due to you too, dearest Claire, for helping to bring this about. God bless you.
    Your affectionate friend,
    Ellen

For some moments Claire was too stunned to take it in, but on rereading the letter discovered she had not been mistaken. Heart full, she felt tears start in her eyes. He had listened after all, but even in her wildest dreams she had never expected he would exert himself so far. For the first time in days her spirits soared. What had made him change his mind? Was it perhaps that he too had come close to death the night Mr Dobson was killed? Or perhaps it was just that, on reflection, he had decided it would not be too difficult to accommodate one more family at Netherclough? Did he understand what happiness he had given to others by his actions? She folded the letter carefully and put it in her pocket. No matter what it cost her she must thank him, too. It was the least she could do.

As it happened she did not need to seek him out because he came to the nursery not long afterwards. Lucy saw him first and the child's face was lit with a smile.

'Uncle Marcus!'

'Hello, Brat.' He lifted her into his arms so that their faces were level. 'I hope you've been behaving yourself.'

'I know all my letters now.'

'I don't believe you.'

'I do, don't I, Miss Davenport?'

Claire smiled. 'Perhaps you should say them.'

Marcus assumed an expression of mock severity. 'I quite agree. Otherwise I will only have your word for it.'

Rather self-consciously Lucy proceeded to recite the alphabet faultlessly. Marcus grinned.

'I am amazed! I never thought to have such a clever niece.'

'Miss Davenport is teaching me to read now.'

'Is she so?' He glanced past the child to Claire. 'Then no doubt you will be able to read to me very soon.'

'Yes, I shall,' Lucy replied, the tone suggesting total confidence. 'Shan't I, Miss Davenport?'

'I am quite sure of it,' said Claire.

'Very well, then. Far be it from me to hinder your progress.'

Lucy eyed him speculatively. 'Are you going away again, Uncle Marcus?'

'Going away? No, why?'

'I haven't seen you for days and days.'

'I know. That is why I wondered if you would like to go riding with me this afternoon?'

'Oh, yes, please!'

'All right, then.' He set the child down. Then he looked at Claire. 'I will see you in the stable yard at two o'clock.'

It was evident that she was to be included in the expedition. Outwardly then everything would appear the same. Only the two of them knew it was not. However, if he could keep up his part of the pretence, she could do no less. It would also give her an opportunity to thank him for his intervention in the Dobson affair. But there was more to it than that, as she quickly acknowledged: she was looking forward to seeing him, to being in his company again. In spite of herself she had missed him in these last few days.

They rode out as usual that afternoon. Claire took care to let Lucy monopolise his attention, and watched the interaction between the two of them. He kept his horse to a slow walk to allow for the pony's shorter paces and, whenever the child spoke to him, he gave her his full attention. Now that she was gaining competence he allowed her a gentle canter, a development that brought a glow of excitement to her eyes.

'Will you let me ride to hounds one day, Uncle Marcus?'

'One day,' he replied, 'when you are more competent. Then I will take you out myself.'

Lucy's smile widened. 'You can come too, Miss Davenport.'

Claire smiled in return. 'Well, thank you very much.'

'Then we can all go together.'

'We'll see.'

As Lucy turned to impart the news to the groom, Marcus reined his horse alongside Claire's.

'She is making excellent progress,' he observed.

'Yes, she is a natural rider.'

'I did not mean in horsemanship alone. She is making progress in every way. More indeed than I could have hoped.' He threw her a sideways glance. 'And that is due to you.'

Claire felt her cheeks grow warm. 'She is a delightful pupil, bright and eager to learn.'

'She has grown much attached to you in the last two months.'

'And I to her.'

For a moment or two they rode on in silence. Then she turned towards him.

'I wanted to thank you for what you have done to help the Dobson family. Ellen wrote and told me.'

'Did she?'

'Yes. You cannot know how much it means to them. To all concerned.'

'Do not cast me in the role of hero. It was done with extraordinarily little effort on my part.'

'You underplay it, sir. If it were not for your intervention, their situation would be dire indeed.'

'Well, at least now they won't end in the workhouse.'

'I should not have said that.'

'Yes, you should.' He paused, surveying her keenly. 'And you were quite right, of course. But do not be under any illusions— my actions were not the result of altruism.'

'What, then?'

'I believe I acted in the hope of pleasing you.'

She met his gaze, but could detect no sign of teasing. On the contrary there was an expression there that made her heart beat a little faster.

'Then you succeeded.'

'I'm glad to hear it. I could not long withstand your disapproval.'

Her colour deepened. 'I am far too outspoken.'

'Yes,' he replied, 'but like the voice of my conscience, hard to ignore.'

She smiled ruefully. 'It was most presumptuous of me and I am sorry for it.'

'Since you are in such a penitent mood I shall take full advantage of the fact. I intend to hold a ball at Netherclough three weeks from now. I would like you to attend.'

Claire's stomach turned over. 'A ball?'

'Yes, it is a genteel entertainment involving a lot of dancing.' Seeing the speaking look that greeted his sally, he grinned.

'I must refuse, sir, though I am grateful for the invitation. It would not be appropriate.'

His smile vanished. 'Damn it, Claire, I don't want your gratitude, and I'll decide what's appropriate and what is not.'

'I cannot, sir.'

'Cannot or will not?' he demanded.

'Cannot, sir. You must see that. The more people who see me, the more likely that my uncle will get to hear of my whereabouts.'

Seeing the anxiety in her face, he felt some of his annoyance ebb. 'Your uncle has no acquaintance here who might tell him. There can be no danger, I think.'

Claire shook her head, unconvinced. 'All the same…'

'Even if he did discover your whereabouts, I would not let him take you from Netherclough.'

'He would have the law on his side.'

'True, but litigation takes time, and by then you would have achieved your majority.'

'How I wish I had.'

The words were delivered with quiet passion and struck him forcibly. What kind of brute was this uncle that he should inspire such feelings of dread?

'You have not long to wait now,' he replied. 'In the meantime it will do you good to enjoy yourself. Come to the ball, Claire.'

'I have no gown.'

'I'll buy you one.'

'No, sir.'

He threw up a hand in despair. 'I am thwarted at every turn.'

'I am truly sorry, sir.'

She really was, but knew that she could not yield the point.

'Think about it,' he said. 'I'll not press you for a final answer now.'

In the event all thoughts of the ball were driven out of her head for a while, because two days later Lucy contracted a feverish cold and was confined to bed. Initially it was thought to be merely a childish ailment that would probably cure itself in a day or two. However, the little girl grew more listless and lethargic and her appetite disappeared altogether. Claire grew concerned enough to go and see Marcus.

'I think we should have a medical opinion, sir.'

He reached for the bell pull. 'I shall have Dr Greystoke summoned immediately.'

The physician was not long in coming but though he examined the child thoroughly he could find nothing more seriously wrong than a bad cold.

'Will she be all right?' asked Marcus as they walked together down the stairs.

'Yes, though she may feel poorly for a few days yet.'

'What brought it on?'

'It is hard to say. A slight chill perhaps,' Greystoke replied.

'Keep her warm and quiet and see that she drinks plenty of fluids. For the time being she must have no excitement or exertion.'

'Very well.'

'I will call again tomorrow to see if there has been any improvement in her condition.'

After the physician had left, Marcus returned to the sickroom to find Claire there already. He came over to stand by the bedside.

'How is she?'

'Sleeping now. I'll sit with her for a while.'

'Are you sure? One of the maids could do it.'

'I would rather stay—for the time being.'

'As you wish.' He regarded her keenly for a moment. 'Is there anything you need?'

'Thank you, no.'

'If you think of something, just let one of the servants know.'

'I will.'

'Very well. I will come back later and see how she does.'

After he had left Claire watched the child sleeping for a while and then moved to the window. For some minutes she stood there, looking out onto the garden. It had been raining earlier and the fallen leaves lay dark and sodden on the pathways and flower beds where a few late blooms drooped over the dark earth. A lowering sky promised more rain. She shivered. The place seemed strangely bleak and forlorn after the previous weeks of autumn sunshine.

Turning away from the scene, she took a glance at Lucy and, seeing that the child still slept, returned briefly to her own chamber to fetch her book. It would help to pass the time. Having accomplished her goal, she settled herself in a chair and began to read.

Lucy woke about an hour later and complained of thirst so Claire gave her some water. Then she read to her for a while until the child dozed again. Marcus returned not long after, moving quietly across the room to join her.

'How is she?'

Claire gave him a summary of the situation.

'I think the sleep will do her good.' He paused. 'As for you, I think some luncheon is in order. You must be hungry by now. I've told Mrs Hughes to prepare something. Meanwhile, one of the maids will sit with Lucy.'

His thoughtfulness touched her and she was glad to obey. Much to her surprise he led her to a small dining room where a table had been set for two. He intended to join her then. She looked around, taking in the cheerful fire and cosy furnishings. It was far more intimate than the main dining room, and at this season much warmer, too. It occurred to her that she should not be here alone with him like this, that it could only lead to further complications, but somehow she didn't care.

If he thought anything amiss it wasn't apparent in his manner or expression. On the contrary, he seemed to enjoy her company and her conversation. For a while the latter turned on general topics but then, gradually, to matters closer to home.

'I spoke to Trubshaw yesterday about the oldest Dobson boy. It seems he has an affinity with horses and has the makings of a fine stable lad.'

Claire smiled. 'I am so glad.'

'The younger brother has yet to find his métier, but no doubt that will become clearer with time.'

'Thank you for all you are doing for them.'

'I am doing nothing at all. I mention the matter only because I thought it would interest you.'

'It does, very much, and you are too modest about your role in bringing it all about.'

'Now the conversation grows dull. Let us speak of other topics, I beg you.'

'Then may I ask whether you have got any further with your

plan to apprehend the men responsible for the attack on Harlston's loom?'

'Yes, matters are in train. With the aid of the militia I intend to arrange a trap.'

'You, sir?'

'Who else? This matter is dear to my heart.'

'You must have been very close to your brother.'

'When we were growing up I thought he was one step removed from God. Wherever he led, I followed. Usually into another scrape.'

'I can imagine. You must have missed him when you went abroad.'

'I did, but India provided enough excitement and challenge to keep me busy.'

'And romance, too.'

'Yes, that, too.'

His fingers tightened on the stem of his glass and for a moment there was silence. For a moment she was tempted to ask, but quickly stifled the impulse. Presently the conversation moved in other directions for the remainder of the meal. At length Claire laid down her napkin.

'I should go back and see how Lucy is faring.'

'Let us go along together,' he replied.

She had not expected it, but merely inclined her head in acquiescence. They walked together back to Lucy's chamber. He did not speak again and she would not break into his private thoughts, though the very air between them seemed charged somehow.

Lucy was awake but clearly feverish. Marcus frowned and laid a hand on her forehead. It was hot to the touch and there was hectic colour in her cheeks. The tray of food nearby was untouched. He turned to the maid.

'Fetch a cup of warm milk.'

As the woman hastened to obey, Marcus peeled off his coat and hung it on the chair she had vacated. Having done so, he wrung out a cloth in the basin on the washstand and laid it on the child's forehead.

'It's nice and cool,' he told her. 'It will help your headache.'

Lucy regarded him with solemn eyes. 'Shall I be better soon, Uncle Marcus?'

'Of course you will.'

'I want to go out riding.'

'And you shall, but not today.'

The words brought welling tears and seeing them Claire came to sit on the other side of the bed.

'It is raining today, dear,' she explained. 'If you took Misty out he might catch a cold, too. You wouldn't want that, would you?'

Lucy looked thoughtful and then slowly shook her head. 'No. He must stay in his stable.'

'That's right,' Claire went on. 'All the horses are staying in today.'

'Even yours, Uncle Marcus?'

'Even mine,' he replied. 'Miss Davenport is right. I should not like them to catch cold. It's even worse for horses than for humans.'

'Is it?'

'Very much so. You have to take great care of them.'

The threatened tears subsided and he gave Claire a grateful look. She had a light touch, he thought. Where had she learned it? All at once he felt curious about her earlier life. Although he knew the broad outline now, she had remained reticent about much of it. Yet was he not reticent also? On some matters anyway. Recalling their earlier conversation he felt a twinge of guilt. He could hardly demand frankness when he was not prepared to give the same.

A few moments later the maid returned with the milk. At first Lucy refused to touch it, but by a mixture of joking and cajolery they persuaded her to drink half of it. After that she began to doze again.

'I think she'll sleep for a while now,' he said.

Claire nodded. 'It's the best thing for her.'

'I'll stay awhile. Just until she drops off. Then the maid can take over for a while.'

'As you wish, sir.'

She took her leave of him and, not wanting to return to her own chamber, made her way to the library. It was her favourite room and one she visited often for, among other things, it contained a handsome collection of novels. Having selected a new book she ensconced herself on the sofa by the fire. Outside the wind flung a squall of rain at the window. Claire smiled. In here it was warm and cosy. She curled up and settled down to read.

However, after a few minutes she found her attention wandering and instead of the printed pages it was Marcus's face she saw. She could not forget the gentleness and concern he showed for his young ward. It was an aspect of his character that she had not expected—such matters were usually considered a woman's domain, beneath the notice of men. Yet he had made it his business to know how matters stood and was not above getting involved either. He must have felt a great affection for his late brother. Did he see something of Greville when he looked at Lucy?

The thought of Greville led to others, less welcome. Marcus had told her that he had a plan for the apprehension and arrest of those responsible for his brother's murder. It disturbed her to discover he meant to be directly involved but, knowing him as she did, she could not imagine that he would stand on the sidelines while others took the risks. What if something were to happen to him? He had been lucky once, but he might not be a second time. She shivered at the implications, unable to conceive of a world where he was not. She could endure to live without him if she had to, provided she knew he was safe and well. It was all that mattered.

Chapter Ten

As the doctor had predicted, Lucy soon rallied from her cold and, within another couple of days, was sitting up in bed playing with her doll. She was impatient to get up, but Marcus would not allow it and refused to be swayed by pleas or tears.

'When your fever is down at night as well as the mornings then you may get up,' he said. 'Not until.'

To sugar the pill he devoted considerable time to her amusement, telling her stories and playing simple card games. When he could not be with her Claire took over. Between them they kept the child calm and entertained.

Once or twice when Lucy was resting Claire took the opportunity to go for a walk round the gardens. Having spent several days cooped up indoors, she felt the need for some fresh air and exercise. It was while she was returning from one of these excursions that she was waylaid by one of the servants who slipped out of a side door as she was passing. With some surprise she recognised the face.

'Mrs Dobson! What a pleasant surprise. How are you?'

'I am very well, ma'am, I thank you.'

'And your children?'

'Well too, ma'am.'

'I am glad to hear it.'

'I've been watching out for a chance to speak to you, Miss Davenport. I want to thank you for all that you've done for me and mine. Miss Greystoke told me as how you'd spoken to His Lordship on our behalf.'

'I was glad to do so.' Claire smiled. 'I hope that you and your family are comfortably settled now.'

'It's like a dream come true, ma'am. Sometimes I have to pinch myself to make sure I'm really awake. If it wasn't for you we'd have had to go on t'parish.'

'Thank goodness it didn't come to that.'

'I thank God for it every day. It must have been divine providence brought you to us.'

More like Ellen Greystoke, thought Claire. Her friend was subtle in achieving her ends.

'I beg you will not mention it, Mrs Dobson. My part in the matter was very small. Lord Destermere must take all the credit.'

'We're beholden to His Lordship and no mistake, but I want you to know that I and my family won't forget what you did. Not ever.'

After they parted Claire returned to her room to divest herself of bonnet and gloves. However, she had not taken two paces into the room when she stopped short with a gasp of surprise. Lying on the bed was the most beautiful ball gown she had ever seen. Made of spangled white sarsnet, it was trimmed with silver ribbons. On the floor lay a pair of white satin slippers. For a moment she could only stare. Then she realised how it had come there and her hand stole to her cheek. If a necklace was an inappropriate gift from a gentleman, how much more was this gown? And yet it was so lovely.

Reverentially she lifted it off the bed and held it up against her. The fabric shimmered with every movement. It needed only a glance to see it became her well. For a few more seconds she wrestled with temptation. Then she was struggling out of her muslin gown. The ball dress was a perfect fit, almost as if it had been made for her. It fitted close to the waist, but was cut low to reveal her shoulders and the soft swell of her breasts. The dress floated away in graceful folds to her feet. It was altogether a more daring gown than any she had ever worn in her life, shocking and wonderful together. The slippers fitted perfectly, too. For a moment or two she pirouetted in front of the glass, turning this way and that to gauge the effect. It was glorious, a gown fit for a queen. *Yes,* said an inner voice, *but not for a governess.* Claire went hot and cold by turns as the implications of the scene dawned on her. She could not accept this gown any more than she could have accepted the amethyst necklace, and Marcus knew it. They must have this out, and soon.

Dressed again in her plain muslin frock she felt more equal to the task of confronting him. Enquiries as to his whereabouts led her to the library. He was sitting at a small table, apparently studying some ledgers, but he rose as she entered. Ignoring the offer of a chair, she stood instead.

'You should not have done it, sir.'

'Done what?' he asked.

'I refer to the new gown.'

'Ah. It seemed necessary.'

'How so?'

'You said you had not got a ball gown.'

'I may have said so, but that did not mean I wished you to buy me one.'

'No, I wished to do that.'

'It's all wrong, sir.'

'Oh? I rather thought the style would suit you very well. Perhaps the gown does not fit?'

Claire controlled herself with an effort. 'There is nothing wrong with the style or the fit.'

The grey eyes gleamed. 'Ah, you tried it on, then? Good.'

'I said I wasn't going to the ball.'

'Yes, I heard you,' he replied, unperturbed. 'However, it is my wish that you should attend.'

For a moment she was speechless, but only for a moment. 'You have no right to insist.'

'No,' he admitted. 'It's a total abuse of power.'

'And knowing that you will still do it?'

'Absolutely. It's one of the great advantages of position.'

'Sometimes, you are quite odious!'

His lips twitched. 'I wonder that you can bear with me at all.'

'Now you are roasting me.'

'You look even more attractive when you are annoyed, you see.'

'Will you be serious for a moment?'

'If you insist.'

She made a vague gesture with her hand. 'How can I make you understand?'

'All I understand is that I want you to be present. It is a ball, not a punishment.'

'I do not think of it as a punishment. You know my reasons for refusing.'

'Yes, just as I know they are groundless. I want you to come and enjoy yourself. Please say you will.'

He paused, his gaze searching her face. She sighed, knowing he wasn't going to yield on this.

'All right, I'll come, but it is for this once only.'

'Thank you.' He rose then and took her shoulders in a gentle clasp. 'It makes me happy to hear you say that.'

'Sir, I…'

'You know my feelings for you, Claire.'

It was so tempting to take the words at face value. How much she would have liked to believe them. The warmth of his hands through her gown, his nearness, filled her with a deep longing, but it was a feeling she didn't dare give in to. Apart from the impossibility of it leading to anything but pain and disaster, she would never accept second place in any man's affections. With an effort of will she detached herself from his hold.

The dark brows drew together. 'What is it, Claire? What's wrong?'

'Why are you doing this? Why pretend you care for me when we both know you love another?'

He stared at her, thunderstruck. 'What are you talking about?'

'Lakshmi,' she replied.

There followed a moment of complete silence in which the hawk-like gaze searched her face. Then, very steadily, he said, 'How do you come to know that name?'

'You spoke it in delirium. Not once, but several times.'

'I see.'

She watched him turn away as though wrestling with some powerful emotion, and she felt her throat tighten. It was as she had suspected. Lakshmi ruled his heart still. The knowledge hurt, but it was better than pretence. At least now the matter was out in the open.

'It is something I have never discussed with anyone,' he said then. 'Not even George Greystoke, but you deserve the truth if anyone does.' He turned again to face her. 'Do you want my story, Claire? I warn you now it is not pleasant.'

Her heart beat a little faster for there was an expression on his face that she had not seen there before. It sent a shiver down her spine. Feeling suddenly in need of support, she sank into a chair. Nevertheless, she knew she must listen.

'I will hear it, if you are willing to tell me.'

'Very well.' He paused, eyeing her keenly. 'The events I am about to relate took place some eight years ago. Lakshmi was an Indian princess, a young woman of extraordinary beauty and goodness. We met by chance when I was able to do her a trifling service. From the first there was a powerful alchemy between us. Our time together was brief, a matter of days only, but I knew then that she was the woman I wanted to marry and spend the rest of my life with. My feelings were returned. However, because of our respective positions there were obstacles to our being together. I should have followed my instinct and taken her away while I had the chance. There would have been all manner of trouble, but we could have surmounted it. Instead I hesitated, fearing to embroil her in a major scandal.

'While I hesitated, her father married her off to the rajah of a neighbouring state, a man old enough to be her grandfather. My despair at losing her was equalled only by the rage I felt for my earlier procrastination. So I threw myself into my work in an attempt to forget her. However, about a year later I had news of her again. Her elderly husband had sickened and died. In accordance with the traditions of that country the old prince's body was to be cremated. His widow was to commit suttee. In other words, she must go to the fire with her husband.'

Claire regarded him in horror. She had heard of the custom. Until now it had seemed unreal, part of the exotic fabric of a foreign culture. Seeing her expression, Marcus nodded.

'You may imagine my feelings on learning that. At any rate I was determined to save her and, taking a detachment of men, left immediately for Kathor. It was three days' ride away, but we travelled fast, pausing only to rest the horses when we had to. We cut half a day off the time but, even so, we came too late. When we reached the burning ground the ceremony had already begun.' He paused, taking a deep breath, seeing again the pyre and the flames. 'I tried to fight my way through the crowd, but it was too dense and prevented me. It also got ugly, for the people of that place believe the custom to be holy and resent interference. I was dragged from my horse and would have died too had my men not intervened and got me away.' One hand went to the scar on his cheek. 'I carry this as a permanent reminder of that day.'

Claire paled, appalled, for this calm relation of events was worse than any deliberate dramatisation could ever have been.

'Oh, Marcus. I'm so sorry. What a terrible thing.'

He was struck less by her evident sympathy than by the use of his name. It was the first time she had ever done so and was all the more telling for being entirely unconscious. In that moment he felt as though a barrier had come down.

'As I said, it was a long time ago.'

'I think it would not matter how many years passed by. Such a thing could never be forgotten.'

'No, we just learn to live with the memories.'

Claire was very still. Suddenly a lot of things had become clear. She was both honoured and moved by his confidence, for she could never have supposed he would open up to her in that way. At the same time it raised other questions. Almost as if he heard the thought, Marcus regarded her steadily.

'I shall never forget her, but one cannot cling to the past, Claire. Life goes on and time lessens the intensity of pain. Lakshmi is not your rival.'

'I see that now.'

'I hope you do.'

She returned his gaze. 'Besides, there are newer hurts to salve, are there not?'

'If by that you mean my brother, then, yes.'

'Can hurts be salved in blood?'

'This one will be, I promise you.'

Looking at the expression in the grey eyes, Claire shivered. This was a side to his character that she had only glimpsed before, but there could be no mistaking its deadly intensity. He would do what he set out to do, no matter how long it took, and his enemies could expect no quarter.

Much later, as she lay in bed, she reflected on that conversation and the story he had told her, unable to sleep for the images it evoked. She could only imagine the horror of it, the horror and the terror. Such things left an indelible impression upon the memory. No wonder Marcus had been so reluctant to speak of it. And yet perversely it was a part of him, a part of who he was. Having been afforded a glimpse of his past and the events that had shaped him, she found herself eager to know more. For all that air of quiet strength and invincibility there was also a hidden vulnerability about him, the person who all his life had wanted to be loved— and to love in return. Yet through some malign fate he had always lost those he cared for. How much she would have liked to be the woman who made him whole, the woman who had his heart. What he had offered her was passion, but she knew it was not enough and never could be. Without love there could be nothing.

As Marcus had intimated, Lucy was able to leave her room the next day and she and Claire re-established their usual routine soon after. In the meantime preparations were in train for the forthcoming ball and an endless stream of carts and wagons arrived at Netherclough Hall delivering everything from candles to chalk. Mrs Hughes spent several hours closeted with the Viscount while the arrangements were discussed in detail. Everyone who had been invited had returned an acceptance. Clearly it was to be the social event of the year in Yorkshire.

As the day came closer Claire found herself looking forward to the occasion and became caught up in the excitement around her. Though she had attended various social functions when she lived at her uncle's house, none had been as splendid as this promised to be. In all probability this was the only chance she would ever have to experience such a glittering event. The thought of the spangled sarsnet gown filled her with guilty pleasure. It would be perfect for the occasion, as Marcus had known when he ordered it. Would he still approve his choice when he saw her wearing it? The thought of his approbation brought a glow of warmth.

Lucy begged to be allowed to attend the ball, but to no avail.

Marcus was adamant. However, he did promise that he and Claire would come and say goodnight before the guests arrived that evening. With that she had to be content. Meanwhile she was making excellent progress in the schoolroom, for she was a keen and conscientious pupil, soaking up information like a sponge. In teaching Lucy, Claire had followed similar principles to the ones that had been used in her own early education, before the stifling regime she had endured in her teens. She wanted the child to learn to think for herself and to be able to apply her knowledge. Along with the basic school work were the practical lessons in music and art, dancing and deportment. Where possible Claire tried to make the lessons fun, and devised all manner of different strategies until she found the ones that suited her pupil. She was devoutly thankful that the task was rendered much easier by having an able and willing mind to deal with.

Marcus, watching it all in his quietly observant manner, was impressed. He had taken a gamble when he had hired Claire, but it had paid off. The three-month probationary period had been a safety clause, but he knew now he wouldn't need to apply it. He couldn't visualise anyone else in the role. Though he had met her only three months earlier, it seemed in many ways a lot longer. She had become such a part of everyday life that he felt as though she had always been there. Somehow he couldn't imagine life without her, a future without her.

However, before he could contemplate the long-term there were matters closer to hand that must be attended to. The ball would be a pleasant interlude, but more importantly it would announce to the world that a new master was in residence at Netherclough. It would emphasise his presence and the role he intended to play in local affairs. All the main players would be present. It behoved him to know them better for they would also have an influence on what would follow.

After his travels abroad he had come to see the importance of every section of society, not merely the aristocracy. Men like John Harlston, with his association in trade, might be viewed with disdain by the upper classes, but they created the wealth that made the country strong. When trade resumed its normal levels again Marcus knew that the mills would come into their own, like the mines and the iron foundries. They were fundamental to the life of the county and of the country. As he told Claire, he could not isolate himself from them in an ivory tower of privilege.

They had gone out riding and, while Lucy trotted on ahead a little way, he had reined his horse alongside Claire's. It seemed entirely natural to him now that he should talk to her about his ideas for the future. Unlike many of the women he had met in the past, she had a sharp mind that was concerned with more than fashion and lap dogs. She was quick to assimilate ideas and was a good listener too, but she could also hold her own in conversation and he often used her now as a sounding board for ideas he wanted to explore.

'Netherclough is at the heart of things,' he said. 'I want this gathering to reflect that, for the county families to rub shoulders with professional men. Society is changing, Claire. We must change with it or be left behind like so many fossils in the social bedrock.'

She returned him a wry smile. 'If the French had understood that they might never have had a revolution.'

'We have our revolution too, though it might be termed industrial.'

'It is proving bloody, too, in its way.'

'Blood will have blood, Claire.' He turned his head to meet her gaze. 'I am coming to understand how the lure of profit may turn ordinary men into killers.'

She frowned. 'I don't follow.'

'It is my belief that Greville was killed because of something he learned, not only because he was a government agent.'

'You think he knew the identities of the wrecker gang?'

'Possibly, though they are just the tools employed to do a job. I think he may have discovered who they worked for.'

'Then you think someone is orchestrating the attacks?'

'I'm certain of it. Just as I'm certain that the wrecking of machines in this locality is about more than workers' wages.'

'But what else is there?'

'I told you—profit.' He paused. 'When one cannot make progress in an investigation a good rule is to follow the money.'

'That's a rather cynical philosophy, is it not?'

'Cynical but accurate. Someone stands to make a great deal out of the misery of others and he has manipulated events to suit his purpose.'

'But who would do such a thing?'

'A ruthless and dangerous man.'

'Have you proof?'

'Not yet, but I *will* get it.' He regarded her steadily for a moment. 'Not just for Greville, but for all those other poor fellows who have been murdered in the name of greed and ambition.'

'And so you will spring your trap.'

'Yes. When the sprats are caught I'll find out what I want to know. Then I'll go after the big fish.'

As the ramifications dawned, she paled a little. Seeing it, he surveyed her shrewdly. 'I cannot watch from the sidelines while others take the risks on my behalf, Claire. I knew the danger when I undertook this mission, and I must see it through. Besides, soldiering is my business.'

'Even so…' she began.

'There is only one way to lead, Claire, and that is from the front.'

Chapter Eleven

'You look beautiful, Miss Davenport!' Lucy's gaze took in every detail of the white sarsnet gown with unqualified approval.

Claire smiled. 'Thank you. I'm glad you like it.'

In truth she had taken a lot of time and trouble over her appearance this evening. One of the maids had helped to dress her hair so that the dark curls were piled high before falling in graceful ringlets over her shoulders. The white gown was a perfect foil for her warm colouring. Around her neck she wore the silver locket. Long gloves and satin slippers completed the outfit.

'You look like a princess in a fairy tale.'

'It's kind of you to say so.'

'It's true.' Lucy looked over Claire's shoulder. 'Isn't it, Uncle Marcus?'

She had not heard him come in and turned to see the tall figure in the doorway.

'You have excellent taste, child,' he replied. For a moment his gaze swept across Claire and the grey eyes warmed. 'A princess indeed.'

Her cheeks went pink. 'Thank you, sir.'

Under that close scrutiny she was more than ever aware of that charismatic figure and the raw, sensual power he exuded. Dressed in immaculate evening dress he looked every inch the aristocrat that he was. The dark coat might have been moulded to fit those broad shoulders. Pale breeches, snowy linen and cream-coloured waistcoat were plain almost to the point of austerity, and yet the overall effect was breathtaking. Once again it would have been impossible to find a more elegant or eye-catching figure.

He bent to give his ward a goodnight hug and tucked her in. Then he turned to Claire and offered his arm.

'Shall we?'

As they walked toward the staircase she glanced up at him once or twice, but could gain no clue from his expression as to the thoughts that lay behind the facade. Yet she somehow sensed his approval and her heart sang. No matter what came after, there would always be this night to remember, the night when for a few hours anyway she had been transported into another world where there was no ugliness or sorrow, only beauty and light and music. A world where he was.

In fact, Marcus was supremely conscious of the young woman beside him. He had not been exaggerating when he had likened her to a princess. She looked all of that and more. As he had imagined, the gown was stunning, serving as a glorious foil for the beauty of the wearer. It showed off every curve and line to perfection while tantalising him with the thought of what lay beneath. Did she know how lovely she was, or how powerful an impression she was making? He glanced down at her, but there was not the least trace of flirtation or coquetry in her manner, and she appeared quite unconscious of the effect she was having. It was probably just as well, he reflected. If she knew what was going through his mind that expression of calm serenity would vanish in an instant.

His attention was eventually diverted by the arrival of the first guests, and Claire slipped away into the salon, hoping that Ellen and her brother would arrive very soon. In fact, she had not many minutes to wait before she heard their names announced. With them was Sir Alan Weatherby. George Greystoke performed the introductions.

Weatherby beamed at her. 'A pleasure to make your acquaintance, Miss Davenport, and how pretty you look! By Jove, I wish I were thirty years younger.'

Claire smiled and blushed at the compliment. Greystoke smiled. 'You look wonderful,' he said. 'That really is a beautiful gown.' 'Thank you, sir.'

Ellen smiled at her friend. 'It suits you very well, my dear.'

'It's enough to make every woman here green with envy,' said Weatherby.

'If Miss Davenport will favour me with the first dance, I'll make a few men envious too,' replied Greystoke.

When eventually the orchestra struck up, he led her out onto the floor. After that, introductions were sought by several other gentlemen, including Major Barstow, who solicited the next two dances. A handsome moustachioed figure in a dashing uniform, he had caught the eye of many ladies present. Claire put him in his mid-thirties. He had easy, unaffected manners and she found herself taking an instant liking to him.

From across the room Marcus watched their progress. Both of them danced well, he saw, and they made a striking couple. From the Major's expression it seemed that Claire had made quite an impression. Forcing his gaze away from the pair, the Viscount gave his attention to his own partner. The girl was not unattractive, but every time he spoke to her she seemed able to reply only in monosyllables and soon he gave up the attempt at conversation. By the end of the dance he was glad to relinquish her hand to her next partner. A glance at the other participants revealed that Barstow had retained Claire for the cotillion. It appeared she had no objection to offer. Indeed, from her smile it seemed to be most agreeable to her. The Viscount's grey eyes narrowed and his smouldering gaze followed them across the floor.

Claire was enjoying herself enormously. Major Barstow was an excellent partner and a witty conversationalist, which made him excellent company. However, knowing it would expose her to gossip if she permitted him any more dances, she pleaded thirst.

'Of course, how thoughtless of me,' he replied. 'I'll find you some refreshment at once.'

He hurried off to execute the commission. While she waited she heard her own name being spoken nearby. It was a woman's voice, one of the party accompanying Lord and Lady Frobisher.

'She's the governess apparently. One wonders what Lord Destermere can be thinking of.'

'I beg your pardon,' replied her male companion, 'but I should say it's very easy to understand what he is thinking of. She's a very attractive young woman.'

The words were followed by others in a murmured undertone. The latter elicited a gasp and a rap on the arm with a fan.

'Shocking, Henry! I am sure it is no such thing. Destermere would never lower himself so far.'

'Of course not, I spoke in jest. I had it from Weatherby that she's connected in some way to the Greystokes,' replied her companion. 'It seems the good doctor is a particular friend of Destermere's. From India, don't you know?'

'Oh, I see.' The woman's tone was suggestive of disappointment. 'All the same, it is rather singular, is it not? I mean, she's little more than a servant after all.'

Claire's jaw tightened and she had to fight the desire to turn round. She would not give them the satisfaction of revealing she had overheard them. Fortunately Major Barstow returned a few moments later with two glasses of punch. They had hardly taken a sip when another voice cut in.

'Major Barstow, won't you introduce me to this delightful creature?'

She looked up to see a stranger. Seemingly in his early fifties, he was a rather stooped figure with sandy-coloured hair. His freckled face was thin and angular, the thin-lipped mouth like a slash. It gave him a slightly reptilian appearance. At his side was a stout young man who bore him a striking facial resemblance.

Barstow stiffened slightly, but then acknowledged them with a polite bow.

'Miss Davenport, may I present Sir James Wraxall and Mr Hugh Wraxall?'

The reptilian mouth widened in a smile that never reached the pale blue eyes. 'Charmed, Miss Davenport.'

Beside him his son echoed the sentiment and smiled too, revealing stained teeth. His gaze travelled from Claire's face to the front of her gown where it lingered. She felt her skin crawl.

'May I have the honour of the next dance?' he asked.

Unable to get out of it, she was forced to accept with a good grace and allow herself to be led away to the ballroom. They took their places in the next set. It soon became clear that Hugh Wraxall was not an accomplished performer and, worse, he kept squeezing her hand in a manner that was both embarrassing and distasteful. Each time the figures brought them together he leered at her cleavage. The music seemed to go on for ever. When it finally stopped she breathed a sigh of relief, wanting nothing more than to escape, but it seemed the ordeal wasn't over yet.

'Don't think I shall release you so soon, Miss Davenport. I claim the next.'

Before she could reply a tall, familiar figure cut in. 'I'm sorry to disappoint you, Wraxall, but this one's mine.'

Hearing that familiar voice Claire felt her heartbeat accelerate and a moment later she was looking up into Marcus's face. For a brief moment an expression of annoyance flitted across Wraxall's features; then it was masked with an unctuous smile. He bowed and retreated, leaving the field to his rival. Claire smiled at her rescuer.

'Thank you.'

'My pleasure,' he replied. Then *sotto voce,* 'How on earth did you get waylaid by that charmless oaf?'

'I wasn't quick enough with an excuse.'

'That's most unlike you.'

She threw him a speaking look, which seemed not to disconcert him in the least. Rather the grey eyes gleamed.

'True sir, but in this instance I am grateful.'

'Good.' He paused. 'How grateful exactly?'

He watched her cheeks turn a delightful shade of pink. 'Odious man!'

He laughed. Then the orchestra struck up the next dance and they took their places in the set. For a little while they were separated by the moves of the dance, but when she rejoined him at last he pursued it.

'You do not answer my question.'

'Nor shall I.'

'Then you must demonstrate the feeling instead.'

Her eyes widened a little. 'How so?'

'By dancing the next with me as well.'

They parted again for a while. Claire, moving through the intricate sequence of steps, was aware of his gaze following her. The knowledge set her pulse racing.

'Well?' he inquired when she returned to him. 'Have you considered my request?'

'I have, sir.'

'And?'

'I accede to it.'

'Excellent. Of course, it would have made no difference at all had you refused.'

The tone was both teasing and provocative, but the expression on that handsome face was less easy to read.

'No, I suppose not,' she agreed. 'You have a habit of getting your own way.'

The grey eyes gleamed appreciatively. 'Indeed I do, ma'am.'

He was as good as his word, for when the dance ended he made no move to lead her aside, but waited while the next set formed around them. Once again Claire was uncomfortably conscious of eyes turning their way. Seeing that fleeting expression, he squeezed her elbow gently.

'Don't let them trouble you, Claire. It will do them good to witness my standards.'

At his words of praise her heart leapt, and she looked up quickly to see him smile. Suddenly all her former anxiety melted away like frost in the sun. As the measure began, Claire forgot everything else and then there were only the two of them and the music and the moment. It felt so right to be here with him, to feel his hand on hers as he led her through the figures of the dance, to see the warmth in his eyes when he looked at her. When she was with him she felt truly alive. This one night was all they would ever have, but she knew it would remain with her as long as she lived.

Marcus had also taken note of the eyes turned their way and was both amused and gratified. Curiosity had been aroused, it seemed. He knew full well every man there would like to be in his shoes, but for this little space at least he had Claire all to himself. The notion was pleasing. It felt right to have her beside him like this. She danced well too, her movements light and graceful, as though it were the most natural thing in the world. Somehow it went against the grain to acknowledge that he would have to yield her up to other partners, but good manners dictated that he must later solicit other young ladies for a dance. After Claire, their company would be at best insipid.

When at length the dance was over he led her aside and paused a moment, looking down into her face. Then he carried her hand to his lips.

'I regret that I am engaged elsewhere, but I leave you in good company this time.' He glanced to where Ellen Greystoke was talking with Sir Alan Weatherby.

Following his look she smiled. 'Very good company, sir.'

Then, having spoken to the others briefly, he reluctantly relinquished her hand and bowed before taking his leave. For a moment
or two she watched his retreating back, then forced herself to look
away and give her attention to her present companions.

Her hand was solicited again several times by other gentlemen
before she eventually sat down to eat supper with the Greystokes,
along with Sir Alan Weatherby and Major Barstow. She found her
companions most agreeable and entertaining, and the conversation
and laughter flowed easily. Once she looked around the room for
Marcus and located him at a table across the room. Among the aristocratic guests gathered there were the Frobishers. Quickly she looked
away again, for seeing him there was a pertinent reminder of who he
was. That was his milieu, the society to which he naturally belonged
and which she could only be part of for this one brief night.

Later she watched him mingle among the other guests, laughing
and talking with his habitual polished ease. She could discern absolutely no difference in his manner whether he spoke to a mill owner
or a lord. If some sections of the company regarded his behaviour
askance, they kept their opinions to themselves. A viscount could
afford eccentricity, and if he saw fit to invite the professions into
his home then he was entitled to do it. However, she knew that
every aspect of this occasion would be discussed in minute detail
on the morrow. She smiled to herself, well able to visualise those
scenes.

Marcus had shown her some attention this evening, more
perhaps than he needed to. Had it aroused jealousy in other female
breasts? Was this going to make her the butt of local gossip for
weeks to come? She ought to feel concerned, but for the life of
her she could not regret it.

Just then his voice broke into her reverie. 'Shall we have some
music? Miss Greystoke, can I persuade you?'

Ellen murmured something in reply and then rose, following

their host to the pianoforte in the corner of the room. Claire watched them select the music and then Ellen seated herself and began to play. The music was gentle and soothing and she listened with close attention until the piece finished, joining the applause enthusiastically. Her friend played two more pieces before relinquishing her place at the instrument to Lady Frobisher's daughter, Mildred. Though Claire had no objection to hearing someone else play, the heat of the room was increasing and she began to feel the need for a little fresh air, so with a smile and a brief word she excused herself. Having slipped away from the crowded reception rooms, she turned into the corridor and headed for the conservatory. It wasn't far and it would be an ideal sanctuary for a while.

Her instinct had been correct, for here among the scented greenery it was blessedly cool and the air sweet and fragrant. She breathed deeply, enjoying it. From somewhere behind her she could hear the music still, though more faintly now, but all the bustle and conversation was absent. The only other sound was of tinkling water from a small fountain. It was restful here, a place to pause awhile and dream. Marcus's face drifted into her consciousness unbidden. He should be pleased tonight: the ball had been an unqualified success. The new Viscount Destermere was well and truly established. She smiled. He looked the part too, every self-assured and arrogant inch of him.

The sound of the door opening drew her back to reality and she turned quickly. Her eyes, accustomed to the dimmer light now, made out a man's figure. For a second her heart leapt. Surely it couldn't be he? The figure made its way towards her.

'Ah, there you are, Miss Davenport.'

She froze, recognising the voice of Hugh Wraxall, and in an instant her former hope was dashed.

'Saw you slip away,' he went on. 'Followed you here.'

Claire regarded him with alarm and distaste. The slurred tones suggested he had been drinking, not enough to render him incapable, but certainly enough to be a nuisance.

'I came in here for some fresh air,' she replied. 'I'm going back now.'

He stood across the path, barring her way. 'What's the hurry?'

'Pray excuse me.'

'Not yet. I think you and I should get to know each other better.'

'I have no desire to know you better, sir.'

Hearing the icy tone his expression changed. 'I'll wager you wouldn't be so damned haughty if the handsome Viscount were here.'

Claire's fists clenched at her sides as she strove to keep control of her temper. 'Please let me pass.'

'Touched a nerve, have I? Thought as much.' He leered at her, wafting a reek of foul breath in her face. 'Had you written down as a fancy little piece from the start.'

His answer was a sharp slap across the face. For a second he reeled, holding his smarting cheek. Then his expression grew ugly.

'You'll pay for that, you haughty little madam.'

He grabbed hold of her arm, dragging her close. Seeing his face looming over hers, she turned her head aside and the intended kiss grazed her cheek instead.

'Let go of me!'

'Oh, no, my dear, I'm not done with you yet.'

His arm tightened around her waist. Pressed against him, Claire could feel his arousal through the thin material of her gown. With each passing moment the danger of her predicament became increasingly obvious and she struggled to free herself from that noxious embrace, but he was strong. She heard him laugh. The sound roused her to renewed effort.

'Get your filthy hands off me! Let me go!'

'You heard the lady,' said a voice from the doorway.

With unmitigated relief Claire recognised Major Barstow.

Taken quite by surprise, Wraxall stared at the newcomer and then his face darkened.

'Mind your own business,' he snarled.

Barstow strode forwards and a second later had him by the throat. With a strangled croak of surprise Wraxall released his hold on Claire. The Major shook him hard, regarding him with contempt the while.

'You nasty little cur! I'll teach you to lay hands on a lady.'

'Mind your own business, soldier boy.'

'This is my business.'

As he spoke Barstow let go of his grip and Wraxall launched a haymaker in reply. It missed by a wide margin, but Barstow's clenched fist hit its intended target and sent the other reeling backwards. As he staggered, Wraxall's heel caught the stone edging round the plant border and he lost his balance to fall sprawling among the greenery in the flower bed. There he groaned once and lay still. Claire stared at him in horror and then looked up at her rescuer.

'Thank you, sir.'

'A pleasure, ma'am, believe me.'

Claire drew in a deep breath to steady herself, trying not to think of what might have happened but for the Major's timely intervention. Seeing her trembling, Barstow put a gentle arm about her.

'It's all right, Miss Davenport. He cannot harm you now.'

This time the bodily contact was comforting, not threatening, and she managed a wan smile. 'I am much in your debt, sir.'

'Nothing of the sort,' he replied. 'Come, let us leave the loathsome brute and find more congenial company. I'll escort you back to the salon.'

She nodded gratefully and allowed herself to be led from the conservatory.

'I am so grateful for your help back there, Major Barstow. If you hadn't come along when you did…'

He stopped and drew her gently round to face him, letting his hand rest lightly on her shoulders. 'Say no more about it, Miss Davenport.'

'How did you know I was there?'

'I didn't. To tell the truth, I thought the conservatory was empty. I wanted a cigar and it seemed like the ideal place.'

'I see.'

He smiled down at her. 'It's a bit of a vice, but perhaps it does have its uses after all.'

'Indeed it does, sir.'

'Will you be all right now?'

'Yes, perfectly.'

He took her hand and carried it to his lips. 'Then I shall adjourn to the terrace for my cigar.'

'I think you have earned it, sir.'

He laughed. Then she became aware that he was looking beyond her and glanced round. As she did so her heart missed a beat to see the tall and familiar figure on the threshold of the lighted doorway. Marcus! For a moment he stood there motionless, his expression thunderous, the grey eyes like chips of agate. His gaze raked her from head to toe.

'I came in search of you,' he said then, 'but evidently too late.' He threw them an icy smile. 'Forgive me. I see I am *de trop*.'

With that he turned on his heel and strode away. Claire paled. Surely he could not have thought that she and Barstow… Almost immediately she knew that was exactly what he did think. Appalled by the implications, she was rooted to the spot. Barstow glanced from her to the Viscount's retreating back. For a moment he seemed nonplussed. Then one eyebrow lifted slightly and he glanced down at his companion. Claire, pale before, had turned pink with mortification. However, he was too much the gentleman to remark upon it.

'I think perhaps I should return you to your friends, Miss Davenport.'

'Thank you, sir, I would be most grateful.'

Together they walked back into the salon. Determined not to reveal her inner turmoil, Claire lifted her chin and fixed a smile on her face. As they entered, the heat hit her at once. The room seemed stifling now, and heavy with the scent of beeswax and perfume and the press of human bodies. All around her conversation and laughter rose in a wave and a feeling of desolation swept over her. Suddenly, her magical evening was ruined.

Marcus returned to the ballroom and found a glass of wine. He tossed it back in one go and then set down the glass with a snap. No one looking at that expressionless face could have guessed at the thoughts behind. However, the grey eyes were more eloquent. He took a deep breath to steady himself. So she preferred the handsome Major, did she? His fists clenched at his sides. If he hadn't had a house full of guests, he'd have run the man through. Part of him still wanted to go back and call the bastard out. And yet why was he surprised? Claire was a lovely young woman. He'd seen the way men looked at her. What red-blooded male wouldn't want her? The handsome Major had lost no time in securing her affections. All too successfully it appeared.

As the evening drew to a close and the guests began to depart Claire was reminded of her social obligations. When her companions announced their intention to go, she accompanied them to the hall. She must smile and bid everyone farewell. Nothing of her inner feelings must be allowed to show in her face either. So far as anyone else was concerned the evening had been a huge success.

Marcus was already there, speaking to some of the departing company and, although his glance acknowledged her presence, she was glad that they didn't have to talk. Her initial mortification had crystallised into anger now; he had been so quick to judge her, so ready apparently to believe the worst. He hadn't even waited to speak to her, or to hear her side of the story.

As she watched him with his guests her chin lifted. If he could play a part, so could she. Accordingly she stepped into role, smiling and laughing, as the people departed. She tried not to think about what would happen when everyone had gone and they were alone together.

The clock was striking three before the last of the carriages rolled away from the door. Claire saw it go with a sense of relief. She was tired now and wanted nothing more than to collapse into bed and fall into a deep and dreamless slumber. However, it appeared that Marcus had other ideas.

'A word with you, Miss Davenport,' he said, glancing past her towards the study.

The imperious tone rekindled her resentment and she made no move to obey. 'I'm very tired, sir. Can it not wait until tomorrow?'

'I will not keep you long.'

Seeing there was nothing for it but to face the coming storm, she nodded. 'Very well.'

He stood aside to let her precede him into the room. Then he closed the door behind them. For a moment they faced each other in silence. Almost she could feel the anger radiating off him. With more calm than she felt, Claire regarded him with a level gaze.

'There was something you wished to say, sir?'

'You know damned well there is. I refer to your unseemly conduct with Major Barstow.'

'Unseemly!' The fragile hold on her temper began to slip. 'How *dare* you?'

He stared at her in disbelief. 'How dare *I?* Can you deny that he held you in his arms?'

'I have no wish to deny it.'

'I see.'

'No, you don't.'

He gave a short, harsh laugh. 'I suppose I imagined that tender scene.'

'Your imagination is greatly overworked.'

'I know what I saw.'

'Major Barstow had just saved me from an unpleasant encounter with Hugh Wraxall. I was still shaken and the Major was merely being kind.'

'That's one way of describing it!' He paused and the dark brows drew together. 'What encounter with Hugh Wraxall?'

'A little earlier I had gone into the conservatory for some fresh air. Unfortunately, Wraxall followed and trapped me there. He was drunk and he…he laid hands on me. Major Barstow came along in time to stop it.'

The hawk-like gaze rested on her face. 'Did Wraxall hurt you?'

'No, it was merely disagreeable.'

The thought of any other man touching her at all was unbearable. That one should have taken liberties filled him with fury. Part of him felt relief that it hadn't gone further, but another part was unwilling to let it go.

'You should not have wandered off alone,' he replied. 'It leads to such misunderstandings.'

'I told you, I needed some air.'

His breast was filled with conflicting emotions: he wanted to take her in his arms; he wanted to shake her. His inner demon refused to lie down and be quiet.

'Some air? How very convenient.'

'What do you mean?'

'Do you really expect me to believe such a tale?'

'But it's the truth.'

He turned, glowering down at her. 'Is it? Or is it rather that Wraxall inconveniently interrupted the tryst you had planned with Major Barstow?'

'What!' Claire glared back. 'You cannot believe that.'

'All the evidence points that way, does it not? Having dealt with the interloper and seen his plans in ruins, the good Major brought you back to the main company, but not before he afforded himself the solace of a comforting embrace.' He paused. 'An embrace which you evidently found most agreeable.'

'It wasn't like that.'

'It looked very much like that from where I was standing.'

'You saw what you wished to see.'

'I had the evidence of my own eyes.'

Claire's chin lifted to a militant angle. 'If Major Barstow and I had wished for intimacy, do you really think that we would have chosen to meet in a public corridor when there are a hundred secluded places in this house?'

His lip curled in a sneer. 'Oh, like the conservatory, for instance?'

'Why are you so determined to think the worst of me? Why will you not hear me, or take my part?'

For a moment there was silence as her gaze searched his face, and for a second there was a flicker of something like pain in his eyes.

'Why do you persist in lying to me?'

'I'm not lying to you.'

'Can I trust you, Claire?'

Her heart thumped painfully hard and a lump formed in her throat. 'If you do not know the answer to that, Marcus, then we have nothing more to say to each other.'

With that she turned on her heel and walked away, leaving him staring in impotent wrath at the empty doorway.

Chapter Twelve

For the next few days Claire barely set eyes on Marcus and when their paths did cross he treated her with a cold civility that was worse than his initial anger. All the ease of their earlier relationship vanished as though it had never been, and overnight they became like distant strangers. His indifference and his apparent belief in her unseemly behaviour confirmed her in the opinion that his feelings had never been as deeply engaged as her own. He had been amusing himself with her company, but nothing more.

When she learned from Mrs Hughes that, in the days following the ball, he had accepted several invitations to call upon his wealthy neighbours, her suspicions were confirmed. It was clear he meant to cast a much wider net. There were many eligible young ladies among the local gentry and several of them were very pretty girls. Perhaps he meant to choose a wife from among their number. At any rate he would never consider a governess for such a position, and she had been a fool to attach any significance to the attention he had shown her.

Her birthday was only a week off, and with it the end of the three-month probationary period. It marked the end of a chapter. After what had happened she knew there was no alternative now but to leave Netherclough for a new position elsewhere and try to forget Marcus Edenbridge. It was a thought that filled her with dread. In spite of everything she could not imagine a life without him, a house where he was not. However, it was impossible to stay here. She felt certain that Ellen would let her stay in the interim if need be, but hoped the gap between this situation and the next would not be too lengthy. She would not want to impose on her friend for long. With a heavy heart she began to scan the advertisement columns in the newspaper.

Her search produced two possibilities, both in London. Before she could apply for them she knew that Marcus would have to be informed. He would need to make alternative arrangements, too. Besides, she would need a character reference. She had to hope that enough goodwill remained for him to provide it. In many ways it would be to his advantage to do so—he would be rid of her and Lucy could start afresh with someone else.

The thought of breaking the news to Lucy caused a sharp pang. In the past weeks she had come to care for the child very deeply and knew it would be desperately hard to leave her behind. It was an additional disruption that the little girl could do without. What signal did it send out when everyone she relied on seemed to abandon her? Claire was saddened to think that she too would be letting Lucy down, and yet there was no other choice now. And if it had to be done, then perhaps the sooner the better. Waiting for Marcus's next visit to the nursery, she steeled herself to speak to him and ask for the necessary interview.

He heard her request in stony silence and she wondered if he would refuse, but at length he favoured her with a nod.

'Very well, Miss Davenport. Come along to the study this evening.'

For the rest of the day she tried not to think about it but somehow it kept intruding on her thoughts, like his face as he looked at her. The grey eyes were bleak with no spark of their former warmth. His voice too was cold. Clearly he still thought the worst.

Heartsick, she knew that the matter was beyond remedy now, that her only recourse was to get away as soon as possible and put the whole sorry business behind her.

She presented herself at the study at the appointed hour. He was seated behind the desk, but rose at her entrance and offered her a chair. She declined it, fearing that if she sat down her legs might refuse to let her stand again after.

'I have come to tell you that I am seeking a new situation and to give you notice, sir.'

His brows twitched together and he shot her a piercing look. 'Indeed?'

'I do not wish you to think me ungrateful for all your past kindness,' she went on, 'but in the light of recent events I feel it is better for all concerned if I go.'

'Go where exactly?' he demanded.

'To London, sir.'

'I see.' He paused. 'Is this what you really want?'

She swallowed hard. 'I feel it is the right thing, sir.'

'Will you not reconsider?' There was another pause. He made a vague gesture with his hand. 'After all, Lucy is growing attached to you, I believe.'

'I am very fond of her, but she is young and will soon form a new attachment.'

For a long moment he said nothing, only regarded her steadily. The grey eyes seemed even bleaker. 'Are you quite resolved to go, then?'

'I believe I must, sir.' She hesitated. 'There is one more thing…the matter of a reference.'

'Oh, yes, of course. Do not concern yourself over that.'

'Thank you, sir.'

Marcus cleared his throat. 'There is also the question of remuneration…'

'You have already advanced me part of my salary. You owe me nothing more.'

For another long moment they regarded each other in silence. Then she made him a polite curtsy and bade him a good evening. With that she hurried back to her room and closed the door, leaning upon it as the tears welled in her eyes.

Marcus rose from the desk grim-faced, and paced the room several times. Eventually he came to a halt by the hearth and stood for a while gazing moodily into the flames. When Claire had asked to speak to him he had not expected that it would be to announce her departure. In anyone else he might have suspected a fit of pique, but her quiet resolution was very different. It left him feeling strangely shaken.

Over the past few days he had had time for calmer reflection and knew that his earlier behaviour had been a complete overreaction. Unusually, he had let his temper get the better of him, but somehow he hadn't been able to help himself. Even now the thought of her in Barstow's arms was enough to goad him to wrath. At the time he hadn't cared to ask himself why. He had thought himself immune to the green-eyed god, but now he realised he was not. Once he had believed he could never care for another woman as he had for Lakshmi. He had believed his heart was dead. Over the past weeks he had been drawn insensibly closer to Claire Davenport: her beauty, her intelligence, her wit, her laughter had all acted on him like sunlight after a lengthy period of darkness. Her strengthening relationship with Lucy was another factor. More than just a gifted teacher, she was genuinely kind and compassionate to boot. Small wonder then if other men should notice her many talents and be charmed in their turn.

For a moment Major Barstow's face impinged upon his consciousness and his fist tightened. The man was personable and good-looking. Why should Claire not find him attractive? It was evident that the feeling was mutual or he wouldn't have gone to the trouble of arranging a tryst. How mortified he must have been to have it all spoiled by a little cockroach like Hugh Wraxall. For a moment Marcus knew a sense of gloating delight. However, it faded almost as quickly as it had come. What replaced it was sweeping desolation.

His mood was not improved when, the following afternoon, Claire did not turn up to ride. He had informed her that morning that he would be accompanying his ward, but only Lucy arrived in the stable yard.

'Miss Davenport has a headache, Uncle Marcus, and begs you will excuse her.'

His hand tightened round the handle of his riding whip. 'Has she?'

'Yes.' Lucy regarded him with solemn eyes. 'Are you all right, Uncle Marcus?'

He forced a smile. 'Of course, never better. Are you ready?'

'Oh, yes.'

'Then let us go.'

He lifted her onto the pony and slid her foot into the stirrup. Then he mounted his own horse, reining in alongside the little grey. Sensing his preoccupation, Lucy remained silent, her solemn gaze going to his face from time to time, but not daring to interrupt his unwontedly sombre mood.

Unaware of her scrutiny, Marcus could think only about Claire. He strongly suspected that the headache was an excuse—she was avoiding him. At first he had been sorely tempted to go back to the house and fetch her himself, but a moment's reflection told him he could not. Besides, as he now acknowledged, she was probably right. The less they saw of each other, the better. The realisation didn't make him feel better though; up until that point he hadn't realised how badly he had wanted her company. It was quite clear that she, on the other hand, didn't wish to see him. Thinking about his behaviour towards her, he could hardly blame her now.

He stayed out with Lucy for an hour and then walked with her back to the house. The child went off with a maidservant to change her clothes and Marcus headed for his own chamber. He was halfway down the corridor when he met Claire. Both of them stopped short and there followed an awkward silence. He was about to make a sarcastic comment about her absence, but one look at her face stopped the words on his tongue. She was pale and the hazel eyes spoke of inner pain. The sight of it filled him with remorse.

'Is your headache better?' he asked.

The tone suggested concern and it took her aback. 'A little better, thank you.' She paused. 'I hope you and Lucy enjoyed your ride.'

'Indeed. We missed you.'

Claire felt her throat tighten. 'I'm sorry.'

'Don't make yourself uneasy about it.'

'Is Lucy gone to her room?'

'I believe so.'

'Then I must go and find her. Please excuse me.'

With that she hurried away. Marcus remained quite still, staring after her, wanting to call her back and yet not knowing how.

Having seen Lucy safe in bed that evening, Claire returned to her room and began drafting out her letters of application for the new governess posts. Now that the decision was made she must expedite it with all speed. However, the words would not flow and it took half a dozen attempts before she had produced something satisfactory. Then she made two fair copies. When they were done she folded and sealed them and wrote out the directions. Finally she took them down to the hallway and placed them on the table, for collection by the footman next day. They would be despatched first thing in the morning.

In many ways it was a relief to have taken some action. If a reference was required, then there was a good chance of her getting one of those posts. She trusted Marcus to write what was fair. In any case it was to his advantage to do so. She glanced once at the study door, but it was firmly closed. With a sigh she made her way back to her room, thinking that an early night would not come amiss.

Needing something to take his mind off present domestic concerns, Marcus took himself off to the library in order to finalise his plans for the capture and arrest of the Luddites. He remained ensconced there for much of the evening, going over the details of the scheme until he was sure that every aspect had been covered. A week from now the trap would be set and, with any luck, well and truly sprung. Then the wrecker crew would be brought to justice for their crimes.

It was late when eventually he left. Retracing his steps, he came at length to the gallery and paused there awhile, looking up at the portrait of his brother. It was a good likeness, he thought, capturing the lithe elegance and the handsome features very well. What it didn't show was the quick mind behind those watchful grey eyes. For a moment he met and held his brother's gaze and in his imagination he heard Greville's voice.

'Don't let me down, Bro.'

Marcus's jaw tightened and he drew in a deep breath, mentally repeating the vow he had made months before. Come what might, he wouldn't fail. With a last glance at the portrait he walked away. A few minutes later he reached the hallway and was heading for the study to collect some papers when he noticed the letters on the table. For a moment their significance didn't register, but a closer inspection revealed that they were addressed to some unknown people in London. His brows twitched together as he recognised the elegant handwriting. For a moment he was quite still. Then, as their significance sank in, he felt a sudden cold chill. Turning away abruptly, he strode to the study, closing the door behind him.

When Claire came down next day the letters were gone. The matter was out of her hands. Breathing a sigh of relief, she made her way to the nursery. She and Lucy spent a productive morning on reading and basic arithmetic and then, the day being fine, they went out for a walk in the afternoon. When they returned it was to see two carriages waiting at the front door. Lucy eyed them with curiosity.

'Visitors, Miss Davenport.'

'For your uncle, I imagine,' Claire replied.

'Who are they?'

'I don't know. Something to do with business perhaps.'

A few moments later she saw John Harlston emerge from the house. She recognised him from the ball. A few paces behind was Sir Alan Weatherby. They didn't notice her or Lucy because they were still some distance off, but instead climbed straight into the waiting coaches and drove away. Watching them depart, Claire found herself wondering at the nature of the visit. She knew his friendship with Weatherby went back years, but Harlston was a different matter. The connection there went back to the time when Marcus had been living under another name, when he had ridden escort on the wagon bringing the new power loom. It brought back unpleasant and frightening memories. She knew instinctively that this visit was related to those events.

Marcus had told her himself that he was devising a trap for the wreckers. He would enlist the help of men like Weatherby and Harlston, and no doubt the local militia. Major Barstow's face flitted into her mind. He too would have a role to play if the plan went ahead. And if it did, what then? Would more men die before it was over? Would Marcus be among them? She glanced down at the child beside her and shivered inwardly.

She and Lucy had taken their afternoon tea by the fire when the footman entered.

'A letter for you, ma'am.'

It was from Ellen and, from the appearance of the scrawled hand, had evidently been written in haste. Claire broke the wafer and opened it.

My Dearest Claire,

Be on your guard. Your uncle has arrived in Helmshaw. He came to the house this morning. You need have no fear that George or I have told him anything. Neither will the servants betray your whereabouts. However, I have since learned from some acquaintances that your uncle has been asking questions in the town. Have a care, I beg you.

Your affectionate friend,

Ellen

Claire's stomach lurched and for several heartbeats she experienced a sensation akin to panic as her uncle's unforgiving countenance imposed itself on her consciousness. She had always known him to be firm of purpose. When no trace of her had been found at the coaching inns on the London road he must have begun to consider other possibilities. Her aunt must have kept Ellen's letters, or at least remembered the address. They must have put two and two together.

Forcing herself to think calmly, Claire studied the note again. Her friend would not betray her. Her uncle had no acquaintance in Yorkshire so far as she was aware and it was highly unlikely he would meet any of Viscount Destermere's circle. Netherclough Hall was the last place he would think of looking.

She was so preoccupied with these thoughts that she failed to hear the door open. Only Lucy's exclamation of delight alerted her to Marcus's presence. Claire returned to the present with a start and hastily refolded the note, shoving it into her pocket. Then she rose to face him. For a moment the hawk-like gaze surveyed her keenly, but with an effort of will she met it, hoping that her demeanour revealed nothing of her inner anxiety.

In fact, very little escaped him where she was concerned and certainly not the ashen colour of her face when he had first entered. She had started, too, as though she had seen a ghost. When he looked into her face he could see the anguish there. It hit him hard for he knew that, in part, he had been the cause of it. The days since the ball had taken a heavy toll on both of them, for he was not immune, either, to the effects of their sudden estrangement. He had tried so hard to hold aloof, to busy himself with work or social calls, but even then he found himself thinking of her, listening for the sound of her step or her voice. In spite of his best efforts he had missed her. He missed their conversations, missed her acute observations, her laughter. He had driven her away because a better man had won her affections. All at once he was sickened by self-contempt.

To cover his feelings he bent down and engaged Lucy in conversation for a while. He listened to her childish prattle as she showed him the work she had been doing and read to him from her primer. Once again he was conscious of how far she had come in a relatively short time, and knew it was due to Claire. His conscience prodded him again. How was he ever going to explain her departure? Lucy would be heartbroken. And it was all so unnecessary. If it hadn't been for his accursed temper it wouldn't have happened. Calling himself all kinds of fool, he knew he must try to put things right as far as possible. That meant making his peace with Major Barstow and with Claire and wishing them well.

His plans for dealing with the wreckers had thus far involved close liaison with Weatherby and Harlston. However, as commander of the militia, Barstow was an important figure in the scheme, an irony that didn't escape Marcus. Knowing he couldn't put the moment off any longer without detriment to his plans and wanting to try to smooth things over anyway, at least as far as possible, the Viscount had requested the Major to dine with him and the others that evening.

To the Major's credit he showed no signs of resentment or ill will over what had happened at the ball. He kept up his part in the conversation at dinner and, when the meal was concluded and they settled down to discuss business, readily agreed to do all he could to assist in the apprehension of the Luddite group.

'My men are at your disposal, sir. The sooner these murdering brutes are caught the better.'

Marcus, already ashamed of his previous behaviour, began to feel distinctly guilty. He knew he owed Barstow an apology and was determined to offer it. His opportunity did not arise until his guests were on the point of departure. Having bidden Weatherby and Harlston a goodnight, he detained Barstow in the hall.

'Would you be so kind as to give me five more minutes of your time, Major?'

There was a fractional hesitation, but then Barstow inclined his head in acquiescence, following his host into a nearby salon. For a moment or two they faced each other in silence. Then Marcus took the initiative.

'I would like to thank you for your help in this current under-taking, Major.' He paused. 'And to apologise to you for my former rudeness.'

'I assure you that I have no recollection of it, sir,' replied the other.

'You are generous. More so than I deserve.'

Barstow regarded him with a speculative eye. 'Is it possible that Your Lordship has formed a mistaken impression?'

'How so?'

'It is a delicate matter because it concerns a lady. One for whom I have the highest regard.' He paused. 'May I speak frankly?'

The Viscount held down his resentment. 'Very well.'

The Major favoured him with a short and unvarnished account of what had happened on the evening of the Netherclough ball. Marcus, listening, might have been turned to stone. Inwardly his heart was thumping. The account tallied in every respect with Claire's. There was no indication at all that the speaker held her in anything other than esteem. He had merely done what any gentleman would have done under the circumstances. Furthermore, there was a soldierly directness about Barstow that Marcus recognised and respected, and he knew the words for truth. As the implications hit him he felt his heart leap.

'Then you're not courting Miss Davenport? She doesn't…'

'My lord, I would be the happiest of men if Miss Davenport ever deigned to look my way. Unfortunately, she has not done so and, I fear, never will.' He looked Marcus straight in the eye. 'I believe her affections are engaged elsewhere.'

With that he bowed and took his leave, though in truth his host was hardly aware of his going. All Marcus's consciousness was drawn inwards to the dawning understanding and magnitude of his own folly. When he thought of the accusations he had flung at Claire, not to mention his subsequent behaviour, he was appalled. She had told him the truth and he, in a fit of jealous pride, had refused to listen. Her words returned to haunt him: *Why are you so determined to believe the worst of me?* He could not forget the look of hurt in her eyes. She had asked for his trust and he had refused to give it. His fists clenched. No wonder she wanted to leave.

Come what may, he knew he couldn't let her go, that she had become as necessary to him as the air he breathed. He had known it since the day she had given her notice. Remembering the letters on the hall table, he knew she meant it. The thought filled him with despair. London be damned, he thought. She belonged here, with him. The question was how to make her see that. Would she hear him? Could she ever forgive him? After what had passed between them he was going to need all his powers of persuasion.

Claire was surprised the next day when a footman delivered a politely worded request to attend her employer in the library that afternoon. Surprise was followed swiftly by misgiving. What now? There was no way of refusing the summons either, as she was at first inclined to do. Then she reflected that it must be important if he felt the need to call her away from her duties. Leaving Lucy with a maidservant, she set off for the library.

He was already there when she arrived and for a moment or two was unaware of her presence. He was leaning upon the mantel above the hearth, one booted foot resting casually upon the fender as he stared down into the fire. Her heart began to beat a little faster. Very deliberately she closed the door.

Hearing the sound, he came out of his reverie and looked up. When he saw her there, his gaze brightened.

'Come in…please.'

He watched her cross the room to join him and asked her to sit down.

Claire took the offered chair and waited. He seemed different today, somehow. The former aloofness in his manner was entirely absent. It had been replaced by a very different expression that was much harder to interpret. If she hadn't known better, she would have said it contained a hint of awkwardness.

'I asked you to come here in the hope of ending the estrangement that has lately existed between us,' he said.

She looked up in surprise, but said nothing.

'You may be aware that several guests came to dine here yesterday,' he continued. 'One of them was Major Barstow.' He saw her cool, quizzical look and hurried on. 'Before he left he favoured me with an account of what happened on the night of the ball. I realise now that I placed entirely the wrong construction on what I saw.'

'*I* told you that.'

'Yes, I know and I'm sorry for doubting you.' He took a deep breath. 'I apologise, Claire.'

Her fists clenched in her lap and for a long moment she was silent. Then she rose stiffly to face him. 'Thank you, sir. And now if you'll excuse me I must return to my duties.'

He regarded her in disbelief. 'Is this all I am to expect?'

'What else would you like me to say, Marcus?' The hazel eyes burned with contained fire. 'You have insulted me, you have doubted my word, and you have told me in the plainest terms that I am not to be trusted. Only when you heard the truth from another man were you prepared to believe it. Only then did it occur to you that you might have been wrong. Why would you not believe *me?*'

His cheeks, warm before, paled a little as the force of the accusation struck him. 'Claire, I'm sorry. I should have believed you, I know that now.' He took a deep breath. 'But I was so jealous that I could scarcely think at all. When I saw you in Barstow's arms, I thought that you and he…well, you know what I thought.'

She stared at him, incredulous. 'Jealous? Of Major Barstow?'

'Yes. I thought that he had succeeded in winning your affections.'

'I had never even met him before!'

He sighed. 'How long does it take to know your own heart? It was not until I saw his arms about you that I woke up to the true nature of my own feelings.' His eyes met hers in anguished appeal. 'I love you, Claire. It has been growing so gradually that I was hardly aware of it.'

'Love? Is that what you call it?' She rounded on him, fury apparent in every line of her body. 'When you believed in my guilt, as you were so ready to do, you could not wait to be rid of me. You positively encouraged my departure. Your only concern was to wonder what you were going to say to Lucy.'

'It wasn't like that, I swear it. I never wanted you to go.'

'You gave a good impression of it, though.'

'A mistaken impression. I need you here.'

'Why?' she retorted. 'Has it just occurred to you that my departure might be inconvenient?'

'Inconvenient! Is that what you think?'

'Yes. After all, there is Lucy to consider.'

'Lucy needs you, it is true, but I need you, too.'

'Why, Marcus?'

'Because you have become so much a part of things that I cannot imagine what life would be like without you.' He paused, watching her closely. 'Did it not occur to you that I might want you to stay for yourself?'

'I could hardly be expected to believe that, could I?'

He sighed. 'I can understand why you might not.'

She turned away from him, trying to conquer the emotion that swept through her.

'Stay here,' he continued. 'Let me protect you. It isn't safe for you to leave.'

The knowledge of her vulnerability was borne upon him even more strongly. Having a good deal more experience of the world than she, he was appalled to think of what might happen if she left Netherclough. She would be easy prey for the unscrupulous, never mind the ever-present threat of her uncle.

'I'm not sure it's a good idea for me to remain, Marcus.'

His heart gave an unpleasant lurch. 'There's no other serious possibility. Surely you see that?'

'London is a big place. One could be anonymous there, I think.'

'I could force you to stay, Claire. I would too if I thought for one minute it would do any good.'

That brought her round in an instant. 'You cannot keep me here.'

He regarded her steadily. 'There are a dozen ways I could do it. Netherclough is remote and I am the law here.'

Her colour fluctuated delightfully. 'You wouldn't dare!'

Even as she spoke she wasn't sure that was true.

'Oh, I'd dare, believe me, but what would be the use?'

'No use at all,' she replied.

'Exactly. I know you too well. Besides, I want you to stay out of choice, not compulsion.'

For the length of a dozen heartbeats they faced each other in silence. Her anger had ebbed now to be replaced with uncertainty and sadness. He saw it in her face. Knowing himself to be the cause, he felt only remorse. He could not blame her, only hope she might forgive him—in time. Meanwhile he had to make her see sense.

'I beg you to reconsider, Claire. Please don't go.'

The tone was humble, almost pleading, unlike any she had heard him use before.

'I don't know, Marcus. I can't think properly.'

'Take all the time you need. Just promise me you'll think it over. That you won't do anything rash.'

She hesitated a moment, then nodded. 'All right.'

He let out the breath he had been holding. 'Thank you.'

She left him then, too rapt in thought to be aware of the gaze that followed her until she was out of sight.

Chapter Thirteen

A sleepless night brought Claire no further help, and she arose next day feeling unrefreshed and heavy-eyed. Being in need of some fresh air, she took Lucy out for a walk later that morning. It also gave her leisure to reflect.

More than anything else she wanted to stay at Netherclough, to be where Marcus was. How much she wanted to believe him when he spoke to her of love, but did the word mean the same thing to both of them? Was his interpretation about passion only? Was it merely a passing fancy that would vanish as soon as it was gratified? Marriage had never been mentioned. She believed now that it never would be. Men of his rank married women of their own class. Anything else was dalliance, mere amusement. That was not the kind of love she sought, although she knew it existed. Instinctively her hand went to the locket round her neck, feeling its reassuring presence.

'Are you all right, Miss Davenport?'

Claire looked down with a start and saw the child's face with its quizzical expression.

'Oh, yes, quite.'

'You looked as if you were far away.'

She smiled. 'Yes, I was for a moment. I'm sorry.'

'Shall we walk down to the river?'

'What a good idea.'

Lucy smiled and tucked her hand into Claire's and together they followed the path through the water meadow. Forcing everything else to the back of her mind, Claire gave the child her full attention. Whatever else, Lucy was not to blame for what had happened.

After an hour in the fresh air they retraced their steps to the house, both of them feeling invigorated and ready for some tea by the nursery fire.

'Will you tell me a story when we get back, Miss Davenport?'

'All right.'

'The one about Cinderella?'

'If you like.'

And so when they returned Claire told her the story again, acting it out and putting on different voices for the different parts, holding her young charge enthralled to the end.

'That's my favourite story.'

'Why that one?'

'I like the bit at the end with the shoe, where the prince realises it's her.' Lucy replied. 'Although I still think he should have known it was her in the first place.'

'Yes, he should,' Claire agreed. 'But perhaps she looked very different. After all, she was wearing a ball gown before.'

'But I can still tell it's you when you're not wearing a ball gown. I think the prince must have been quite stupid.'

'Yes, or else his eyesight wasn't very good.'

Lucy giggled. Then, a movement in the doorway caught her attention.

'Uncle Marcus.'

He came to join them and, smiling at Lucy, received a shy smile in return. Over the child's head Claire met his gaze, but his expression gave nothing away.

'Might I have a word, Miss Davenport?'

They walked aside a few paces.

'There are matters I should like to discuss with you,' he said. 'I would be grateful if you'd meet me in the study this afternoon. Shall we say at three?'

Once again she was conscious of feeling torn, of wanting to be alone with him and at the same time dreading it. Every time she saw him it became harder to try and pretend that her emotions were under control. How easy it would be to surrender, to throw caution to the winds and let her heart rule her head. She had wondered before how women could allow love to overrule common sense. Now she knew.

'As you wish, sir.'

'Until three then,' he said.

As the morning wore on her anxiety increased. Would he press her for an answer? He had told her she might take time to reflect. Perhaps his definition of time meant something different. Knowing the nettle must be grasped, she duly presented herself at the appointed hour. However, on entering the study she checked in surprise. Marcus was dressed to ride. A pair of pistols lay in an open case on the desk. Beside them the light gleamed softly on the hilt of a sheathed cavalry sabre. As the implications dawned she looked from them to him in sudden alarm, all other thoughts driven from her mind.

'You are going after the wreckers tonight.'

'Sooner. I mean to take advantage of the last hour of daylight to ride for the rendezvous with Barstow.'

'I see.'

'If the plan works this district will be rid of the wreckers for good.'

'Yes.'

He heard the determined neutrality in her tone and threw her a shrewd glance. 'It has to be done, Claire.'

'I know, but cannot the authorities deal with the matter?'

'The authorities are dealing with it,' he replied. 'Sir Alan Weatherby is fully apprised of the situation, as are John Harlston and Major Barstow.'

'That is not what I meant and you know it. Surely there can be no necessity for you to go.'

'It is most necessary.'

'I understand why you think so, but there are other considerations now.' She paused. 'What about Lucy? If you are shot and killed, what happens to her? Have you considered that?'

He gave her a wry smile. 'I don't intend to get shot.'

'You didn't intend to last time.'

'On this occasion it is we who are setting the ambush. If the wreckers take the bait and attack the wagon, they won't find a loom beneath the tarpaulin, but a dozen riflemen instead.'

'Will they take the bait?'

'I've arranged for news to leak out that Harlston is bringing in a replacement loom. I'm gambling that the wreckers won't want to let that happen.'

She knew with sick certainty that they would not. The simplicity of the plan could not be faulted, or its potential deadliness doubted.

'More men will die, Marcus. Perhaps you among them.'

He surveyed her with studied nonchalance. 'Would it matter if I were?'

'You know it would.'

For a moment neither of them moved and the only sound in the room was from the crackling logs in the hearth. Then, somehow, his arms were round her and he was clasping her to his heart.

'You don't know what it means to me to hear you say that.'

He bent his head and kissed her gently on the mouth. Claire closed her eyes, letting her body relax against him. The kiss grew deeper and more passionate, a long, lingering embrace that set her pulse racing and turning her blood to fire. Then he drew back a little.

'I love you, Claire.'

'Then don't go tonight.'

'I must, you know that.'

'Think, Marcus, I beg you. Let the militia deal with this.'

'It is an affair of honour, Claire.'

'What use will honour be if you are killed?'

Forcing his eyes away from hers, he gestured to the mantelpiece and for the first time she saw the letter there.

'I have no intention of getting killed,' he said, 'but I've been in enough battles to know that there is always a chance. You asked me if I had considered the consequences. The answer is yes. For that reason I have left instructions. Should the worst happen, I would be grateful if you would see that they are carried out.'

Claire paled and her throat felt suddenly dry. 'Marcus, I…'

'Will you do it? There is no one I'd trust more.'

At first she wasn't quite sure she had heard him correctly, but there could be no mistaking the look in his eyes. 'I…yes, if you wish.'

'Thank you.' He drew closer and she felt his hands on her shoulders. 'Now kiss me, Claire.' Again the wry smile appeared. 'After all, it may be the last time.'

She shook her head. 'A keepsake for you to take into battle, Marcus? I won't do it.'

For answer he pulled her hard against him. 'Kiss me, you contrary little witch!'

A second later he matched the deed to the words, his arms tightening about her as the kiss grew deeper and more passionate. It seemed to go on for a long time. Then he drew back, looking down into her face.

'If I'm to die, I'll do it as a happy man.'

Anger replaced fear and she pulled free of him. 'Damn you,

Marcus Edenbridge! Damn you to hell! This business with the wreckers means more to you than anything else, doesn't it? More than me or Lucy or Netherclough?'

'That's not true.'

'It is true. You're so caught up in the past you're willing to sacrifice all our futures to it.' She threw him a fulminating look. 'I only hope that if someone tries to shoot you tonight, they aim for your head. It's the only place a shot wouldn't do any damage!'

With that she turned on heel and marched to the door. Marcus bit back an exclamation. He wanted to run after her, to talk to her and try to make her understand, but a glance at the clock revealed that it was half past the hour. It was time to go if he was to make the rendezvous by dark. He didn't want to leave things like this with Claire, but there was no choice now. Reaching for the sword belt, he buckled it on and then shoved the loaded pistols into his belt.

A discreet cough at the door caused him to look up quickly and for a moment his heart leapt, hoping it might be her. Instead a servant entered to say that his horse was saddled and ready at the door.

'Very well, I'll be there directly.'

The man withdrew and Marcus sighed. Taking a last look around to make sure he hadn't forgotten anything, he threw a cloak around his shoulders, donned a hat and strode out into the hall. Minutes later he was mounted and heading the horse up the drive.

When she left him Claire had no clear idea of where she was going, following the corridor blindly, but presently found herself by the exit that led to the rear garden terrace. Opening the door, she slipped out, needing to escape the confines of the house for a while. Marcus's words were still ringing in her ears. Why would he not listen? Why were her powers of persuasion so ineffective? She crossed the terrace and descended the steps, heading off down the gravel path beyond. For a while she walked on, regardless of the chill or the direction until her anger began to abate.

Gradually, it was borne upon her that she and Marcus might never meet again. The men he sought were dangerous. They had almost killed him once before. What if, in the darkness and confusion, a stray shot should find him? *I only hope that if someone tries to shoot you tonight, they aim for your head.* Claire bit her lip. Dear God, what had she said? It was in that second, as the possible ramifications became clear, that pride and anger evaporated and were replaced with anguish. If anything happened to him, it would be like losing a part of herself. Beside that, their argument paled into insignificance. She could not let him go without telling him the truth.

For the first time she looked around, taking stock of her surroundings. Her steps had taken her some distance from the house and brought her to the edge of the herb garden. She could see two figures there at work, an older man and a boy. They straightened on seeing her and touched their caps respectfully. She acknowledged their presence with an inclination of the head, her gaze lingering on the lad. He looked familiar. For a moment she couldn't place him, then memory returned and she smiled.

'You are one of Mrs Dobson's boys, are you not? Is it Peter?'

'Luke, miss. Peter's my older brother. He works in t'stables.'

'I see. And you are learning to become a gardener.'

'Aye.' He gestured to the area he had been working on. 'Clearing t'herb beds today, miss.'

'And do you like the work?'

'I like it well enough, miss.'

'Well, then, I'd better leave you to it.'

He nodded and touched his cap again, before returning to his task. Claire walked away down the path, aware now of the low sun and the chill air. It had been foolish to come out without a pelisse or gloves. Foolish, too, to let Marcus go without a word of support from her. He would do what he thought he must. What mattered now was to wish him well in the endeavour. She could only pray it was not too late.

Her thoughts were rudely interrupted when a man stepped out from behind a hedge and blocked her path. She drew in a sharp breath and looked up quickly. Her heart lurched as she found herself face to face with Jed Stone. Suddenly the sense of cold intensified and she shivered inwardly.

'What are you doing here?'

He gave her an insolent smile. 'I came to look for you, Miss Davenport. In fact, I've been hanging around for a couple of days in t'hope of meeting you.'

'Why?'

'Someone else is looking for you, too.'

'I don't understand.'

'Your uncle?'

Her heart began to beat faster. 'What have you to do with my uncle?'

'Word went out in Helmshaw that he were looking for you.'

'What of it?'

'Seems he's very concerned about you.'

'Is he?'

'Oh, aye. You know you really shouldn't have run away from home. Bein' a minor an' all.'

'My actions are no business of yours.'

'The world's a dangerous place for a young lady alone. It's my duty as a good citizen to see that you're returned to your guardian.'

Claire felt the first prickling of fear, but forced herself to face him down. 'You wouldn't know duty if it leapt up and slapped you in the face.'

His smile never wavered, though it didn't reach his eyes. 'What would the authorities say, if they knew t'Viscount were harbouring a minor without her guardian's knowledge or consent?'

'I neither know nor care. Nor is it any business of yours.'

'It is when there's a handsome reward for t'information.'

His words gave her a real jolt. The possibility that her uncle might offer money for information should have occurred to her. It was a measure of his determination to find her. It was also the greatest misfortune that the matter had been brought to Stone's attention. A chance of easy gain would be irresistible to this man. With far more calm than she felt, Claire met his eye.

'So go and claim it, then.'

She made to pass him, but he sidestepped, blocking the way. For the first time she realised they were out of sight of the house and the light was fading.

'I intend to do better than that,' he said.

'What do you mean?'

'There's a reward for information, but an even bigger one for returning you to your guardian.'

Her heart began to thump. He took a step closer. Seeing his intent, she turned and ran, but he had hold of her in three strides. Claire shrieked. Then a hand closed over her mouth. There followed a brief, unequal struggle before she was gagged and bound, after which her captor swung her up into his arms and carried her away.

She was taken down the path leading to the perimeter hedge and thence out into the lane beyond before being dumped unceremoniously into a waiting cart. Stone climbed in beside her and, favouring her with a nasty smile, threw an old blanket over her, concealing her from public view. His companion whipped up the horse and the vehicle rumbled away. Sick with fury and fright, she struggled to free her hands but the knots held good. Above the rumbling wheels she heard Stone laugh.

From the shadow of the hedge Luke Dobson watched the departing vehicle, wide-eyed. Claire's scream had reached the two workers in the herb garden and his older mentor had sent him to investigate. Knowing he must do something, but not being quite sure what, the boy hesitated. Should he go back and tell his companion what had happened or should he follow the cart? Instinct told him to keep sight of the cart. It held Miss Davenport. His ma would take it much amiss if anything were to happen to the lady she considered to be the family benefactress. Remembering her words on the subject, Luke set off in pursuit of the vehicle.

Marcus rode at a steady pace to the rendezvous on the moor, taking care not to push his horse too hard. The animal was fresh and champing at the bit, but he would not indulge it yet; he might need its strength and speed later. In his mind's eye he went over every detail of the plan and was satisfied that nothing had been overlooked. The only unknown factor was whether the rebels would take the bait. On the other hand, would they let Harlston bring in a replacement for the loom they had smashed before? As he had told Claire, he was gambling that they wouldn't.

This day would see the end of the Luddite threat in this part of Yorkshire. He sighed, wishing he could say as much for his own problems. Claire's face swam into his mind. Almost he could feel the crackling tension of that last encounter. At the same time he could still feel the warmth of her in his arms, the taste of her mouth on his. Just the thought of her excited passions he once thought he would never know again. He wanted her with every particle of his being, needed her, loved her. Somehow he must make her understand that, make her believe him.

These thoughts were uppermost in his mind until he reached the meeting place half an hour later. It was dark now, but by the flaring light of half a dozen torches he could see Major Barstow and a dozen mounted men. Seeing the new arrival, Barstow smiled.

'Good evening, my lord.'

Marcus returned the greeting. 'Are you ready to go hunting, Major?'

'Indeed we are.'

The Viscount glanced toward the wagon some yards in front.

Drawn by four heavy draught horses, its deadly load was concealed by a tarpaulin stretched across a wooden frame. Four armed out-riders waited alongside. Two linkmen stood in front with torches. Looking at them, Marcus experienced a moment of *déjà vu*. It sent a chill along his spine. This time he was determined the boot would be on the other foot. He turned back to Barstow.

'Are your men ready, Major?'

'They are, my lord.'

'Very well. Let's get them on their way.'

The Major gave the order and the lumbering vehicle moved off. Marcus waited until he calculated that it and its escort were a quarter of a mile ahead, then nodded to Barstow. At the signal his men doused the remaining torches and a few moments later the column of mounted men moved forwards.

Claire had long since given up any hope of freeing her hands and lay still now. Half smothered by the dirty blanket and jolted by the movement of the vehicle, she fought the rising tide of panic that threatened to overwhelm her. Where was Stone taking her? In the conversation about her uncle he had mentioned Helmshaw. Would he risk being seen there under these circumstances? Surely if he took her into town she would be able to attract attention somehow. There must be someone who would come to her aid. Miserably she thought of Marcus. By now he would be at the ren-dezvous with Major Barstow's men. When, eventually, he returned to Netherclough she would be long gone. He would have no clue as to her whereabouts. By the time he found out it would be too late. She would never see him again.

Suddenly she became aware that the cart was slowing. Then it stopped altogether. Surely they had not travelled above two miles, not nearly enough to have reached Helmshaw. Before further thought was possible the blanket was thrown aside and for a moment she found herself looking at Stone. She shivered inwardly as he bent towards her. To her considerable surprise he untied the gag round her mouth. She eyed him uneasily.

'Why have we stopped?'

'This is where we part company,' he replied.

'I don't understand.'

'You will soon enough.'

He climbed out of the cart and hauled her out after him, setting her down on the track. Then he untied her wrists. Taking a firm grip on her arm, he led her round the side of the vehicle. Her heart lurched. For the first time she saw the dark mass of the waiting coach partly concealed against the trees at the side of the lane. Stone felt her hesitate and his grip tightened.

'Come, miss. Don't be shy.'

'Where are you taking me?' Even as she spoke she guessed the truth.

'I'm sure your uncle will be glad to see you again,' he said in a conversational tone. 'He's been most anxious to find you.'

Claire hung back, trying unsuccessfully to break his hold. The grip tightened and dragged her on.

'Of course,' he continued, 'I'd like to have spent a bit longer with you myself, for old times' sake, but I don't suppose your uncle would approve of that. In any case I've other matters to attend to this evening and other places to be. Still, it's good to know you'll be in capable hands.'

She stumbled on down the track beside him, knowing it would be useless to try to appeal to his better feelings. Where she was concerned he had none. Moreover, it was clear he was enjoying his revenge.

A few moments later they reached the coach and a familiar dark-clad figure stepped out. Her stomach lurched. Uncle Hector!

Then they were face to face and the cold eyes fixed her with a gimlet stare for a moment before passing on to Stone. The latter smiled.

'The young lady, sir. As promised.'

'You have done well,' her uncle replied.

He produced a leather pouch from the folds of his cloak and tossed it over. Claire heard the clink of coins. Then he jerked his head to the waiting vehicle. Stone dragged her to the door and, when she tried to resist, lifted her off her feet and bundled her unceremoniously inside. Having seen her safely stowed, her uncle climbed in after. She had a glimpse of Stone's grinning face in the gathering dusk before the door slammed and the coach moved away.

Breathing hard from his exertions, Luke Dobson flung himself down behind a bush, staring at the departing vehicle. Presently Stone and his companion returned to the cart. He watched them climb aboard and then they drove off too, taking the fork in the road that led to the moors. The boy frowned, wondering what could possibly take them up there with night almost upon them. When they were out of sight he emerged from his hiding place, knowing now that he had to get back to Netherclough at all costs. Then he would go to the kitchens and find his mother. She would know what to do.

Feeling the coach gather speed, Claire's panic increased. Knowing she must fight it, she drew in a deep breath and tried to think. Somehow she had to get away. Eyeing the far door, she weighed up her chances. If she jumped from the moving coach, she risked a broken ankle or worse, but it was a chance she was prepared to take. There was no other. In desperation she made a lunge towards the door, but a hand like a vice closed on her arm and pulled her roughly back. Then Davenport slapped her hard across the face. She gasped, her hand clutching her burning cheek.

'Don't attempt that again,' he said. 'There's no escape for you now.'

Her stomach knotted. 'What do you mean to do?'

'What I intended to do from the outset. That is to see you married to Sir Charles Mortimer.'

'I will never agree to that.'

He regarded her coldly. 'I rather think you will.'

The knot in her stomach tightened. 'Please, Uncle, I beg you, don't do this.'

'You have made me a public laughing stock and you have caused me to look a fool in the eyes of my friend. I intend to rectify that. Tomorrow you *will* become Lady Mortimer.'

Anger vied with surprise. 'That's impossible. It is at least three days' travel to Northamptonshire.'

'You are not going back to Northamptonshire,' he replied, 'only as far as Sir Charles's country house near Barnsley—where you and he will be married.'

Claire paled. 'Never! I'd rather die than be wed to that disgusting, lascivious old man.'

He slapped her again, harder, across both cheeks this time, rocking her head back and forth and bringing water to her eyes.

'You will marry him,' he replied dispassionately, 'be assured of that. Then I have no doubt your husband will tutor you in the subject of wifely submission. He and I see eye to eye on such things. He will very soon bring you to heel.'

Claire turned cold as the implications dawned. Barnsley was hardly any distance at all. They would arrive the following day. Her stomach churned.

'We cannot be married,' she protested, her voice shaking. 'The banns have not been published.'

'It is of no consequence. Sir Charles has obtained a special licence. His brother is a bishop and will officiate at the ceremony in the private chapel at Mortimer House.'

Claire paled, her hands clenching in her lap. Her uncle surveyed her with a cold and knowing eye.

'In the interim you will have my company and, when we reach

our destination this evening, I intend to teach you about the follies of disobedience and ingratitude. When I'm done with you, my girl, you will be only too glad to marry Sir Charles.'

Marcus scanned the gloom ahead, listening intently, but could detect no sign of human life. They had ridden for several miles now without challenge. In keeping with the plan, the wagon and its escort had been sent along a different road this time, one more open and less susceptible to ambush. He hoped that detail would lend authenticity to the scheme and help convince the wreckers to take the bait. They had to believe Harlston was being extra cautious this time. The information had been deliberately leaked in the appropriate quarter some days since. Marcus smiled grimly. He wished he could have been there, but felt certain that Sir Alan Weatherby had done a good job.

A staccato crack rang out in the darkness up ahead. Barstow held up his hand and the column stopped, every man there straining to hear. The still air carried the sound of two more shots and then shouting voices.

The Major grinned. 'I think they've taken the bait.'

As he spoke the sound of shouting increased and then there was a crash as of something falling and a volley of shots. He drew his sword. The sound was repeated as a dozen more blades were drawn free of their sheaths. Raising the weapon aloft, he ordered the charge.

The horses leapt forwards and the noise of shots was drowned by the sound of galloping hooves. Barely a minute later, the wagon came into view. By the light of the torches Marcus could see several bodies stretched out around the wagon and swaying figures locked in hand-to-hand combat. The mounted force swept down on the attackers. Seeing the arrival of armed reinforcements, the wrecker crew saw too late the full extent of the trap that had been sprung. Seriously outnumbered and on foot, the survivors of the first deadly fusillade were no match for mounted men and swinging sabres. Some abandoned the fight and tried to run, but were pursued in their turn.

Marcus reined in, looking swiftly about him as the militia mopped up the remnants of the rebel force. As he did so he saw a movement out of the corner of his eye and turned his head in time to see a dark figure emerging from the shadow beyond the wagon. And then the man called out.

'Eden!'

Just in time Marcus saw the pistol aimed at him and flung himself sideways as the weapon discharged in a spurt of flame. He felt the breath of the passing ball on his cheek. A moment later he hit the ground and rolled, coming to his feet in time to see the dark form retreating into the darkness. Marcus raced after the fugitive figure, rage lending wings to his feet. He heard the sound of a heavy thud and a muffled curse that told him his enemy had stumbled and fallen. A second later he was on the man and they rolled, locked in a deadly struggle. In the process the other's hat fell off and moments later Marcus's clawing fingers ripped off the handkerchief round the face but even before he saw, he knew who it was.

'I hoped I'd catch up with you, Stone.'

'I've looked forward to it too, Eden.'

A second later Marcus felt a fist connect with his jaw and returned the blow with interest. He heard the other man grunt in pain. But Stone was tough and fighting for his life. He came to his feet, facing his enemy, breathing hard.

'I thought I'd killed you before.'

Marcus smiled grimly. 'You're not a good enough shot.'

He ducked the punch aimed for his head, but took one in the midriff. For a moment he staggered, caught off balance. Stone laughed.

'I promised you'd get yours, you bastard, and I mean to deliver.'

Without warning he bent and drew the knife from his boot, lunging forwards in one fluid movement. Marcus leapt back to avoid the blade, dodging and weaving to evade the savage edge. However, Stone was fast and dangerous and several times it passed close, slashing fabric. Marcus set his jaw, waiting for a chance. In desperation he feinted, pretending to stumble. Stone saw it and lunged for his breast. A moment later, Marcus's hand closed on his opponent's wrist and twisted hard. He heard sinew crack and then a muffled expletive. The knife fell. Before Stone could recover a boot came up into his groin with brutal force, doubling him over in agony. As he slumped forwards Marcus's knee caught him in the face, snapping his head up and pitching him backwards. Stone fell and lay still, groaning. Breathing hard, Marcus lifted his arm and wiped blood and sweat from his face with the sleeve of his coat.

Then he became aware of other figures approaching and looked up to see Major Barstow and four of his men. As the latter moved in to secure the prisoner, Barstow eyed Marcus.

'Are you all right?'

The Viscount nodded. 'I'll live.'

'The rest of the Luddite gang are dead or taken,' said Barstow. He glanced toward Stone and then at his men. 'Sergeant Carter, put this one with the others.'

'Yes, sir. At once.'

As the sergeant moved to obey, Marcus held up a hand.

'One moment. There's something I want to know first.'

'You'll not learn anything from me, Eden,' said Stone.

Marcus stepped in closer. 'Who killed David Gifford?'

A flicker of surprise registered for a moment in the other's face. 'What's it to you?'

'Who killed him?'

Understanding dawned in the other's face. 'You're another bloody government agent.'

'I am many things.' Marcus paused. 'You haven't answered my question.'

'Nor shall I, since I'll hang either way.'

No sooner were the words out than Stone gasped as a powerful hand closed round his tender privates. A second later the point of a blade pierced his breeches and punctured the skin beneath. Sergeant Carter, face thrust close, favoured him with a winning smile.

'The gentleman asked you a question, you murdering bastard. Either you answer him or I cut off your balls.' The blade moved a little deeper.

Stone yelped. 'All right! All right!'

'So talk, scum.'

'It were Sir James Wraxall—he shot him in t'back.'

For a moment there was silence. Marcus fixed Stone with a cold eye.

'Why?'

'He knew Gifford were working for t'government to find out who were behind t'machine breakin'.'

'Wraxall is a magistrate. Why should he work against the man who was trying to stop it?'

'Because it were Wraxall as were behind t'attacks. When t'looms were smashed, some of t'mill owners couldn't sustain t'financial loss and went under.'

'And then Wraxall bought up their mills for a song,' said Marcus.

Stone nodded. 'He's made himself rich.'

'Yes, with your help.'

'What were we supposed to do? Wraxall paid well. You can't feed a family on eight shillings a week.'

'So you turned to murder.'

'Those men took their chances.'

'Yes, and so will you, you bastard. At the end of a rope.'

'Aye, he'll dance to a different tune, my lord,' said Sergeant Carter.

Stone frowned and glared at Marcus. 'My lord? Who? What's he talking about?'

'A matter of identity. Mine, to be precise.'

'Lord Marcus Edenbridge, Viscount Destermere,' Carter explained.

For a second Stone didn't move, his expression registering first incredulity and then anger. Then both were hidden behind a slow smile.

'Viscount Destermere?' he said. 'Well, well, who'd have thought it, eh?'

'Life's full of surprises, isn't it?' Marcus replied.

The insolent smile widened. 'Oh, yes, my lord, it certainly is. More than you know.'

With that he began to laugh. Marcus regarded him with disgust for a moment and then turned to Carter.

'Take him away.'

The soldiers led Stone off to join the other prisoners. Barstow looked at the Viscount.

'There's something else I think you ought to see, my lord.'

He turned his horse and led the way back toward the wagon onto which his men were lifting the injured. The bodies of the slain lay where they had fallen. It was beside one of these that Barstow eventually stopped. Then he turned to Marcus.

'See for yourself.'

The Viscount turned his attention to the corpse and found himself looking down into the face of Hugh Wraxall. A round, dark hole in the forehead told how he had died, the eyes still wide with sightless astonishment. Suddenly sickened, Marcus turned away and met Barstow's gaze.

'He's paid a heavy price for his part in all this.' He glanced across at the prisoners. 'When all is said and done these men were just pawns in a larger game. I think it's time we went to find the main player.'

Chapter Fourteen

When Marcus and the militia arrived at Wraxall's mansion they were met at the gate by Sir Alan Weatherby. Then they went in to confront Wraxall. As Marcus had expected, he first denied all knowledge. Then he blustered for a while and finally, on learning of his son's death and the destruction of all his plans, fell into a tight-lipped silence. Weatherby stepped forward.

'Sir James Wraxall, you are under arrest.'

'For what crimes?'

'For murder, among others.'

'Murder? Don't be ridiculous.'

'I accuse you of murdering the late Viscount Destermere and of being instrumental in the deaths of at least half a dozen other men.'

'Viscount Destermere died in an accident. It's common knowledge,' Wraxall replied. 'Besides, I never laid eyes on the man in my life.'

'Perhaps you knew him better as David Gifford,' said Marcus.

For a moment the cold eyes widened a little.

'I see you know the name.'

'I…it is familiar to me.'

'I know it is. When you discovered he was working for the government, you promised him your support to help break the Luddite group.' Marcus paused. 'Later, when he got too close to the truth, you lured him to a remote spot and killed him.'

Wraxall licked dry lips. 'You can't prove any of it.'

'We have proof and to spare. Not all your underlings were killed tonight. And when they're offered the chance to save their necks they'll testify against you, enough to hang you several times over.'

'I had no part in it. It was all my son's doing.'

Marcus surveyed the cold reptilian face with disgust. 'I have long thought of the moment when I would be face to face with my brother's killer and could run him through. Now it has come and I know I will not dirty my sword with you. Let the law take its course.'

As Wraxall was led away Marcus let out a long breath. His godfather regarded him in silence for a moment, understanding something of the thoughts behind that impassive face.

'So it ends,' he said.

'Yes.' Marcus met his gaze. 'Wraxall will hang, but what of the others?'

'Some of them were guilty of murder, too.'

'But not all. What they did was wrong, but they were also driven to desperation by circumstances over which they had no control.'

Weatherby regarded him in frank astonishment. 'Are you suggesting they deserve mercy?'

'Who am I to say what they deserve? What I do know for certain is that they can't feed their families on eight shillings a week.'

'Many others are in a similar plight and yet did not resort to crime.'

'True, but then everyone has a different breaking point.' Marcus made a vague gesture with his hand. 'Can anything be done to prevent more deaths?'

'I don't know,' Weatherby replied. 'If some of these men are prepared to give evidence against Wraxall, then the death sentence *might* be commuted to transportation instead. But it's a long shot, I warn you.'

'Will you try?'

'I'll try, but I promise nothing.'

'Thank you.'

'Since when did you become so tender-hearted?

Marcus returned him a wry smile. 'Let's just say I must be mellowing with age.'

'I think there is more to this than meets the eye and I'm curious. Will you come back with me and dine?'

'I thank you, no. I must return to Netherclough. There is someone there I must see.'

His godfather grinned. 'Would that someone happen to have dark curls and beautiful hazel eyes?'

'She would.'

'Well, don't let me delay you, my boy.'

They walked together back to Weatherby's carriage and his godson waved him off. Then Marcus remounted his horse and headed for home.

He rode steadily, wanting time to reflect. Besides, weariness was setting in now and the bruises he had acquired earlier were making their presence felt. Yet in spite of that he felt a sense of release as though months of pent-up tension had lifted and gone. His promise to Greville was fulfilled. It was time to move on.

He knew now where his future lay and what he wanted from it. He had seen enough of fighting and bloodshed and death to last a lifetime. What he craved now was peace, the chance to build something worthwhile. He must look to the estate entrusted to him and the people in his care. One day he would pass Netherclough to his own son. That thought led to others and Claire's face drifted into his mind. After all that had passed between them, did he still have a chance? He sighed. Just then, out of nowhere, Greville's voice came to mind again, this time speaking in tones of mild reproof.

'Faint heart never won fair maid. Get to it, Bro.'

Marcus shook his head and smiled. Then, touching his horse's sides with his spurs, he urged it to a canter.

He arrived home half an hour later to find the butler in the hallway waiting for him. From the man's expression it was clear that something was amiss. The Viscount frowned.

'What is it, Mather?'

'It's Miss Davenport, my lord.'

'What about her? Speak, man!'

'She's gone, my lord.'

'Gone where?'

'We don't know, my lord. She's been kidnapped.'

'Kidnapped?' Marcus stared at him. 'Who kidnapped her?'

'I think you should speak to young Dobson, my lord. He saw it.'

'Where is he?'

'I took the liberty of asking him to wait in the small salon. His mother is with him, my lord.'

The Viscount strode into the salon. At his entrance the pair sprang from their seats, regarding him in trepidation.

'I'm sorry, my lord,' Luke burst out. 'I would have stopped 'em if I could, but there were two on 'em.'

Marcus regarded the small tearstained face and then said, 'I'm sure you would have.'

'Are we going to lose us places now?'

'No, of course not.' He took the child gently by the shoulders. 'Just tell me what happened, lad.'

Luke took a deep breath and then began to explain. Marcus heard him first with incredulity and then with mounting anger. With an effort he controlled it. What had happened wasn't the boy's fault and he was already frightened.

'Did you recognise the men who took her?'

'One of 'em were Jed Stone, my lord.'

Recalling the man's laughter earlier that evening, the Viscount was suddenly filled with a sense of foreboding.

'Are you sure?'

'Begging your pardon, my lord,' said Mrs Dobson, 'but Stone once worked in t'same mill as my late husband. We know 'im all right.'

'He's a bad 'un,' said Luke. 'Pa said so.'

'Your father was right,' replied Marcus. 'Did you recognise the man with him?'

'Aye, my lord. It were Jake Harcourt. He lived in t'same street as us before we came here.'

'What about the third man, the one in the carriage?'

'I were too far away to see 'im properly, my lord. An' it were goin' dark.'

'No matter, you've done well, Luke. Now I need you to do one more thing for me.'

'Anything, my lord.'

Marcus looked down at the earnest little face. 'Go to the stables and tell Trubshaw to harness Lightning and Wildfire to my racing curricle. Tell him I want it at the door in ten minutes.'

'At once, my lord.'

When Luke had gone the Viscount strode into the hall, calling for Mather, and then rattled off a series of instructions before heading to the study where he reloaded the pistols. As he worked his mind turned over all he had been told. He knew that the real perpetrator of the kidnap had to be Claire's uncle. Just how he had come to meet Stone was less clear. However, it was a devilish partnership.

He finished what he was doing just as his valet appeared bearing a clean coat and another cloak. Marcus divested himself of his torn and soiled garments and donned the others swiftly. Then he thrust the pistols back into his belt. Pausing only to retrieve a purse from the top drawer of the desk, he strode back into the hallway. The sound of wheels on gravel announced the arrival of the curricle.

Five minutes after that he was heading the horses out of the main gate and onto the highway. He knew full well it would have been faster to ride, but there were Claire's needs to be considered, for he had no intention of returning without her. Davenport would be heading south, but would no doubt put up for the night at an inn along the way. There were not so many places of good repute that it would be hard to find him.

The thought of Claire's terror fuelled his rage. Now he understood why she had been so afraid of her uncle discovering her whereabouts. The man was a ruthless blackguard. While he could understand Davenport wanting to find his niece and secure her return, why would he go to such extreme lengths? Her majority was not far off now. Surely he might more easily have washed his hands of her. What was the point of compelling her to return? Unless, of course, he had another end in view. An unwelcome possibility occurred. Surely the old reprobate wasn't still planning to try and force Claire into the marriage she had shunned before?

The more he thought about it the more likely it seemed. She had said her uncle was of a vengeful nature and not one to tolerate disobedience. Marcus heard her words in his mind: *He is nothing if not tenacious.* The realisation turned him cold. The idea of Claire married to anyone but himself was unthinkable. It came to him then that he loved her beyond all reason, too well to try to compel her to remain at Netherclough if she did not want to. Only let him rescue her from her uncle's clutches, and then he would do whatever she asked.

They had a good hour's start, but the curricle was light and swift and drawn by two of the best horses in his stable. Besides, Davenport would not be expecting pursuit. Marcus smiled grimly. He was confident of his ability to catch them. Focusing all his attention on the team, he settled down to drive.

* * *

Claire had no idea how long they travelled for time had lost all meaning. All she had been able to glimpse in the darkness was the verge speeding away beyond the window and each minute carrying her further from Netherclough and from Marcus. What would he think when he returned to find her gone? What if he did not return at all? What if he had been injured or killed? She shut her eyes, trying not to succumb to the terror that lurked on the edges of thought.

Having delivered that dire account of his intentions, her uncle had not spoken since. Nor did she wish for conversation, preferring to be alone with her thoughts. Her cheeks still smarted from the blows he had struck. They were merely an earnest of what was to come. At the thought her stomach churned, for she knew him well enough to know he meant every word. Could she withstand such a beating? Recalling how he had dealt with even the slightest transgressions before, her throat tightened. This would be far worse. Dear God, let her have the courage to endure it. The knowledge of what submission meant made her feel physically sick. Better to die than be bound for life to a man like Sir Charles Mortimer, to be compelled to yield her body to him whenever he chose. For a moment Marcus's face flashed into her mind. In despair she closed her eyes and leaned back against the padded upholstery.

At some point she must have dozed off, for she came to later to find that the coach was slowing. As the vehicle stopped she could see a building set back off the road. It didn't look much like an inn, but more like a private house. Her heart thumped. Was this where they would be staying? It seemed so, for the door of the carriage opened and her uncle got out, commanding her to follow. There was nothing for it but to obey. Trembling she stepped down, shivering as the chill air insinuated itself through her clothes, looking fearfully around. The house was in darkness save for a light burning in an upper window. She could see no other vehicles or any sign of life. Further reflection was denied for her arm was seized in a firm grip and she was led toward the house.

'Where is this place?' she asked.

'It belongs to an acquaintance,' he replied. 'However, he has had to go away on business so we shall be quite alone.'

Claire swallowed hard, her steps lagging. The hold on her arm tightened and she was drawn inexorably toward the door. It was opened by a hard-faced woman in a mob cap and shawl. It was clear that she recognised Hector Davenport and the thin lips formed a smile.

'Good evening, sir.'

He returned the greeting brusquely and strode inside, drawing his niece with him. The woman glanced at Claire, taking in her slightly dishevelled appearance and the lack of bonnet and cloak, but if she was surprised she made no comment.

'Is my niece's room prepared?' Davenport demanded.

'Quite ready, sir.'

'And the meal too?'

'Everything is ready, sir, just as you ordered.'

'Good. Then you may go. I shall not require you again tonight.' He paused. 'Nor do I wish to be disturbed under any circumstances. Do you understand?'

'Very well, sir.'

The woman bobbed a curtsy and withdrew. Hector Davenport strode to the stairs, dragging Claire with him. With thumping heart she stumbled up the flight to the next floor and along a passageway with several rooms leading off. Her uncle stopped by one of these, opened the door and thrust her inside. Claire stumbled again, only just retaining her balance. He followed her over the threshold. Trembling, she looked around. The room was quite large, but cold and spartan in appearance. The walls and floor were bare of covering or ornament, the only furnishings a narrow bed, a single chair and a washstand with basin and ewer. Her eyes flicked to the window. Her uncle noted the direction of her gaze.

'Do not imagine that you will escape this time, Niece. The window is barred and the door will be securely locked. I shall go and sup now and leave you at leisure to repent of your folly.' He paused. 'When I return, we shall discuss that subject further.'

With that he left her, locking the door behind him. Claire listened to his retreating footsteps and heard him descend the stairs. With pounding heart she flew to the door and tried the handle. It yielded not a whit. She turned next to the window but, as he had told her, it was barred with stout iron rods. She had no hope of moving them. Disconsolately she turned back to the room, wrapping her arms about her to ward off the chill, and then sank down onto the bed in despair. She was lost. Even if Marcus were to follow he would never find her. Unbidden, the tears welled in her eyes. It was hopeless. Her uncle had outwitted every chance of rescue by using a private dwelling. Furthermore, the place was remote and set back off the road. Even if she screamed for help, no one would come.

As time passed the room seemed to grow colder and Claire began to walk up and down in an attempt to keep warm. The hearth was empty save for a few blackened embers and a heap of ash. From the look of it, it hadn't been used for some time. She knew the lack of fire and food was no oversight. Her uncle had never intended to provide any. He intended to make her pay for every bit of the inconvenience and embarrassment she had caused him. This waiting was no mere chance either. It was designed to give her time to speculate on the punishment to come, a deliberate and sadistic ploy to increase her fear and soften her will. It was a calculated piece of cruelty, and that knowledge reignited her anger and resentment. Instead of weakening her resolve, it strengthened it. She would not let him win, could not let him win when the whole of her future hung in the balance.

She stopped pacing and looked round the room again, this time with a sharp, analytical eye. Clearly the window and door afforded no chance of escape. Which left just one possibility. She crossed to the hearth and, bending under the mantel, looked up the chimney. At the bottom anyway the flue was wide enough to take a person. Stepping into the hearth, she straightened and then began to explore the brickwork. After perhaps half a minute her questing hands found what she was looking for, the jutting bricks inside the flue that provided footholds for the sweeps and their boys. She had no idea how long ago this particular chimney might have been swept, but a bit of dirt was a cheap price to pay for freedom. Taking a deep breath, she began to climb.

Chapter Fifteen

The flue was dark and cold and smelled strongly of damp and soot. The footholds were small and she tried them gingerly, feeling her way for the next one. Her fingers sank into soft powder and little falls of it rustled past her shoulders. She prayed it wouldn't be enough to be noticeable among the ashes below. As she moved upwards the chimney soon began to narrow. There was no chance of being able to climb to the top, but she didn't need to. All that was required was to get clear of the hearth so as to be invisible from the room below. When she was sure that she had gone high enough she braced herself against the sides of the flue and waited.

The clock on the landing struck nine. As the last note died away, a door opened downstairs. A moment later footsteps sounded on the stairs. Claire's heart pounded. Straining to catch every sound, she waited dry-mouthed. The footsteps stopped outside the door and she heard the key turn in the lock. Someone took two paces into the room and checked. Then she heard an exclamation. Her uncle! She heard him move further into the room, probably to look under the bed. It was the only place someone could be concealed. Apart, of course, from her present hiding place. She bit her lip, her muscles trembling with reaction and the effort of maintaining her precarious position. A few seconds later she heard a soft oath and then he strode out of the room and back along the passage. His footsteps clattered on the stairs and she heard his angry tones calling for the housekeeper.

Heart pounding now Claire climbed down from her hiding place, regaining the hearth. A glance across the room revealed the open doorway. Her heart leapt in silent exultation. In moments she had crossed the intervening space and was peering cautiously into the passageway. It was empty. She made her way to the far end, praying that her guess was right and there would be a back stair-case, one the servants would use. Her luck held. Furthermore, it was in darkness. She made her way down, guiding herself with the banister rail. A few moments later she was on the ground floor. A high window afforded enough light to make out a nearby doorway. From the far end of the house she heard voices, her uncle's and that of a woman: the housekeeper. Claire's heart thumped pain-fully. Turning the handle of the door, she slipped through it into the room beyond.

Stale cooking smells announced a kitchen. A swift glance around revealed the dark bulk of the outer door opposite. She moved towards it and lifted the latch, but the door didn't move. Locked! For a moment she fought panic. Her fumbling fingers felt for the key and discovered it, still in the lock. She turned it and tried the latch again. Still the door refused to open. There must be a bolt somewhere. Reaching upwards, she felt for it. Sure enough it was there. Stealthily she slid it back. This time when she tried the latch the door opened. A swift look around revealed there was no one in sight, so she slipped out and pulled the door to behind her. She was free.

With slow care she made her way to the corner of the building and peered round. A second later she caught her breath and flat-tened herself back against the wall, for her uncle was standing on the driveway, lantern in hand, speaking to his coachman. The housekeeper stood just a few feet behind him. Claire swallowed hard, scarcely daring to breathe. A few moments later the crunch of gravel announced movement and someone heading her way. Heart in mouth she waited, motionless. The footsteps came closer. She could make out the man's dark shape only feet away. Praying he wouldn't look round, she watched with bated breath as he strode on past, heading for the buildings opposite. Claire let out the breath she had been holding and then peered round the corner again. The coast was clear. She began to move cautiously away from the house.

Moments later a woman's voice called out a ringing challenge. Claire threw a horrified glance over her shoulder and saw the housekeeper standing in the doorway. Knowing the shout would bring her uncle in seconds, she picked up her skirts and ran, tearing along the drive and out onto the road. Behind her she could hear running feet. The sound spurred her to renewed effort; if her uncle caught up with her now it was all over.

Knowing the centre of the road was muddy and slippery, she tried to keep to the sides, ignoring the twigs and brambles that slashed at her and snagged on her clothes. Several times she stumbled and nearly went down, but fear kept her going. She could no longer hear the sounds of pursuit, but knew better than to stop, for any minute now the coach would be following in her wake and much more quickly, too.

She was perhaps half a mile up the road when her parched lungs and pounding heart forced her to pause. The night was very still, the cold, damp air carrying every sound. For a second or two she could hear nothing. Then her ears caught the muffled thud of hoof-beats that could only be a carriage driven at speed. It was coming her way. In desperation she looked wildly around and then plunged off the road into the bushes at the side. Half a dozen paces later she hit a stone wall. Stifling a cry, she stumbled along it, turning her ankles on the uneven ground. Then her foot met something big and solid, and she half fell across the fallen tree. Behind her the sound of hoofbeats grew louder. A few more seconds and the carriage would be on her. Claire threw herself flat along the length of the tree trunk so that she was between it and the wall.

The carriage thundered past. Claire remained quite still, listening to the sound diminishing in the distance. Then, cautiously she raised herself on one elbow and peered over the top of the tree trunk. The night was still again, but she knew she couldn't leave her hiding place yet. When her uncle found no trace of her in the next mile or so he would return and cover the ground again, more slowly this time. She took a deep breath, forcing herself to think. Her uncle couldn't search properly in the darkness and this stretch of road was lined with trees and undergrowth. If she held her nerve, she might evade him yet. And so she waited. For the first time she began to feel cold, for the damp had soaked through her clothes and shoes and the chill was biting. She had never felt so alone in her life.

For the first time since her escape she had time to think about Marcus and her throat tightened. She knew now that he was the reason she could never submit to an arranged marriage with another man. There could never *be* another man. The thought of their last meeting weighed doubly heavy on her heart. How much she regretted the angry words she had flung at him and how much she would have given to have felt his arms around her again.

The sound of hooves and wheels invaded her consciousness and she stiffened, listening. There could be no mistake; the carriage was returning as she had guessed it would. Her uncle knew full well the sort of distance she would be able to cover on foot in the time available and, having found no trace of her further along the road, was now going over the ground again. For one brief moment she felt a surge of pleasure at the thought of having foiled his plans yet again. His rage and frustration must be at boiling point and she was glad of it. What she felt for him now was hatred and that was stronger than fear.

The vehicle drew nearer, but now it was moving at a walking

pace. Peering over the fallen tree, she glimpsed the light of the carriage lamps through the trees. The window was down and her uncle was leaning out, his gaze scanning the darkness, his face a mask of cold fury. Claire dropped low again, listening intently. The carriage drew level with her position and stopped. She held her breath. Her heart beat so loudly she was certain her uncle must hear it. For fully half a minute nothing moved and the night was silent. Then the vehicle began to move forwards again at the same pace. Claire remained still. Fifty yards further on, the carriage stopped again. She could visualise her uncle's angry gaze peering into the undergrowth, looking for any trace of movement, listening for any sound that might reveal the presence of his quarry. How long before he realised there was little chance of finding her in the darkness? Trying to anticipate his next move, she suspected it would be to wait until first light. How far would she be able to get? She was alone, penniless and on foot. He must rate his chances of recapturing her very highly.

At last the carriage moved on and was lost to view. When she was sure it was out of earshot she stood up and with infinite care made her way through the bushes to the road. Then she was off and running again, determined to put as much distance as possible between herself and that awful house.

After two more miles the trees and bushes died away and only stone walls bounded the highway. No wonder her uncle had turned back so quickly. There was no place to hide here and the walls were too high to be climbed easily. On either side was only yawning darkness. There was a pain in her side now and her wet dress clung round her legs, impeding her progress. Yet she couldn't stay here. She had to find somewhere to take shelter if need be.

The stitch got worse and forced her to a walk, but she kept moving nevertheless. However, the road was climbing and beyond isolated trees there was still no sign of any kind of cover. Then her ears caught a sound. She paused, listening intently, and her heart missed a beat. There could be no mistaking the sound of hoof falls. In a moment of terror she froze, unable to go forwards or back. Her uncle had not given up after all!

It was several seconds before she realised that the vehicle was coming towards her, not from behind. The relief was almost overwhelming, so much so that she remained where she was in the middle of the road. The driver was almost on her before he saw the pale figure looming out of the darkness. He reined in hard. She heard a muffled expletive and then there was a confusion of flying hooves as he brought the startled and plunging horses under control.

'What the hell do you think you're doing, walking in the middle of the road like that?' demanded a furious voice. 'I might have killed you, you bloody idiot!'

Claire's heart leapt for she recognised the voice instantly.

'Marcus!'

The driver of the vehicle stared at the filthy and dishevelled figure now pooled in the lamplight at the side of the vehicle.

'Christ! Claire?'

The relief of hearing his voice was so great that she began to shake. Then he was beside her and she was being swathed in the warm folds of a huge cloak and held very close to a broad chest.

'Oh, my love, my sweet Claire, I thought I'd lost you.'

'He came for me, Marcus. He made me go with him.'

'My poor darling. My dearest love.'

At the sound of those endearments her throat tightened, making speech impossible, and she began to shiver violently with cold and reaction. Wasting no time on further speech, he swept her into his arms and lifted her onto the seat of the curricle before climbing up himself. Then, with the practised ease of a skilled whip, he turned the vehicle round and began to retrace his route.

* * *

Afterwards Claire had only a hazy memory of that part of the affair. Some time later she was carried into what appeared to be an inn, and there followed a confused impression of voices and hurrying footsteps. Then she was put down gently in a chair by a cheerful fire and two large warm hands were chafing her cold ones.

'Drink this.'

A mug of hot and fragrant liquid was held to her lips. She took a sip and felt it carve a path to her stomach. As the spiced wine warmed her she became aware of a familiar figure seated on the stool at her side.

'I was afraid you'd been killed,' she said. 'But you're all right. You're all right.'

His jaw tightened. 'Never mind me. It's you I'm concerned about just now.'

In truth he was appalled by the sight of her physical condition, revealed in ghastly detail by the lit room. Appalled and deeply angered. To judge by appearances she had been confined in a coal cellar. What the hell had happened in the time before he found her? What kind of a brute was that uncle of hers? He fought down the vengeful feelings rising in his breast, knowing he'd have to wait to learn the truth. What mattered now was to get her warm and clean again and safely tucked up in bed.

A few minutes later the landlord appeared to say that the room was ready. Hearing that, Claire got shakily to her feet, feeling both the effects of fatigue and spiced wine and wondering if there was sufficient strength in her legs to get her up the stairs. The answer was never known because Marcus had no intention of putting the matter to the test. Lifting her with casual ease, he carried her to an upper room and set her down before a cheerful fire. Glancing round, she was aware of a large bed and, blessedly, a tub of hot water.

She was vaguely aware of the door closing, but when she looked over her shoulder it was to see that Marcus was still this side of it. Surely that couldn't be? Before she could say a word he moved closer.

'Come here. We need to get you out of those wet things.'

Her eyes widened a little. 'We?'

'That's right.'

Under her astonished gaze he shrugged off his coat and rolled up his shirtsleeves. The implications sent a rush of warmth from her neck to the roots of her hair.

'But, Marcus, you can't…'

It seemed however that he could, for a moment later the cloak was plucked from her shoulders and tossed aside. Then his hands were on her shoulders again, this time turning her gently round. Their warmth through the damp fabric sent a shiver along her skin. The voice of her conscience said this was wrong. That he should not be here doing this. And yet perversely it felt right. His touch should have frightened or disgusted her, but it did not. The feeling it aroused was quite different. He drew the torn and filthy gown off her shoulders and down over her breasts, freeing her arms from the sleeves, and let it fall. Then he undid her petticoat and stays with the practised ease of a man completely at home with female clothing. Moments later she was standing in her shift. The grey gaze warmed. Following its downward glance she was suddenly aware that the sodden fabric was clinging to her flesh and revealing a great deal more than it concealed. She saw him smile and then reach for a chair, pushing her gently down into it. Then he knelt and lifting her feet in turn, removed her shoes. She felt his hand brush her leg as he unfastened the garters that held her stockings and rolled them down, drawing them off her feet.

'Come,' he said.

He led her to the tub, and paused a moment to remove the pins from her hair. It tumbled in disordered curls about her shoulders.

Finally he reached for the fastening of her chemise. When she was completely naked he lifted her into the tub. In an instant she was enveloped in delicious warmth.

Kneeling beside her, he took a cloth and soaped it thoroughly. Then he wiped her face, cleansing away the dirt. Claire winced. For the first time he noticed the dark bruise along her cheekbone. His brows drew together. Immediately his gaze looked for further evidence of abuse, but mercifully found none. He rinsed the skin clean and then washed her hair, vigorously at first to remove the dirt, then gently the second time, massaging her scalp with his fingers, loosening the tension in her neck. Then he rinsed her hair with clean water from the jug. Soaping the cloth again, he moved on to her arms and hands, cleansing away the mud and grime, and thence to the smooth, soft skin of her neck and shoulders and back. Her body was beautiful, he thought, more so than he had envisaged, and he had thought about it often.

Under the soothing strokes of the cloth and the pervading warmth of the water Claire, at first as tense as a bow, began insensibly to relax. The spiced wine, taken on an empty stomach, made her feel pleasantly light-headed. In one part of her mind the voice told her this was shocking and deeply immoral, but another, stronger voice, replied that she didn't care. All that mattered now was to be here with him, to feel his hands on her skin and to revel in the new and wonderful sensations they aroused. Every particle of her body felt deliciously alive, as though she had been asleep before and was only now awakening to a dimension hitherto unguessed at.

A firm hand closed round her ankle and, lifting her leg, drew it straight. The cloth soaped its length, beginning at her foot and moving slowly along her calf to her knee and thence to her thigh, repeating the exercise with the other leg. Laying the cloth aside, he soaped his hands and began to massage the skin of her neck and shoulders. Gradually, as the skilful fingers continued their work, the knotted muscle relaxed and became pliant. Claire sighed in contentment. It felt blissfully good.

His hands moved down, gently stroking her breasts, brushing the nipples to tautness. Claire drew in a sharp breath for the touch sent a shiver of pleasure rippling through her entire being. Deep within, a familiar spark rekindled and glowed into life and became flame. The shiver along her flesh intensified. And then his mouth was on hers in a soft kiss, gentle and tender, offering only itself, demanding nothing. Her lips parted beneath that soft pressure, her mouth yielding itself to his.

Then he drew away and took the cloth again and rinsed the soap off her. When it was done he drew her to her feet and lifted her from the tub, wrapping her in a warm towel. Without any evidence of haste he dried her hair and then moved on to the rest, moving his hands over her body with slow and deliberate thoroughness. Her flesh, warm from the bath, burned beneath his touch. He turned her to face him, drawing her against him in a warm and gentle embrace, and kissed her again. Her arms stole around his neck and then she was kissing him back, pressing closer, drawing his face down to hers.

Marcus felt the flaring warmth in his groin, instantly aroused, wanting her. A week ago, a day even, and he would have lain her down on the rug by the fire and followed his desire to its conclusion. It was still very tempting, but he knew now it wasn't enough. With a supreme effort of will he drew back a little and looked into her face.

'Are you sure, Claire? I cannot pretend I don't want you, but nothing is going to happen without your consent.'

'I love you, Marcus.'

His heart leapt, for he had never thought to hear those words from her.

'And I you,' he replied. 'I think I did not know how much until I had almost lost you. Yet when I remember some of the things I said before, I feel only shame.' He paused, looking into her eyes. 'Can you ever forgive me for doubting you?'

She put a finger to his lips to silence him. 'I told you, there is nothing to forgive. Besides, my own angry pride was much at fault.'

'You had every right to be angry after the way I have behaved. I cannot think of it now without abhorrence.'

'We both said things in haste that we did not mean.'

'Do you really want to leave Netherclough, Claire? If you do, I'll not prevent you or blame you, even though losing you would be like losing a part of myself.'

She shook her head. 'I don't want to leave. I never did.'

'Then stay, I beg you, and for good this time.' He looked down into her face. 'Marry me, Claire.'

Her heart performed an erratic manoeuvre in her breast that was followed a moment later by flooding happiness.

'Yes,' she replied. 'Oh, yes.'

For a while after that no speech was possible. Afterwards it was unnecessary. He carried her to the bed and, stripping off the remainder of his clothing, joined her there. Then he made love to her, continuing what he had begun before, fanning the embers of the banked fire, restraining his own desire to increase hers, wanting it to be perfect for both of them. He wanted her, but he wanted all of her, not out of fear or compulsion but of her own free will, and so he was gentle and infinitely patient, exploring her anew, making his ultimate possession an act of homage.

No longer afraid of the feelings she had hidden for so long, Claire returned his passion, knowing that this was what she had both desired and refused to acknowledge. Now she yielded herself up to his lovemaking with every part of herself, holding nothing back, wanting to be part of him. Her lips sought his now, teasing, provocative, and passionate by turns, her arms twined about him, her entire being revelling in the nearness of the body pressed against hers. She quivered, feeling his lips travel from her mouth to cheek and temple, ear and throat and breast, kindling her flesh until it seemed that every part of her glowed like a brand. Awareness became a fusion of different sensations: the coarse linen sheet beneath her back, the smell of woollen blankets and tallow candles mingled with wood smoke and the warmth of flesh on flesh, the hardness of the muscles in his arms and shoulders, the erotic, musky scent of sweat on his skin.

She felt his hand slide from her waist along her hip to her thigh and thence to the hidden cleft between, gently stroking. The movement sent a delicious shudder through her body. As he continued stroking, sensation intensified and she gasped, feeling a sudden shockwave of pleasure. Then his weight was pressing her down into the bed, his knee parting her thighs and he entered her, gently at first until the initial resistance was past and then more strongly, the rhythmic strokes thrusting deeper, sending pleasure coursing through every fibre of her being, her body arching against him in ecstasy. She felt him shudder and heard him cry out and then the sudden exhalation of breath as the tension left him afterwards.

And then she lay in his arms, feeling his body curled around hers, both of them drowsing and deliciously sated, protected by a cocoon of warmth. Here with him there was no fear or disgust, only delight, for this was where she belonged. With him she had found the love she had dreamed of for so long.

Claire woke the following morning with a delicious sense of well being. She yawned and stretched lazily, opening her eyes to the new day. As memory returned her heart leapt. He had come for her. Against all the odds he had found her. Just knowing he was near made her feel absurdly happy and all the adventures of the previous evening seemed like an evil dream now from which she had awoken. Recalling too the wonderful sensations of his love-making, she reached out for him.

Her hand found only empty space. Coming to full wakefulness, she sat up and looked around. He had gone. Her heart began to beat a little more quickly. Climbing out of bed, she realised suddenly that she had no clothes. The ones she had been wearing yesterday were good for nothing but rags now and the rest of her things were at Netherclough. She reached for a blanket and wrapped it around herself.

A knock on the door diverted her attention. A few seconds later Marcus entered the room. For a moment he surveyed her keenly, his gaze taking in every detail of her appearance, from the dark curls tumbled about her shoulders to the small bare feet just visible below the hem of the blanket. Then he grinned.

'Good morning. You're looking much better.'

'I feel much better,' she replied, very much aware of the sudden acceleration of her heartbeat.

'I've brought you these.' He held up the garments on his arm. 'They're not exactly in the first style, but they're all I could get hold of. They're more or less your size, I think.'

The grey eyes rested on her critically and she was conscious of warm colour rising from her neck.

'Thank you,' she replied.

He laid the clothes over the back of a chair and crossed the intervening space, taking her in his arms and following the gesture with a lingering kiss. Then he looked down into her face.

'Are you hungry?'

'Yes.'

'Good. I've ordered some breakfast downstairs. Then, when we've eaten, we'll go home.'

'Oh, Marcus, I thought yesterday that I would never see you or Netherclough again.'

He smiled. 'I'm not so easy to get rid of. Nor would I let another man steal you away from me.'

'I was so afraid.'

He drew her close to his breast, letting his lips brush her hair.

'There is no need to be afraid, my darling. I won't let him hurt you again.'

Thinking of the narrowness of her escape and of the consequences if she had failed, Claire shuddered. Marcus felt that tremor and frowned, vowing silently that nothing should hurt her again if he could prevent it.

When eventually he left her she dressed hurriedly in the borrowed garments. As he had said, they were hardly stylish but they were at least clean and serviceable. Then she arranged her hair as best she could. Having made herself as presentable as possible under the circumstances, she made her way downstairs. A servant directed her to a small private breakfast parlour.

Marcus had been looking out of the window, but turned when he heard the door open, and then smiled. Feeling oddly self-conscious, she allowed him to lead her to the table and ply her with ham and eggs and hot coffee. Only when they had finished eating did he bring the conversation round to the events of the previous evening.

Claire gave him a summary of all that had taken place. He listened without interruption, only his expression revealing the anger he felt. Only the part about her eventual escape brought a smile to his lips.

'You're as courageous as you are beautiful,' he said.

She could detect not the least trace of mockery in his tone and the look in the grey eyes reflected only sincerity.

'It wasn't bravery,' she replied. 'Only self-preservation.'

'Your uncle should be horsewhipped. He may yet be if we ever meet.'

Claire paled. 'He will come after me, I know it.'

'Let him. It will avail him nothing. He will not lay hands on you ever again, I swear it.'

Unaccountably a lump formed in her throat.

'Don't be afraid, Claire.'

'I'm not—now.'

'If I had been there, this whole sorry business would never have happened.'

'It wasn't your fault,' she replied. 'Just bad timing, that's all.' She paused. 'But you have not told me your story yet. What happened last night? Did your plan work?'

'Yes. The Luddite group is finished. In that neck of the woods anyway.'

She listened intently and in mounting horror as he outlined what had taken place. It was almost inconceivable that a man in Wraxall's position should stoop to such baseness, and she could feel no pity for his impending fate.

'So your brother is avenged,' she said. 'And you have fulfilled your promise.'

He nodded. 'Yes. It's a strange feeling in many ways, and a relief too that it is over.' He paused. 'Now I can think about the future, our future. I want to build something worthwhile, Claire, and that will only be possible with you beside me.'

Her heart leapt, both for the tone of the words and the intensity of his expression. 'We will build a future together, Marcus. A wonderful future. I know it.'

He raised her hand to his lips. 'You do me a greater honour than I deserve.'

'Let's look forward, not back.' She smiled up at him. 'After all, there is so much to look forward to.'

Chapter Sixteen

Marcus was just about to hand her into the curricle when another carriage pulled up outside the inn. She recognised it in a moment, and the familiar figure that got out. Her cheeks paled.

'My uncle,' she murmured.

Marcus, following the direction of her gaze, frowned and laid a hand over hers, but before he had time to say anything, Davenport's gaze came to rest on the handsome racing curricle and the tall, elegantly clad man beside it. For a second or two he didn't recognise his niece in the young woman with him. Then he saw her and his expression lit with triumph. Claire swallowed hard. Moments later her uncle was crossing the intervening space. She glanced from him to Marcus, who seemed not to be in the least perturbed, but merely watched as Davenport strode towards them. Having reached the curricle, he threw a cold glance at his niece and then another at her companion.

'Forgive me, sir,' he said, 'but I must ask you to hand that young woman into my custody.'

Marcus raised an eyebrow and raked Davenport from head to toe with a haughty look. 'And who might you be, sir?'

'I am Hector Davenport and the girl is my niece.'

He was favoured with the briefest of bows. 'Lord Destermere, at your service.'

For a second Davenport didn't move. His cold eyes registered surprise, but he recovered at once and bestowed on the other a thin smile.

'Your servant, my lord. May I say how much I regret the trouble that you have been put to by this wayward wretch?'

'Your niece has been no trouble. On the contrary.'

'You are generous, my lord.'

'Not in the least. My only concern is that you should have caused the lady to be removed from my house in such an underhand manner.'

'It was necessary, my lord.'

'Indeed?'

'You have been grievously imposed upon. I do not know what tale the girl has told you in order to trick her way into your house, but she is as devious as she is headstrong.'

The Viscount's grey eyes grew colder. 'Devious? How so?'

'She left home some months ago, without my knowledge or permission.'

'Ah, she ran away? Why would she do that, I wonder?'

Davenport's cheeks reddened a little. 'She is a disobedient and ungrateful girl. A most advantageous match had been arranged for her but she, in a fit of contrariness, saw fit to go against the judgement of her elders and betters.'

Marcus shook his head. 'Dear me, I can hardly credit it.'

Claire threw him a speaking look, which he affected not to notice. Evidently, though, her uncle took the words at face value.

'It is indeed difficult to grasp the extent of such wilful folly,' he continued. 'The girl has put me to a good deal of trouble, but now that I have found her again, I shall take her off your hands.'

'As you did yesterday,' replied Marcus.

'She gave me the slip yesterday, but she will not do so again, I assure you. I shall have the knot tied by tomorrow night.'

'And what has the lady to say to this?' asked Marcus, glancing at Claire. 'It seems from her behaviour that she still does not desire this marriage.'

'I will never agree to it,' she replied.

Marcus looked at Davenport. 'There you have it. It looks to me to be a hopeless case. The lady does not wish to marry your choice of husband.'

Davenport stared, as though he could not believe his ears. 'I beg your pardon?'

'In fact,' Marcus went on, 'I don't wish her to either. You see, I intend to marry her myself.'

'You intend…'

'That's right, and she has done me the honour of accepting my proposal.'

Davenport's face suffused with colour when he saw the smile that passed between the other two and he controlled himself with a visible effort. 'Your ruse will not work, my lord. I am the girl's legal guardian and until she comes of age she is mine to dispose of as I see fit.'

Claire, who had been listening to the exchange in mounting concern, felt her stomach give a strange lurch as another realisation struck her. Then a smile lifted the corners of her lips and she turned to Marcus.

'What is the date today?'

'The thirtieth, why?'

'It's my birthday!'

Marcus grinned and turned to her uncle. 'It looks as though your guardianship has just lapsed, sir.'

For a moment there was an awful silence in which Davenport surveyed them in impotent wrath.

'Very well, then, you have made your choice, Claire. I'm done with you. I wash my hands of you.'

'Is that a promise, Uncle?'

'Wicked, ungrateful wretch!'

Seeing him raise his hand, Claire shut her eyes instinctively, anticipating the blow. However, it never reached her for the fist was

arrested in mid-air by a grip of iron and held there. In utter astonishment Davenport found himself looking into a pair of cold grey
eyes.

'I have always disliked men who abuse women,' said Marcus,
'and you, sir, are one of the most contemptible examples of the
species. The only reason I don't thrash you as you deserve is out
of consideration for the lady, who I know would dislike a public
scene.' He paused, lowering his voice. 'But understand this—if you
ever lay a hand on her again, I'll kill you.'

Looking at that flinty expression, Davenport was left in no
doubt that he meant it. His face, red before, went pale, but he
vouchsafed no answer. Marcus's lip curled, but he released his
hold.

'Get out.'

Pausing only to cast upon them a look of loathing, Davenport
turned on his heel and strode back to his carriage. He flung in and
slammed the door. Moments later the vehicle was drawing away.
As Claire watched him go, she was conscious of a huge weight
being lifted off her shoulders. She glanced up at Marcus, who was
still staring wrathfully after the departing carriage.

'God help me,' he said, 'I have never wanted to knock a man
down half so much in my life.'

'He's not worth the effort,' she replied.

'No, you're right. All the same it would have given me immense
satisfaction.' He turned and folded her in his arms. 'His tyranny
over you is at an end.' Then he grinned. 'Mine, however, is only
just beginning.'

'I believe I shall be better able to withstand yours.'

'Can you really bear the thought of a lifetime of me, to say
nothing of my wretched temper?'

'There is no one else I would rather share my life with.'

'The sentiment is returned.' Then another thought occurred to
him. 'I haven't even wished you a happy birthday yet.' His mouth

descended on hers in a long and lingering kiss that set her heart thumping. Then he looked into her face. 'What would you like as a present?'

'I already have what I want.'

'It seems a poor reward to me,' he replied.

Dashed poor, agreed Greville. *Have to do better than that, Bro.*

Marcus grinned. 'How about a diamond ring?'

Claire returned the smile. 'All right, I'm persuaded.'

'I hope it's going to be this easy to get my own way after we're married.'

'Don't count on it.'

'I was afraid you'd say that.'

Clasping her fingers in his, he helped her into the curricle and then climbed up beside her, taking hold of the reins and the whip. Then he glanced down at his companion.

'Home, my lady?' he asked.

'Home, my lord,' she replied.

HISTORICAL

Novels coming in November 2009

TALL, DARK AND DISREPUTABLE
Deb Marlowe

Mateo Cardea's dark good-looks filled Portia Tofton's girlish dreams – dreams that were shattered when Mateo rejected her hand in marriage. Now Portia's home has been gambled away, and Mateo is the only man who can help. However, she has in her possession something he wants – so she strikes a deal with the devil himself!

THE MISTRESS OF HANOVER SQUARE
Anne Herries

Forever generous, matchmaker Amelia Royston will do anything to help others' dreams come true – yet will her own feet ever be swept off the ground? Then the charismatic Earl of Ravenshead returns to tip her world upside down! He finally declares his intention to marry her – but is he only wanting a convenient bride…?

THE ACCIDENTAL COUNTESS
Michelle Willingham

When Stephen Chesterfield, the Earl of Whitmore, awakes to find a beautiful woman berating him, he knows he is in trouble! He cannot recall the last three months of his life, never mind having a wife! What's more, someone is trying to silence him before his memory returns… Can he find trust and love before it is too late?

MILLS & BOON

HISTORICAL

Another exciting novel available this month is:

COMPROMISED MISS

Anne O'Brien

**He remembers luminous grey eyes…
and a mysterious gentle touch…**

Despite being unconscious for most of the night, Lucius has been
accused of compromising a lady. She may not be an obvious
beauty, dressed as she is in seaman's garb, but his rescuer is all
woman – and now he must marry Miss Harriette Lydyard.

The Earl of Venmore is lethally attractive, and Harriette knows
she should refuse him. Only with her reputation in tatters
Harriette must face the consequences of her actions – by making
a pact with this disreputable, dangerous devil of a man!

HISTORICAL

**Another exciting novel available
this month is:**

RUNAWAY LADY, CONQUERING LORD
Carol Townend

Taming his runaway lady!

Raised a lady, Emma of Fulford is a fallen woman with a young
son as proof. He is all she has in the world, and now the boy's
brutal father has returned… Desperate and afraid, she needs to
escape, and fast, so approaches Sir Richard of Asculf. She begs
this honourable Norman knight for help – and offers the
only thing she has left…herself.

Honourable he may be, but Sir Richard is only human, and
Lady Emma tempts his resolve. Can this conquering knight
tame his runaway lady and stop her running for good?

**Wessex Weddings
Normans and Saxons, conflict and desire**

 MILLS & BOON